The Pharaoh's Curse

C.J. Boomer

In fond memory of my grandfather, Edward Morgan Ford, the greatest storyteller I'll ever know.

Chapter 1

Fleeing back to the safety of the charioteering class was no longer an option. The thrill of the imminent hunt pulsated unpleasantly in Merkhet's ears.

If he was going to survive beyond the next week of gruelling preparation, he needed to silence the surging guilt. His brother was right to convince him to abandon their class. Merkhet was not ready for what was to come, not even close.

Ahead, beyond a clump of towering palm trees, shadows darted across the shimmering heat haze.

Peronikh held out his arm. Merkhet accepted his brother's signal, pulling hard on the reins. His mare obeyed, stopping without so much as a whimper. He hopped down, securing her with a coil of rope to a nearby palm. Hundreds of them, set back from the Nile's bends, sheltered the way to the river's banks.

Trailing Peronikh through the trees, Merkhet was careful not to scuff his sandals on the sand. A single false step would betray their presence and alert the herd of gazelles breaking their afternoon thirst. For some of the most rapid creatures in the lands, they were easy to fright. Their pointy ears and curved black horns were always reaching for the sky, even as they slurped the flowing brown-green liquid. His brother crept closer towards the muddier terrain stretching out from the river.

Merkhet suspended his advance, so that he could wipe away the sweat lining his brow. Resting his arm there, the dangling linen protected his eyes from the harsh sun that pierced through the palm trees. The herd was almost within range, less than one hundred feet away now. Suddenly, coarse heat swallowed his feet, scratching and suffocating them. His sandals sunk so far beneath the surface that the scolding sand became cool, almost welcoming. Merkhet groaned as quietly as he could.

Peronikh halted, turning around. He flashed a daring smirk, then bounded away, ending their stealthy approach. The gazelles responded, scattering while Merkhet attempted to free himself. Buried almost to the knee, his legs could not escape their sand prison. Powerless to stop his brother from scoring the first kill, he slammed the sand around him.

Forcing a few calming breaths, the foggy helplessness cleared away. Bursting upward, Merkhet unleashed one trapped leg, and then the other. He chased after Peronikh but trudging through the dwindling desert wouldn't cut it. He needed powerful strides because his brother was already lining up his third target.

Merkhet fumbled for the bow flung across his back. Clutching it, he struggled to snatch an arrow from the quiver strung over his shoulder. His fingers continually slipped on the feathery fletching as a gazelle, one of the few still within reach, strayed near him. Frustrated, he ripped at the quiver, snapping its leather strap. Once he latched onto an arrow, everything but that and the bow was discarded behind him.

As he nocked the arrow, Merkhet fixed his attention on the gazelle. Tugging on the bowstring, the creature held steady before him, its bright eyes almost staring straight through him. All he had to do was pull tight, steady his aim, and then release. Yet its eyes widened, pleading for mercy, and his arm was shaking so much that the bowstring flexed forward. A fresh wave of grit stole over him, and his trembling settled. Bowstring fully drawn, Merkhet raised his back elbow a touch and relaxed his fingers.

The arrow, mesmerising twirls of black and white feather, whizzed through the air. His aim was true. It could not miss.

A mere moment from the arrow hitting its mark, the gazelle had crumpled to the ground, Peronikh's shot protruding from its head. Merkhet slumped into the dried mud's hard embrace. He may not have made the first kill, but he would still have at least made one. What now?

Peronikh did not smile, nor did he frown, as he pulled out *the* arrow that cheated Merkhet of a kill. 'Why do you gaze skyward for answers, brother? The gods cannot help those who are too afraid to help

3

themselves.'

Why couldn't Peronikh have given him a chance to shoot, just this once? It wouldn't have killed him. And what did his brother possibly know about the workings of the gods, anyway? He was too busy being perfect at everything else. Whether it was hunting or swordplay, it did not matter. Peronikh would flaunt his skill, just so he could torment his younger brother.

Merkhet fought against the rigid reluctance in his weary limbs and forced himself up. He retrieved his wayward arrow. 'I've had enough for today,' he said, hoping he could mask the bitter defeat in his voice. 'Let's go.'

Merkhet and Peronikh returned to their horses and untied them. They drew their cloaks over their head and slung their bows across their back, ready to depart. Peronikh was already mounted atop Tendrence, and with a hefty slap on the side of his steed, was galloping towards Thebes—the City of a Hundred Gates.

Merkhet hesitated, as painful memories were stirred. He received Abacca as a gift from his father five years earlier. She had thrived in that time, developing a magnificent brown colouring and a gentle soul that matched his own. Together, they were great companions, but Merkhet struggled to be around her. The anguish of losing his first mare still lingered. Abacca brushed against him with her luscious coat and that was enough to set aside his unease.

Cantering through the burgeoning sandstone capital, Peronikh was annoyingly gleeful. He always was after a successful hunt, which made the ride even more unbearable. At least none of the stall owners hassled them as they cut through the markets and the administration precinct. Finally, they were closing in on the gleam of the royal palace. Constructed upon a desert dune, its sandstone walls shone like a star in the fading daylight.

Merkhet could perch himself on the palace's terrace for hours, looking down upon the world and never growing restless. The birds frolicking as they dipped in and out the Nile. The steady hum of worship echoing from the temples. Seldom did he get chances to savour those delights anymore. Too strenuous were the demands of a prince when maturity beckoned him.

'Same again tomorrow?' Merkhet asked with a sigh.

'Yeah,' his brother said, making way to leave. 'You need all the practice you can get.'

'Not so fast, my dear princes,' someone called out. One of the royal guards had abandoned his entrance post and was striding over to them. 'Pharaoh Nekhet requires you both in the throne room.'

Peronikh groaned. 'What, now?'

'Yes, *now*.'

The guilt returned in a flood, and Merkhet's stomach churned to the tune of a hundred days' hunger. Father already knew of his and Peronikh's afternoon exploits. As could be expected—he was the Pharaoh of Egypt. Deserting a royal class for a hunting expedition was bad enough, and now, with nothing to show for it …

Looking up at his father, the Double Crown of Egypt atop his head, how could Merkhet possibly explain himself?

Chapter 2

Merkhet resisted the urge to shake. Awaiting the verdict of his father was torture.

Pharaoh Nekhet was collecting his thoughts but looked just about ready to deliver them. 'Wandering through the desert,' he said, 'without a royal escort. What were you thinking?' Speaking from his seat upon the Golden Throne, a single brazier flickered on the wall above him, working against the encroaching gloom. His voice was even, controlled, but his stern gaze bore right through Merkhet. 'Explain yourselves.'

Merkhet couldn't. He lowered his head, no longer able to maintain eye contact. The hieroglyphic wall decorations in his peripherals were now a blur, courtesy of the threatening tears. The disappointment in his father's tone was palpable, like a hostile wind tunnel, rooting him on the spot. He could scarce recall a time when such passion consumed the pharaoh.

'You are Egyptian princes, heirs to this very throne. Our enemies never rest. They are everywhere, always seeking opportunities to hurt us. We cannot afford to present them with any.'

'Sorry, Father,' Merkhet said, glancing sideways at Peronikh, who offered nothing, not even so much as a morsel of remorse on his vacant face.

'You must understand that my love for you is equal,' the pharaoh said. 'Your mothers understand this, and you must, too. Whichever of you succeeds me, it matters not, as long as Egypt comes before self, before all.' He paused, collecting his breath. 'From this day forward and for the rest of your living days, I charge you to place Egypt's needs above your own. Do you accept this charge?'

'I do,' Merkhet said.

Peronikh grunted into his chest.

A deep furrow appeared across his father's face, and he opened his mouth to challenge the feigned response but must have reconsidered, for he said, 'As for your royal classes, they will be cancelled until Merkhet's trial is complete.'

'But—'

'But nothing, Merkhet. Alternative arrangements will be made for the other pupils. If it means I must delegate my duties in order to oversee your final preparations, then I will.'

'You will?'

'Yes. Tomorrow we will venture into the desert in search of worthy prey.'

Peronikh snorted. 'Maybe we should find something already dead. Even then, it might still need to be bound up.'

'If you weren't so greedy, I would have had that gazelle.'

'Enough,' commanded their father. 'Tomorrow morning, we hunt. In the afternoons, too, if we must.'

Merkhet bowed before the pharaoh. Peronikh had already vacated the throne room.

Recovering between hunts, Merkhet leant against the acacia tree. Its bushy foliage covered the palace's entire courtyard in shade. Nursing his flagging spirit and spent body, he would have his father to thank if he did perish at the hands of his mounting woes.

Blisters smothered Merkhet's hands. Soreness riddled his joints and muscles, in places he never fathomed could ache. His death wouldn't be intentional, but that would do little to comfort his mother. Merep had opposed the escalation of her son's preparations from the outset. As gruelling as multiple daily hunts were, two thousand years of Egyptian law supported his father's uncompromising stance—a prince must attempt the Pharaonic Trial on his sixteenth birthday.

Merkhet shuddered. Tomorrow morning, he would be the first recorded failure. The scribes would not spare him, no matter his nobility. They would scrawl and scribble their *truths* until all hope of him ever becoming an esteemed diplomat evaporated in the searing desert heat. At least if he didn't survive the ordeal, he would be spared their demoralising accounts of his ungallant attempt.

He tried to read one of his grandfather's many diplomatic texts to calm himself. This particular text—written by Pharaoh Turkhet, the Master Diplomat—which he had already read in its entirety four times, and it still required further examination to yield all its wisdom. How Merkhet wished he could have met his grandfather, to learn from him.

His reading efforts were futile, the methods for establishing relations with new states did not sink in. He could not concentrate on the words, no more than he could prevent the creeping desire for the trial to disappear and for everything to return to normal. But no matter how many prayers he whispered beneath the acacia that would not happen. He would have to face it, like all the princes that came before him, including his brother. Merkhet set the scroll beside him, closing his eyes. Just another moment's rest before his final preparatory hunting expedition.

'Never delay what can be done right now.'

Startled, Merkhet sat up. A young servant girl, piled under a stack of bronze cooking pots, passed under the tree's sweeping branches. Merkhet couldn't even offer her assistance because she scurried inside the palace without turning to elaborate or explain. Whom was she talking to? And delay what? Merkhet shrugged. The girl must have been voicing her own concerns aloud. Once again, he laid down and shut off the world around him.

He snapped to alertness, knowing that he had

dozed and perhaps for longer than he should have. The sun was glaring high above him now. It must be time. Merkhet stood up, stretched his aching arms and legs, and headed down the slope. The royal chariot, distinguishable by its woven canopy and gold-rimmed wheels, awaited him. He was the last to arrive. After weathering the disappointment—a lecture on responsibility and punctuality from his father—he clambered into the back, and the chariot departed.

Huddled between Nekhet and Peronikh, they roared past the ibises that lurked on the Nile's banks. Weaving their way along the river's curves, their three-chariot convoy journeyed across the hardened surface where the dark mud kissed the red desert sand. As they raced along the uneven track, he was jolted into his brother. Mistake. Before he could protect himself, Merkhet suffered a rib-crushing elbow. The air was sucked from him, leaving him gasping for each breath, as if he had just sprinted the length of the Nile. Such was the life of the younger brother, at least this one.

'For Amun's sake, will you sit still! The next one will be twice as hard.'

'Peronikh, do not tempt the gods' wrath with your immoral speech,' his father said.

'Alright, alright.'

Their voices were distant—audible, even when competing with the river's steady flow and the chariots' rattling wheels—yet still distant.

'Are you even with us, Merk? Don't fret, your stubby fingers couldn't possibly fail you again.'

Worried that his hunting skills were lacking? Understatement of the Eighteenth Dynasty. Terrified, more like. Not for the afternoon's routine hunt but for the trial that awaited him on Ra's next solar rising. And who wouldn't be terrified when confronted with the prospect of taking down a four-thousand-pound hippopotamus? Strangely, that wasn't troubling him as much right now as it had done earlier. Instead, his mind kept drifting to a question, one to which he had no answer. Maybe there wasn't one.

'Father,' Merkhet said, ignoring Peronikh's taunt, 'can you please explain Ma'at to me?'

'Again? My poor baby brother must be desperate to avoid any consideration for his doomed trial.'

'I confess my surprise, Merkhet. As my most intelligent son —'

'I'm still here,' Peronikh muttered.

'We all have our strengths. And you will discover the full extent of mine should you interrupt me again.'

His brother mumbled something resembling an apology, averting his gaze as he grovelled. Their father was the only person who could strip away his confidence with such ease. Strong, handsome, assured, and Peronikh remembered birthdays—if only because of the trial and the torture he could inflict in its approach. No wonder everyone thought he was the perfect prince, the rightful heir to the Golden Throne. Why shouldn't they—the pretty noble girls lusted for him and the government officials sang their praises all the way from the administration precinct to the temple district.

However, Merkhet's mother was the Great Royal Wife, not Peronikh's.

Even as the younger brother, if Merkhet passed his trial tomorrow, he would be the next pharaoh. But when pitted against Peronikh, his fortune ended there.

Maybe that was for the best. The burden of ruling was unforgiving, unrelenting. It weighed heavy upon his father and would weigh even heavier upon him. Merkhet could happily fail to defeat the hippopotamus and fade into obscurity …

Except the shame of disappointing the pharaoh would be too great, and to cheat himself of an illustrious career as a diplomat, too unbearable.

'Sorry, Son, what were we speaking about?'

'Ma'at.'

'What would you hear of it?'

'How does it work?'

'If we are good—' his father said, pausing. 'Why do you concern yourself with such matters, anyway? It is the pharaoh's duty, *my* duty, to maintain Ma'at.'

'I don't.'

They didn't understand. A prince at the top of his royal classes yet Merkhet could not grasp the principles of Ma'at, the very foundation of their society. Why did the gods intervene in some matters and not others?

'Good. You have enough to prepare for without burdening yourself further. Focus on passing your trial. That starts with a hefty haul on today's hunt.'

'I will not let you down, Father. Thank you.'

Merkhet stared out at the limestone cliffs rising on his left, searching for the small, almost hidden, opening between the jutting precipices. A single untimely blink and he would miss the passageway that led into the Valley of the Kings, the burial ground of all past pharaohs. Would a mangled prince, who succumbed to the will of a rampaging hippopotamus, be laid to rest there, too?

A pair of royal guards, dressed in red, handled the

reins of their chariot as it clattered on. Before long, Merkhet was scouring the distant dunes for gazelles. Cradling his bow, moulded by the finest Egyptian craftsmen available, he willed one to appear. He traced its lone carving with his finger, as he did before every hunting expedition. His bow Horakhty—or *Horus on the Horizon*—was named so for the Eye of Horus that he etched into its wooden frame, granting him the favour and protection of the gods. He could never blame Horakhty for his own flaws. It was accurate, reliable.

'What is it with you and Horus, Merk?'

Embarrassed, he stopped mid-trace. 'Who better to watch over us than the all-seeing falcon god soaring across the skies above.'

'My brother the philosopher, how insightful! Reminds me, you will never believe what happened the other day.'

'Are you sure? Your brother once thought that mummified corpses were rising from beneath his bed.'

'Father! That was one time.'

'One time this harvest, maybe,' the pharaoh said.

Peronikh howled with laughter. A rare smirk even appeared from under the Double Crown of Egypt. The cobra figurine, attached to the front of the red and white striped head cloth, was poised ready to strike. His father's delayed chuckle meant the serpent did strike, repeatedly. Thick strands of his black ponytail, as dark as a starless night, escaped from beneath the crown and fell along the length of his spine.

'Well, are you going to tell us?' asked Merkhet.

'No.'

'Why—'

'Shh!' Peronikh gestured for quiet, determination

spreading on his olive-tanned face. 'Can't you hear that?'

Merkhet titled his head to listen. Nothing at first. Then a distant noise, faint and unclear, reached him. A yelp? No. Unmistakable this time, a high-pitched scream echoed across the valley. The royal guards instinctively slowed the chariot, turning to the pharaoh for guidance. Another shriek, more urgent now, hung in the air. Someone was in dire trouble.

His father commanded the guards to a halt, perhaps worried the chariot would become bogged if it strayed from the compact sand-mud. But Merkhet didn't hang around for any more instructions. Following Peronikh's lead, he jumped out of the slowing chariot. His chance had finally arrived—the moment he could prove to everyone he was ready for the Pharaonic Trial. His brother dashed ahead, and even though Merkhet pursued him with vigour, he did not catch him. Peronikh sped over the dune and out of sight.

Merkhet scrambled up the dune, his knee-length shirt impeding him, but not nearly as much as his swaying loincloth. Still, Merkhet narrowed in on the frenzied screams. At the peak, he launched himself down the far side, gliding on the slippery underside of his sandals. A girl lay on her back, struggling. From behind long messes of dark hair, she was frantically trying to fend off a small clan of hyenas. Even though she scuttled backwards, the savage beasts were ripping shreds in her dress and closing in on her exposed calves.

Stumbling out of the slide, Merkhet sprawled face-first into the desert's scorching surface. He wiped his face clear and regained his feet. He was rearing to enter the fray and remove himself from the enormous shadow of Peronikh's flawless aim. The hyenas, all four of them, were so fixated on the girl that he and his brother's arrival went unnoticed. Merkhet attempted to retrieve an arrow from the quiver draped over his back, but his fingers were clumsy, unresponsive.

The beasts continued to encircle the girl in a flurry of fang-bared snarls. Panicking now, he managed to grasp an arrow before a ghastly whimper caught hold of him. A hyena crumpled to the ground. Blood gushed from its snout and the fatal wound, where the arrow struck its head. Peronikh's arrow. Once again, his brother had beaten him to the opening kill. Disheartened but not defeated, Merkhet shook free the fleeting incapacity. He had to redeem himself. If not for the impending audience of his father, then for the girl.

The remaining beasts, now alert to the imminent threat the hunting party posed, abandoned the girl with a final menacing growl and lunged towards them. They snarled and snapped their jaws as they ran, signalling their lust for flesh. By the time the pharaoh arrived, the hyenas were already upon the princes. Merkhet crouched low as one of the beasts leapt at his face. He propped up Horakhty and turned his head, anticipating heavy impact.

When it didn't come, he chanced a glimpse between slitted eyes. The hyena's rotten, yellow teeth had locked onto his bow's frame—instead of his face—but barely inches from his fingers. Slimy spittle soaked him and seeped into his eyes, stinging them. But then there was the horrid stench. Soon the beast would devour his precious face, and his final memory would be of its vile carcass breath.

Praise Horus his bow's frame had lasted this long. The end was near though; Horakhty was starting to bend inward. Slowly to begin with, and then the strain intensified. It was almost about to snap when a stone thudded into the hyena's ribs. The beast whirled around. Confused, it unhinged its jaws from the bow. Merkhet seized his opportunity, snatching an arrow from his quiver and plunging it deep into the beast's neck. The arrow sank into soft flesh and warm blood bubbled around his clenched fist. The hyena fell, twitching in the sand next to him.

Panting and shaken, he let go of the arrow and dropped beside the felled beast, which was facing … the girl. Had she thrown the stone that saved his face from certain mutilation? What was she doing out here all by herself?

Merkhet didn't get a chance to ponder any further, his attention drawn to his brother and father. Peronikh was on the ground, unarmed, as a hyena sprung itself at him.

Farther away, Nekhet delivered a devastating blow with Thekla to the beast pestering him. It stood no chance against the might of the legendary golden war hammer. He transitioned from his prized weapon to his bow with ease, simultaneously firing two arrows. Merkhet admired the skill of his father, a trick he had yet to attempt, let alone master.

The arrows whizzed through the stifling desert air, both puncturing the throat of the hyena in mid-air. It crashed to the sand in a snout-first tumble. The creature gasped and wheezed, but its efforts were futile.

Nekhet appreciated his successful shot while a

sweaty, grateful Peronikh got back to his feet.

The hyena, pounded by Thekla, had somehow recovered. And it was angry. Furious.

'FATHER!' Merkhet bellowed. Quicker than he had ever done before, he plucked an arrow from his quiver, nocked it, and tugged on the bowstring until it was on the verge of snapping.

Lining up his shot, the string cut deep into his fingers. The hyena was almost upon his father—too late to heed the warning—and that was when Merkhet's dreadful battle nerves seized him. He delayed his release a fraction of a moment, but when he finally did, his elbow had slumped. The bowstring lurched forward, searing his inner forearm. The arrow whistled in the air, wedging in the beast's side, but not before its teeth had sunk into the tender flesh of the pharaoh's hamstring.

His father groaned in agony, dropping his bow beside him and withdrawing a dagger from his belt. He swiped backwards with the sharp blade. The dagger connected with the hyena's head, but not even its bony skull could repel his immense strength. The pharaoh pried its limp jaw from his leg and heaved the beast away, the blade still lodged in its head, forgotten.

Merkhet sprinted towards Nekhet, eyeing his bloodied leg. 'Father?'

'It's nothing,' he said, grimacing.

The hunting party collapsed around the pharaoh, exhausted and relieved. The mysterious girl joined them, her dress torn and tattered.

'What are you doing out here by yourself?' his father asked, half scolding, half enquiring into her wellbeing.

She didn't respond. She didn't even acknowledge them. The poor girl would not be venturing into the desert again anytime soon. If ever.

The guards appeared, puffing. 'Your Worship, we came as quick as we could. Are you hurt?'

'Never mind me. Did you stop to cast a line in the Nile?'

Merkhet had never seen six faces turn such a violent shade of red, a colour not too dissimilar to their uniform. They were just about to babble an excuse, but the pharaoh cut them off.

'Prepare the chariot for departure,' his father said. 'We will be with you in a moment.'

'Do you require any assistance, Your Worship?'

'No. Ready the chariots.'

The guards showed tremendous hustle—perhaps fearing the pharaoh's delayed wrath—disappearing much quicker than they had arrived.

'Well, young lady, what's it going to be?' his father asked, persisting.

Finally, she made eye contact and what eyes they were. The sweetest light blue, shimmering like an oasis amid an endless desert. Those sparkling spheres and the divine way they complemented her glowing pink-tinged skin. Even the sombre expression she wore reminded Merkhet of every Nile sunset he had ever seen. He couldn't look away.

'Th-th-thank you,' she said, before glancing downward again, sullen and withdrawn.

'At the very least, you must tell us where you live.'

She nodded, as if she was ready to speak, but she never got the chance.

A sudden outcry heralded an unwelcome arrival,

and a volley of arrows filled the sky. The first wave, some thirty arrows, thudded in a perfect straight line, twenty feet shy of them. When Merkhet looked up, the assailants were already fast approaching, somehow sprinting in their long black cloaks.

'Hittites!' his father cursed from the ground.

Their bone-chilling cries were worse than the legends gave them credit for. Merkhet was ready to deliver his final prayers as the pharaoh tried to get up but couldn't. After another failed attempt, he said, 'Take the girl. Retreat to the chariots.'

'We cannot leave you, Father,' Merkhet said, a tremble in his voice.

'Go, now!' the pharaoh bellowed, climbing to his haunches. 'We must protect our dynasty.'

'Peronikh should go, I will—'

'All of you! Now!'

Another wave of arrows landed, almost on top of them this time. But a forceful grip was already dragging Merkhet away. The rare show of courage he had mustered was useless. He wanted to break away from Peronikh and run back to his father. But he was unable.

Wet splotches started to blur his vision. He could only just make out the pharaoh, crouching on his knees as he drew two arrows. Fifty feet separated his father from the converging Hittites. Diving to avoid something, the Double Crown fell from his head. It tumbled across the sand, and then Merkhet lost sight of everything, swallowed by a swathe of red. Two royal guards whisked him over the sand dune and away from harm. His frenzied pleas to leave him and rescue his father were lost in the fabric of their uniforms.

Merkhet was forced into the back of the royal chariot with Peronikh and the girl. He was vaguely aware of the chariot gaining speed as his mind raced for a solution. The other guards *had* to be going to his father's aid. Would they be quick enough to save him from the marauders? The pharaoh was an elite hunter and warrior, and the royal guards were privileged to have undertaken rigorous military training, the best in all of Egypt. Maybe they could hold off the Hittites long enough to retreat.

By the time the chariot reached full-pelt, dreadful screams chased them down the Nile. Merkhet shivered. Five against thirty. What chance did the pharaoh and his guards stand? All Merkhet could do was stare at the Eye of Horus, silently pleading with the sky god.

The mystifying question burned anew.

Why did the gods intervene in some matters and not others?

Chapter 3

The Gongs of Sorrow reverberated around Thebes, keeping her awake all night. Pharaoh Nekhet was dead.

How Llora wished she'd possessed the courage to tell him of her family's woes—now she would be forever denied that chance.

Hugging herself tight, her chin dug into her knees. Numbing needles stabbed at Llora from the waist down. Unforgiving sunlight attacked her through the tiny slits between the mudbrick hut's walls and ceiling, ensuring that the sweet relief of slumber would continue to elude her. Yet she couldn't desert her reed sleeping mat. The safety of her family's home was all that remained.

Just one glance was it all took. Just one glance at that stained and tattered dress. Discarded on the ground, it had Llora reliving the most chilling day of her life. Was the blood hers, or the hyenas? Did that even matter?

Llora tried all morning to muster some sympathy for the murdered pharaoh. Something, anything. The heroic actions of him and his sons were the reason she was still alive. Actually, as far as the gods would be concerned, she had already repaid that debt. Llora had saved the chubby prince with a well-timed throw, and good fortune was destined to find her because of that.

But what gods, worthy of worship, would reward her with a little brother so famished that he could scarcely function?

Wuntu was eleven, growing fast. Hunger in a boy of his age was the worst of injustices. Their mother, Tiaa, toiled hard to receive their food allowance from the state. The menial work of harvesting wheat and corn provided them the barest of bread rations. It was seldom enough, and without a father to contribute, the strain fell on Llora.

Wanting to ease her family's pain, that was why she found herself in the desert. Well, and the other reason. She heard the officials coming—Laseb didn't. She didn't get a chance to warn him, either. All she could do was escape and run. It wasn't until a pack of hyenas surrounded her, that Llora noticed where she was. Thankfully, her mother and brother knew nothing of the misery of the day before. It was better that way.

They had enough on their plates, without having her problems added to theirs. Llora shivered, a dagger of ice clawing its way down her spine and sending sharp tingles through her legs. Her family rarely had anything on their plates.

Following her reckless scamper through the desert, the hours blended together, but Laseb's detainment stayed with her. The torment didn't ease through the night. His face and voice were everywhere. Eyes shut, hands jammed across her ears. Nothing made any difference. His accusing stare continued to haunt her.

Laseb was far from innocent though. He was all too eager to trade any goods that made their way into his greasy palms. Knowing he would have done the exact same as her, given the chance, did little to stifle her rising uneasiness. Still, why should she wither away in hiding?

Entering Thebes' bustling market district—wearing her only remaining dress—everything hit her at once. The sweet, sweet hum of hundreds and hundreds of trades.

Food was the most exchanged good, but far from the only. There was also makeup for the vain, so pungent it seeped into your dress and hair; exotic vases for the lavish, painted in bright dyes and of all different sizes; potent alcohol for the drunkards; foreign cured meats; idols and amulets of the gods; and clothes and garments for all trades and classes.

The market district was much busier than usual, as many people were trading the necessary ritual accessories that would assist Pharaoh Nekhet in reaching the Afterlife. With great thanks to the swarms of those pious mourners, they afforded her the perfect cover to skip along the inner market lanes. After a halting moment of weakness, where a black dress with the most striking golden embroidery caught her eye,

Llora reminded herself of why she was there.

A pretty dress wouldn't provide for her family, but Egypt's finest jewellery would. She didn't *like* stealing, and it wasn't as if the thrill of theft sent Llora into a blissful romp, where everything else seemed trivial, unimportant. The jewellery taunted her, dangling on display in the various market stalls, sparkling and gleaming.

Llora made sure that she smiled at all the merchants as she passed them. The deviants were quite happy to scan the full scope of her goods without paying. So why couldn't she—*why shouldn't she*—return the favour? Was there truly a difference between browsing and sampling?

Over time, she discovered the trick was to always be moving, distracting the merchants and citizens as she went. A wave with one hand could cleverly disguise a swipe with the other. She learnt this quickly—had to—after a few too many risky encounters. If she kept herself busy, they wouldn't notice her devious, wandering hands. Her routine was simple: skip, skip, smile, skip, wave, *snatch*, wave, *conceal*, skip, skip. Then just keep on skipping.

After the first wave, one rather stocky merchant returned the gesture, and Llora sprung back half a step in surprise, just as she was readying to make her snatch.

'Not you, girl,' he said. 'It's always me, me, me with you young ones, isn't it?'

Twisting around, she could see a lady waving at the merchant. How dare he accuse her of being self-absorbed. The nerve of the man and his terrible timing. What could he know, sitting behind his stall all day and trading jewellery at extortionate rates? Llora would target him another time. Would serve him right for his snide manner. One final glare at the rude merchant, and she skulked down the alley.

As Llora made for her second attempt at a first snatch, her heart was thumping hard against her chest, but she composed herself, steadying her breathing. Her hand was just about closed around the most magnificent emerald encrusted necklace—

'Desert girl! Desert girl!'

The husky voice came from behind her. A voice she recognised. One she had encountered recently, in the heat of the desert. Shocked, Llora recoiled, tucking her outstretched hand awkwardly at her side. Pivoting on the spot, a young bare-chested man came bounding over to her. Not just any young man, either. Peronikh. A name she'd learnt in the course of yesterday's traumatic afternoon, courtesy of the exchanges between the distressed princes in the retreating chariot.

'It is you,' he said, smiling. Peronikh stepped forward, away from his escort of guards. 'I knew it was! What are you doing here?'

'Same as everyone else.'

'Oh, right, stocking up for the rituals—' He trailed away, as if he had forgotten all about his father's death. Pain briefly flickered across his handsome face. But it was not weary and dishevelled, as her own must surely be. How had he managed to sleep?

'Sorry,' she said. 'I didn't mean to.'

'I know you didn't. Listen, Llora, what are you doing tomorrow?'

'I'm not sure. Wait, how do you know my—'

'Come to my coronation banquet. The viziers have

decided that I will ascend the throne tomorrow after attuning myself with the needs of the city.'

Llora could sense her face flushing. She would need to say something quickly. Yet, still, she pondered. What reason could the prince have for wanting her, a humble girl from the peasant villages, to appear at his banquet? 'But what about your father's funerary preparations?'

'The Hittites will vanquish Thebes if we wait the customary seventy days, not stopping until there is nothing left but mudbrick and limestone ruins. You know, it was fortunate that both viziers were here to witness what would've been Merkhet's Pharaonic Trial today and could decide on a swift course of action. I'll see you at the feast then.'

'Yeah, sure,' she said, not wanting to harp on about his father. 'Where is it?'

'Base of the royal palace. Sundown.'

'I'll see you—'

Peronikh was already gone. When Llora was certain he would not make a sudden reappearance, she cleared her mind and started over. Third time's a charm, people often said. She would see.

Weaving her way through the crowded market lane, she reached its end in what must have been a new record. Hiding in plain sight, she made four snatches without arousing any suspicion, and the troubles of the desert and her survivor guilt were fading fast.

Llora couldn't wait to exchange the necklaces and rings. She would need to find somewhere new in the villages to trade the valuables though. None of the merchants at the markets would deal with her. Despite that, Llora could feel her cheeks stretching, an odd and rare sensation. She was smiling again, brimming with energy, almost as if she were exuding happiness from her pores.

She bounced down the nearest alleyway—almost out of the market district—when a hand grabbed her on the shoulder, jerking her to a jarring standstill.

'Where do you think you are going, young lady?' a masculine voice demanded in her ear.

'Uh …' Llora swivelled around to a shadowy face, concealed beneath the hood of a dark cloak. 'Home. I'm going home.'

'That's rather interesting, Llora,' he said.

The man wrapped his hands around her mouth as quick as a viper strike and dragged her from the alley into an abandoned hovel. Llora screamed and screamed, but no good came of it. His brutish hands muffled her cries. As she tried to wriggle her way to freedom, she was distracted by the overbearing spices invading her nostrils.

Remembering her situation, Llora kicked and squirmed. But the man was too strong, the cinnamon strangely soothing, and …

He also knew her name.

Chapter 4

After what endured to be the most depressing birthday, Merkhet could be thankful for one thing. The burden was Peronikh's, not his.

Watching the citizens pour into the administration precinct, he was overcome with the biggest relieving sigh of his life. Then the instant crippling guilt stripped him bare of his gratitude. Why his father, why now?

The Thebans were gathering between the many government buildings that lined the open, paved space. The square—where agricultural, economic, civic, and architectural matters were decided—had attracted thousands. People of all trades and class were present, wishing to witness the inbound pharaoh commence his reign. Weary labourers, delighted for an interruption to their immense schedule; meticulous scribes, thankful to record a new era of Egyptian history; and artisans, eager to complete the construction of his father's tomb and sarcophagus.

Tired and bleary eyes were rare among them. Not many furrows. Few bore the dejected demeanour that smothered his own face. Instead, they merrily chirped to one another. Other than his mother, who could scarcely dress or feed herself, it seemed one day of mourning was enough for the rest of them. A day that had been reserved for Merkhet's trial, which could never happen now.

The royal chariot arrived, Abacca and Tendrence easing to a gentle trot before stopping near the altar. Peronikh disembarked the chariot—accompanied by his mother, Samena—smiling and waving at the crowd.

Merkhet trembled with rage. His brother was no different than the Theban citizens. Nekhet, the Third Pharaoh of the Eighteenth Dynasty, may as well have already been mummified and sealed in his tomb for all anyone cared.

Giving Samena a peck on the cheek, Peronikh made his way onto the tiered altar. He should have been nervous, but he didn't appear to resemble anything of the sort. Calm and collected in his white ceremonial robe, he ascended the sandstone steps and joined the viziers. Lufu and Prahmun were also dressed in white robes. However, silver feathers around their necks—the Amulet of Ma'at—distinguished them.

From his vantage point beside the altar, Merkhet watched the proceedings. Everyone was awaiting the start of the Walking of the Walls, where the gods would accept, or deny, Peronikh's claim to the Golden Throne.

His brother stood resolute between the viziers. Without doubt, Peronikh would retain the services of their father's loyal advisers. Any state task could be delegated to them, and his brother would thrive under those conditions. The viziers' already haggard faces were not fated to improve anytime soon.

Prahmun—Vizier of Upper Egypt—managed tax collection, food distribution, and the empire's various constructions and water sources. Merkhet didn't know much about the role of Lufu, the other adviser. Having only met him once before, the prince understood he was a dear childhood friend of his father. Lufu resided in Memphis and handled matters in Lower Egypt, whatever those were. With their assistance, the pharaoh was free to oversee the judicial and military arrangements in Thebes.

Raina, one of Egypt's most talented scribes, was also on the flat platform being used to initiate the ceremony. Many believed she was a gift from Thoth, the god of knowledge and writing. Lurking in the corner, with her trusty scribal kit slung over her shoulder, Raina's reed pen flicked up and down in smooth, entrancing movements as she recorded the events on a papyrus scroll. Her words were every bit as compelling as those of his grandfather.

She was a female excelling in a profession reserved for noble men, and her proficiency in the art had begun to change that perception. Raina had eclipsed even his own progress as a scribe. Strangely, Merkhet had never heard her talk. Observing the world through her keen hazel eyes, maybe no one had ever heard her speak. But the way in which she crafted her words with such compelling elegance and lavish detail, what could she possibly have left to say?

Lufu addressed the gathered crowd, his voice loud and clear. 'Nekhet, the Tireless Warrior-Builder, has left us for the Fields of Paradise. However, before the coronation of Peronikh can become official, he must face another test—the Walking of the Walls. May the gods imbue the esteemed son of our resting pharaoh with their divine will and all-knowing judgement.'

The crowd listened, a great hush cast over them. Merkhet's legs tingled, as if he were the one about to undertake the ceremonial walk.

'During this rite,' Prahmun announced, 'Peronikh must skirt the city walls, becoming one with the needs of our lands and people. Only then will the gods accept him as the rightful—'

'Stop!' a robed man shouted from the edge of the altar. The High Priest of Amun approached Peronikh and the viziers, speaking for all to hear. 'In the name of Amun, the King of the Gods and the God of the Winds, this ceremony must not proceed.'

'What is the meaning of this?' Lufu asked the priest.

'A terrible mistake is about to occur. The wrong prince stands before you.'

Merkhet stiffened, his throat contracting so quick that the sides rasped together.

'If you continue talking, something terrible will occur,' Peronikh snarled.

Silence enveloped the administration precinct. The altar and crowd alike were reduced to a hush.

'We cannot dismiss the High Priest of Amun so hastily,' Prahmun said, signalling for calm with open hands. 'But we will require you to clarify your statement.'

The priest, weary with wrinkles, bowed before Prahmun and Lufu. He stooped as low as his frail frame would allow him and much longer than necessary, almost as if he was enjoying his own theatrics. Merkhet was still struggling to breathe, and Peronikh's fingers instinctively twitched at his side, searching for a weapon. But his brother did not latch on to one because there wasn't one there. The priest could be appreciative of that. Peronikh would gut him in a second, reddening the white robe and leopard skin shawl that clung to his figure.

'The gods work in mysterious ways, none more so than the glorious hidden one, Amun. I have received a vision from him, praise him in his greatness. Amun the hidden, Amun the pure, hear us! He has informed me, his most faithful servant, that Merkhet must be crowned Pharaoh of Egypt.'

'Who will entertain such ravings? My brother is sixteen and has not passed his Pharaonic Trial. I have. I am to be pharaoh. Guards, remove the priest at once!'

'Enough, Peronikh.' Lufu cautioned him.

'But—'

'Enough, I said.'

Merkhet spotted Raina, furiously scribbling the unfolding events. So very lucky Peronikh's sword was in the palace. Lufu whispered in his brother's ear. Peronikh said nothing, but the toxic red fury that consumed his face, spoke for him. He charged off the altar, blazing into the back of the chariot, which departed promptly.

Lufu informed the thronging crowd that the senior administrators must confer at once; a new pharaoh could not be initiated until they had clarity. Then he, Prahmun, and the High Priest shuffled from the sandstone platform themselves. The crowd parted for them as they disappeared into the viziers' quarters for further discussions. What decision would they arrive at? When would they make it?

Merkhet's deprived lungs forced him to inhale, and he did so, deeply. First, the gods had taken his father, and now, they were conspiring again to place him upon the throne he'd sworn off since the day he could think for himself.

It couldn't happen. He refused to believe the gods could be so cruel.

Chapter 5

What were the gods thinking? Merkhet didn't want to be pharaoh.

The High Priest should have known better than to intervene. It all had to be some grand misunderstanding. Maybe a cruel joke, orchestrated by his brother, who was waiting patiently for Merkhet to accept it, so that he could rip it away from him in some horrible display of public humiliation. That did seem to align with Peronikh's unusual sense of humour. Yet, the viziers—after lengthy consultation with the priest— were adamant of their decision.

Just as soon as the preparations could be arranged, Merkhet would become the first pharaoh to grace the Golden Throne without ever having completed the

Pharaonic Trial.

But he couldn't rule Egypt, not after his failure resulted in his father being bitten and then …

Merkhet stared at his forearm, where the bowstring had lashed him in the desert. The braziers flickered, and each time they did, the angry red splotch was illuminated in orange. It wept. Just like he did, and had done, ever since he was escorted back to the royal palace after that harrowing hunt. But it didn't matter. He would not remain in Thebes much longer. A city of a hundred gates and all of them were screaming at him to leave.

The true hurt befell him—not in the scorching desert—but when the throne gleamed at him in the tormenting hours that ensued. Thekla and the crown lay discarded at its base, having somehow been retrieved during the ambush. They reminded him all too well of the usual vibrancy and purpose that resided there.

Holding his beloved Horakhty in one hand, Merkhet rummaged through his leather travel bag, shifting aside a hardened bread stick. After placing a bulging water skin inside, he tightened the bag's flax strap and slung it over his shoulder. Behind the throne, the hieroglyphic dedication to Bastet, the goddess aligned with protecting the pharaoh, caught his eye. Maybe she had shirked her duties in the desert, or was it that Osiris could not be cheated from claiming his victims?

Still, the question that could not be answered, bothered him the most. Why did the gods intervene in some matters and not others? They had no objection to convincing the Amun High Priest of Merkhet's obligation to the throne. But when it came to preventing the death of his father, where were they?

The hieroglyphs featured Bastet in her most common depiction: a gentle woman with the head of a cat. Right on cue, Beebee brushed against his leg, meowing. No one knew the cat's true origins, but Nekhet had always expressed his suspicions. Supposedly, the day the royal palace's construction was finished, Beebee appeared. She seldom ventured out of the throne room, and even rarer did she leave the unknown wonders of her slumber. As common as her markings were, Beebee was no ordinary black cat with a patchy white underside. His father was adamant that she was a gift from the gods, the physical spirit of Bastet. Timeless and unaffected by the years, she had been Pharaoh Nekhet's personal guardian.

Had. Merkhet exhaled, long and heavy. He gave Beebee the best reassuring pat he could muster for the loyal feline had not eaten or slept since …

He had to leave. One final scan of the room—absorbing the hieroglyphic scenes that detailed his father's greatest conquests; his war table, where he planned his famous victories; his crown and prized war hammer; and the bare throne itself. Then he left.

Striding through the courtyard, Merkhet brushed his hand against the acacia's furry bark trunk and whispered goodbye to the palace. Another of his father's achievements. The guards on duty did not question his descent, or his intentions. If it weren't for his bow and travel bag, he could easily be mistaken for a grieving prince, needing some fresh air and a long walk.

Exiting the walled complex, Merkhet looped

around its base and set his course for the royal stables. The city's paths were eerily quiet. Walking past the harem village, where Peronikh lived, he neared the stables. Tethered in their stalls, most of the horses were faring poorly after a recent escalation with the Hyksos forces. Urged beyond their limits, now they required nurturing. Merkhet was glad to tend to them. He didn't even take off his travel bag, just placed his bow on the ground and begun treatment. One final gesture before he would leave Egypt forever.

Usually, Merkhet would assist the overwhelmed stable master between the strict schedule of his royal education. He would miss diplomacy, writing, foreign languages, charioteering, astrology. The ever-tedious geometry class, which even the aspiring architects loathed at times, too. Especially, since all studies were denied to him in the lead up to his Pharaonic Trial. If Merkhet ascended the throne, as was expected of him, it would remain that way. Egypt, the country he loved as dear as his own family, would never be the same for him again.

He settled on treating his own mare, Abacca. Even though she escaped the Hittite ambush without injury, some of her earlier wounds and cuts required attention. 'There, there,' he said, dabbing a stubborn wound near her back-left hoof with water from the Nile.

'My friend, where are you going with that bag?'

Merkhet stopped dabbing and turned around. Taharva stood before him, wearing the royal guard red, which was very red against his barren, scarred scalp. The colossus Nubian's voice matched his appearance, rugged and powerful. Yet somehow, it also radiated calmness. The prince didn't want comforting though.

He wanted to disappear.

All *that* eternal evening, after the Hittite marauders had come, the Gongs of Sorrow banged incessantly. Each emphatic chime penetrated his mind, ensuring that he would never forget. Could never forget.

Gong!

His father was dead.

Gong!

The pharaoh would be embarking on a perilous journey to the Afterlife, *alone*.

Gong!

It was all Merkhet's fault!

In the aftermath of the gongs, the days and nights jumbled together. But their resounding clamour never left him, even when Merkhet tried to sleep. Especially, when he tried to sleep. How long had it been? Three days, four?

The tears came in waves of sobs. His guilt ebbed and flowed with the hours, yet one constant stayed with him: the injustice. How could the gods will the pharaoh's death, allow it to happen? Where was the justice of Ma'at?

'Did you hear me, boy? Set down that pack of yours.'

When the prince looked up to meet the gentle giant's warm eyes, they tore away the shroud of anger that surrounded him. His resolve softened but not enough for him to put down his bag. Merkhet could not deny him. Taharva had guided him on as many, if not more, occasions as his father had. Once they had scoured their way through the Nubian lands together, with Peronikh, in search of a lion cub. A harrowing conclusion to that quest meant Merkhet was sometimes tentative and wistful around Abacca. Despite those memories stirring, he would give the Captain of the Royal Guard a chance.

Merkhet stood up. 'Ma'at,' he said, his voice low and wispy, full of anguish.

'What of it?'

'How could he be taken from us?'

'I don't know.'

'You must,' Merkhet said.

'I do not. If we are good, the gods bless us with the life-giving flood, steer the plagues away, and provide us with strength to defend our lands.'

'If we can't appease them—what happens then? They allow our enemies to murder the pharaoh?'

'No, the gods cannot control our enemies. If order is not maintained, Ra would stop his daily journey on the solar barge and the sun would vanish. Hapi, the river guardian, would deny us the flood and the crops would wither.'

'I didn't even get the chance to meet all of my siblings. Who knows where they are, who they are? It's not fair. I'm leaving!'

'Without saying goodbye to your mother?'

'What other choice do I have?'

'May I speak my mind?' Taharva asked, rubbing the inside of his wrist.

'Please stop letting that ghastly hunting bow scar undermine you. I don't care for your slavery status. My father may have tainted you with his horrid seal, but he also trusted you as our family's protector. I trust you, too.'

Taharva stopped, bowing. 'Where are you headed then, Scrollworm?'

'Anywhere but here. How can I show my face around Thebes? I'm the reason he's dead.'

'How can you say that?'

'Because it's true!' Fresh tears welled in the corners of Merkhet's eyes. 'I faltered. And the hyena bit him.'

'I wasn't there, and I will bear that thorn for as long as I live,' Taharva said, his voice tinged with sadness yet still soothing. 'But I've heard the reports from the charioteers themselves. A hyena didn't kill your father, the Hittites did. We could not have anticipated an attack so soon after we'd just repelled the Hyksos.'

'Then why were the Hittites able to swarm us? I didn't take down the hyena, that's why! If I did, we would have already been feasting on their rugged, stringy meat in the palace halls.'

'Listen and listen well.' Taharva paused, long enough for Merkhet to wipe his linen top across the bridge of his nose, soaking up his tears. 'Your self-pity,' the Nubian said, 'is the most disrespectful way to mourn. You cannot blame yourself. You already said it, our enemies murdered your father. It is time you let Mura go.'

'W-wh-what of her?' Merkhet choked, thinking back on that wonderful white horse.

'That was nothing more than an error of judgement, yet it follows you everywhere. The indecision. The unease. We are not in Nubia anymore.'

'But—'

'Discard your *buts*. All of them. They will not serve you well as pharaoh.'

'I don't care for the throne. I was set to follow in my grandfather's tread and travel the world as a diplomat.'

'Don't you want your father's legacy to be fulfilled?'

Merkhet stifled a sniffle. 'Of course, I do, but—'

'But what, my prince? The pharaoh is the country's most influential diplomat.'

'All I care about is making my father proud.'

'He already is, but I know you will not hear it now. Command Egypt yourself and make damn sure of it.'

'I miss him so much,' Merkhet said.

'Pharaoh Nekhet is watching over you. He will be watching all of us.'

'Do you really think so?'

'Yes.'

Merkhet went quiet. The hollowness from his chest receded a little. Not completely, but enough for him to set down his bag, with the immediate intention of leaving Thebes gone.

'But you must grieve first,' Taharva said. 'When you are ready, we will begin your real training.'

Merkhet nodded.

'Go now to your mother. Comfort her. Be the strong son she needs. Be the pharaoh Egypt needs.'

Chapter 6

Merkhet reeled out of days of endless contemplation, dizzy and uncertain. He came to as he was assisted, by a chatty pair of servant girls, into his pure white ceremonial robe.

One week after his father's death, they were readying him to ascend the Golden Throne. But was he ready? He wanted to convince himself more than anything that he was, but his clammy hands said otherwise.

The royal makeup artists came bustling in next and began to fuss over his appearance. They were delighted to be back in work after Pharaoh Nekhet had long refused their trade. Padding and dabbing, they buried him under several powdered layers of kohl, until his face matched his mood. Irritated. After what seemed longer than the agonising prelude to his abandoned trial, they departed. At least the robe was comfortable, maybe the freshest fabric that had ever graced his skin, and it soothed him. Soon, he would be sworn in as the Fourth Pharaoh of the Eighteenth Dynasty.

The chariot transported him to the administration precinct, but from that moment on, the ceremony's introduction was a haze. Merkhet didn't hear either of the viziers address the crowd. The square was not teeming, as it had been for Peronikh. Looking around, only a few hundred faces stared back at him, and all of them were his father's. The pharaoh's stern expression pierced him from the bodies of children, men, and women alike.

Merkhet didn't regather his senses until Lufu tapped him on the shoulder. Confused, he stepped down from the altar, where his brother had stood only days earlier, and which now seemed as high as the Great Pyramid of Giza. The atmosphere was tense, hanging heavy in the air. Merkhet could almost taste the sweaty apprehension of those gathered. They were braving the heat for a second time, courtesy of the High Priest's disruption.

The Walking of the Walls—where legend had it that a man became a god, living and ruling on their behalf. But the tales never spoke of boys—did they become gods?

Taking care not to stumble over his white robe with each stride, another unhelpful, irrational thought struck him. The sand would part and swallow him whole for cheating his way to the throne. Instantly, his steps became laboured as he plodded along. The crowd followed him out of the administration precinct, but maintained their distance, mindful of his solitary fulfilment. Exiting through the main gate facing the river, he walked a few paces, then turned around to face Thebes. Filing along the ramparts, the crowd clustered at interval viewpoints to watch the proceedings. He saw Peronikh among them, disbelief and dejection smeared across his face, as if he were eating something sour.

At a time when all Merkhet craved was the space to grieve and to comfort his mother, instead, he was pressured by the administration to act. He had not even passed his Pharaonic Trial, but they would not hear his appeals. Of a hundred different fates drawn before him in the sands, Merkhet would never choose this one. Why would the gods intervene when they never had before? The High Priest had to be mistaken.

That all-consuming helplessness, that horrible feeling you get when you are certain there is no way to win, stayed with Merkhet as he commenced the ceremonial rite. Before he could even tread past the first gate, new doubts surfaced. Would the gods imbue him with their powers? He could not know for sure. But he had to try and establish a connection with them. He slowed his breathing to focus on opening the deep, hidden recesses of his mind. Nothing, not yet.

Could he possibly live up to the greatness of his father? A tactician, a leader, a warrior. Merkhet possessed none of those traits, at least not in their entirety or with enough conviction to rule a country. Already halfway around the walls of Thebes, he pleaded with the gods for guidance. A sign, anything, to let him know he was following the path of his true destiny. His call went unanswered and discouragement blossomed in the form of a bitter truth at the pit of his stomach, heavy and unrelenting. His brother's footprints should be paving their way around the city. He was the obvious choice to lead Egypt. Confident in mind and powerful in body, Peronikh had the mettle of a gallant pharaoh.

Merkhet walked and walked. Nearing the hundredth gate, a sudden, blustery gust surrounded him. His feet were riveted. His arms and legs tingled as a strange mix of cold and warmth spread over him. The wind whirled and whirled around him, lifting his body until he was supported by just the tips of his toes. But as quick as the gust had come, it released him, and he landed flat on his feet. Staring down at his hands in awe—had he just received the blessing of the gods? What else could explain such a strange occurrence?

Speaking to only the air, the sand, and the gods themselves, Merkhet said, 'Thank you. I will maintain Ma'at, as all the pharaohs before me have done. I will protect Egypt from harm and never put myself above my country or its continued prosperity.'

Giddy, Merkhet rushed on. He was eager to report his mysterious encounter with the gods to the viziers and vowed to train with Taharva, the real training that the Nubian promised him.

Around the last corner, the citizens gathered outside the city gate, buzzing with the mind-numbing drone of ten thousand cicadas. But rather than greeting him, they faced Thebes. Merkhet pushed through their ranks. He stopped so abruptly the hem of his robe caught beneath his sandals, and he almost tripped. A large hieratic scrawl confronted him. Its message, written large and red, dominated the wall just beside the gateway.

With Ma'at's blessing, the Cursed Pharaoh will rise, unleashing chaos upon Egypt.

When the Thebans eventually noticed his presence among them, the chattering crowd dispersed. Snippets of their whispers reached him. *A prophecy. The Cursed Pharaoh.*

Merkhet, motionless, was on the verge of faltering. He had just completed the Walking of the Walls, where the gods connected with him, accepting him as their living embodiment. His coronation banquet awaited him. Yet how could he celebrate when unknown people were already conspiring against his reign?

Ruling Egypt would not be easy. The role would have its challenges. He was already expecting that. But this, and so soon …

Merkhet pleaded to the gods and his father for strength, for courage. Where else would he find the confidence to be decisive and defiant in the face of such oppressive evil?

Chapter 7

Thebes was awash with chatter about pharaonic prophecies and curses. Llora caught wind of all this — and more — without even leaving her village.

She had been too afraid to venture out anyway. The vile man from the markets could be waiting for her anywhere. Llora wanted to ignore what happened in that shady hovel, just off the alley. But she couldn't.

So what — he knew her name — what were the chances of him finding her again in a bustling city like Thebes? If the man did report her to the administration, Llora would join Laseb at the Judgements. The gods would deem her guilty and a fatal stoning would be one of the least brutal punishments she could wish for.

But she also couldn't spend the rest of her days confined to the villages, living in constant fear.

Llora approached the base of the royal palace, where the feast was prepared on a hardened plateau. Soldiers and royal guards formed a perimeter around the festivities, and between them, braziers were pitched in the ground. An unfamiliar nausea lurked within her. What was she even doing here, mixing with the Egyptian nobles and administrative officials? Besides, Peronikh invited her, not his brother. Would her name even be on the list? She doubted it.

'Excuse me. Hey, young lady, are you in the line?'

The man, possibly part of the administration, was polite enough, gesturing for her to join the queue into the festivities. Llora, irritated that she was so oblivious to her surroundings, quickly returned a forced smile, and then shuffled in behind a couple.

She had to try her luck—just in case Peronikh was there. He may not even attend, not after his public shaming. Llora couldn't blame him if he was hiding, but she hoped it wasn't so as the queue dwindled in front of her.

'Name?' the royal guard asked her when she reached the front.

'Llora,' she said, hoping she would be saved the indignity of being turned away.

The man ruffled through several papyri sheafs, before saying, 'Proceed.'

She did as the official commanded, stepping into the life of the lavish and luxurious. An entire world away from the stale bread she knew, were overstocked platters of assorted breads, local fish, meats from distant lands, and overflowing bowls of vegetables.

These lined the banquet tables and the guests lined up to sample them.

By the time Llora was done drooling, most guests were already seated. She skirted around many of the tables, planting herself on a free bench farthest from the royal table. Even from a distance, the aromas converged together in a harmony that drew her into a salivating romp. No one at her table bothered to speak to her, which suited Llora just fine.

Enormous pots of beer were strewn every few steps around the inner perimeter and clay flagons of red wine were scattered among the feast. Everyone was catered for. Lack of food or drink would not be a dilemma this evening. As the feast was on the brink of capacity, the sun's dying rays languished across the land. All seats were filled except for one—the pharaoh's. A persistent clinking, which rang out from the royal table, grew louder with each clink, until all the laughter and conversations quietened.

'Thank you, everyone,' the grey-haired vizier said. 'I won't take much of your time. I thought it would be fitting to truly welcome our new pharaoh. In many ways, Merkhet reminds me of his father, my dear, departed friend, Nekhet. In others, he is his own man. Because of this, I know we are in safe hands. May he rule with the interests of Egypt always before his own and with the guidance of the gods above.'

The vizier finished his short speech, raising his mug high above his head. 'To Merkhet!'

Everyone mimicked him and began a cheerful chorus in honour of the new pharaoh. 'Merkhet! Merkhet! Merkhet!' they chanted.

Merkhet descended from the peak of the palace,

dressed in a white robe. A hushed stillness lay over the feast. Everyone craned to see him—the Fourth Pharaoh of the Eighteenth Dynasty—while Llora searched for Peronikh. Where was he?

Merkhet lumbered into the banquet, and the crowd gasped and muttered. His head was clean shaven. The dark and fluffy tufts were gone. He looked strange—what was the pharaoh thinking? Lingering at the head of the main table, a miserable woman was behind him. By the look of her sunken cheeks and heavy eyelids, she was probably his mother, grieving the loss of her husband.

The viziers stood either side of the pharaoh. The older one held up the Double Crown of Egypt, placing it atop Merkhet's head. The other displayed an Eye of Horus insignia of some sort, handing it to Merkhet. Llora didn't know what the seal was for, but both acts were met with resounding cheers.

Then the crowd broke into rapturous applause. 'All hail, Pharaoh Merkhet!'

Merkhet, shadows surrounding his eyes, straightened himself in preparation to speak. He gestured for the crowd to settle, but the pharaoh was swaying on the spot. He removed the Double Crown. 'Th-th-thank you. Thank you all for coming,' the pharaoh managed. 'May the gods bestow you all with good fortune.'

The crowd clapped for him. Would they have clapped louder for Peronikh? Where was he? She still couldn't see him.

'I—' Merkhet faltered. 'I wi-wish that this moment had not come so soon, but I assure you that I am ready for the challenge. How many of you here, saw the *prophecy* outside the city walls today?'

Murmurs spread through the banquet.

'Forget it. For during the Walking of the Walls, the gods connected with me. I am honoured to announce that they have accepted me as Pharaoh of Egypt, the fourth of the Eighteenth Dynasty. I repay them with a declaration of my commitment to maintain Ma'at.'

Unease spread across Merkhet's face as he forged on, 'I am dedicated to continuing the work of my father. Rest assured, the Egyptian Empire will continue to flourish. Our emboldened enemies will cower beneath our will once again.'

More applause, thunderous this time.

'I know that all this and more will be possible with Lufu, Prahmun, and the rest of the administration at my side. But for now, enjoy the food and drink on offer. Go forth, be merry!'

'Merkhet!' the crowd praised in unison.

As the last chant bounced off the surrounding valley dunes, the attendees bowed before the pharaoh and the harpists began to pluck their strings. Their sweet melody enchanted the celebration, and the banquet sprang to life. Beer flowed from the pots and wine from the flagons. The guests consumed them in rapid succession, not afraid to pounce on the platters, either. Social celebrations of this calibre were rare, and it seemed the Theban nobility were eager to forget the uncertainty the prophecy had sparked.

Besides a chance to see Peronikh, there was another reason she attended a banquet full of nobles: the mounds of food begging to be eaten and possibly even stolen. Guilt-free theft—what more could a girl and her hungry family ask for?

No one else was near Llora, the guests all swaying to the flute's jovial tune. She grabbed handfuls of fruit and vegetables, hiding them beneath her undergarments. She found it hard not to scold herself. If Llora had just had the sense and foresight to wait for these celebrations rather than getting caught thieving at the markets. When she feared she might be mistaken for a lady late into her pregnancy, a voice startled her.

'How good it is to see you again, Llora. As busy as ever, I see.'

A familiar voice, but it didn't warm her, not as a friend's might. A tall man faced her, and he was shrouded by the same dark hood. The faint outline of his cadaverous cheeks was both distracting and alarming.

Oh, no. Not again. Llora wanted to run, but she was rooted to the spot. Causing a scene at an official event was rather low on her priorities. Did no one else object to a man concealing his identity at a private banquet, such as this?

'Your hair looks immaculate tonight,' he said. 'Not bad for a girl hailing from the peasant villages.'

Llora swallowed hard, but the air caught in her throat. He knew her name, and he knew where she lived. How?

'Can I help you?'

'We had an agreement, young lady. Are you so quick to forget our arrangement?'

'My memory is a little hazy,' she said.

'No, my dear girl, your memory is just fine. We only bumped into each other a few days ago at the markets.' His cackle echoed in her ears. 'Come closer. Where do you think you are going? I told you I would find you.'

Nowhere. She was going nowhere. She couldn't move—fear gripped her. The man found her, just like he promised he would. What else was he capable of?

'I can have you sentenced to death for your crimes. What do you think Pharaoh Merkhet would make of your misdeeds?'

'Maybe we'll solve that mystery, and I will tell him myself. Death would be a lesser punishment than staring at your vile hidden face any longer!'

'How feisty you are. But enough of this play. Do you recall our agreement yet?'

Llora nodded, the muscles in her neck betraying her. 'I've not had a chance to speak with him.'

'Nonsense. You've had ample time to act. You had no objections when the elder prince was set to be crowned pharaoh.'

She didn't respond. Her silence said everything. Of course, she was happy to distract the handsome pharaoh and avoid being stoned to death for her cooperation. Except now the handsome prince wasn't the pharaoh. It was his brother.

'I knew it,' he said, unable to contain his smugness, which spread the width of his face. 'I was right to assume you would require more convincing.'

'Excuse me?'

'You will do exactly as I say.'

'Why should I?'

'Are you so unworldly to believe that a pharaoh can be ambushed on the outskirts of their very own capital? This is far bigger than you, a paltry village girl.'

Llora sunk inside herself, the desire to defy him diminishing. Who was she dealing with, and why couldn't he have at least one discerning feature? Something that could identify him from the thousands of others in Thebes with a similar build. A limp, a hunch. Anything. She was ready to give up right then, but the man had other ideas, holding up an object in his hand. A weathered toy lion. He took one massive stride towards her, placing it in her hands. She flipped the toy over, searching for the carved symbol. Not that she needed to. Llora would recognise that lion anywhere.

Her heart plummeted. *His* symbol was there, carved exactly as she remembered it.

'Where is he?' Llora begged, ready to cry. 'What have you done with my brother?'

'Don't worry, he's safe, providing you serve me.'

'Why are you doing this?'

'I need to keep you motivated. Your focus has been on the wrong prince, but no longer will it be that way.'

'But—' She faltered.

'I'll be in touch soon. Here, take this,' he said, handing her something else.

Llora paid it no heed. Speechless, her eyes were still fixed on the wooden lion: Wuntu's favourite toy.

'Give that to Pharaoh Merkhet. Keep him busy, don't allow him to settle into his duties. Remember, don't do anything rash if you ever want to see your brother alive again.'

Llora shivered. She was cold.

And alone. So very alone.

Chapter 8

The citizens' daring whispers of the *Cursed Pharaoh* were exhilarating. They spurred Peronikh all the way through the city and back to the harem village.

Hours later, a single flame torch, buried in the sand, illuminated his hut in sweeping flutters of yellow and orange. Unlike the recent brooding days, this evening would be different. Peronikh had good reason to celebrate. More than just because he would finally banish the moment the High Priest made a blatant mockery of him in front of the gathered masses, too.

When Merkhet returned from his walk and saw the graffiti, questioning his claim to the throne, dismay crippled his poor brother's hapless face. All Peronikh's fury faded, and a strange blend of curiosity and joy spread over him.

The blank faces from his interrupted ceremony no longer leered up at him at every chance. Even the smug expression of the wretched priest, convincing everyone of his raving delusions, appeared less often in the flames. Peronikh would never forget the snivelling old fool's slight, not even as he gasped for his final breaths. According to him—on behalf of the patron god of Thebes—he was not capable of commanding Egypt. But it didn't matter anymore. Someone, somewhere, understood the injustice of it all. Just knowing that, released so much undeserving tension.

Slumped against the hut's wall, the constant echo of the festivities thrummed deep into Peronikh's mind, his very existence. He couldn't bring himself to attend Merkhet's celebration. His only consideration for attending the banquet—the one that should have been held in *his* honour—taunted him from his hut. A strong aroma wafted from the feast. The spices, as they danced around his nostrils, were reminiscent of every feast the royal kitchen had ever prepared. Merkhet had introduced Peronikh to the cooks, and now they served him food at any time of day—or night—even allowing him to make special requests.

The perks of royalty were endless, and Peronikh, happy to abuse his privileges, would never have it any other way. Merkhet did too, but his unfortunate brother was not able to conceal his fondness very well. It sat plump around his midriff. Thinking of him and how he would soon be seated heavy upon the Golden Throne, snapped Peronikh back to focus, where his embarrassing snub burned at the fore once again.

The nip would help him forget how wronged he was. At least until such a time he could learn the identity of the vandal, and whether they truly supported his right to rule. After all, how could they not? He had passed his trial. It was he, Peronikh, who confronted the horrifying river beast, not Merkhet. Four-thousand-pounds of hippopotamus aggression steaming at him.

Peronikh was victorious, not his brother.

The nip never failed him, having helped him to numb everything so far. His father was gone and so were their impromptu hunting trips. The childish jokes. The stern lessons. His inspiring shrewdness and physical grit were lost forever. At least in this life.

Peronikh scratched at the scars that lined his feet and between his toes. After a deep sigh, he was slipping on the thick leather gloves that sat beside him. Across the room, a small sandstone enclosure contained his cherished escape. Reed matting prevented it from burrowing beneath the sand. The black-tailed scorpion lashed out as he leant over to pick it up, clamping its pincers together and striking at his gloves with its stinger. The gloves absorbed the scorpion's aggression as he lowered himself to the ground again.

He didn't need to grapple with nerves. They didn't appear anymore. Peronikh guided the beast towards his feet, not even flinching as it struck with remarkable speed. As he returned the scorpion to its enclosure and removed the leather gloves, already his foot was swelling, darkening to an ominous shade of purple. When he sat again, his muscles were relaxed, free of strain and burden. Sweet blissful serenity coursed through him.

That was when Peronikh remembered the

invitation. The one for attending the banquet that he had extended to the lovely Llora. Unable to move, he cursed inwardly. So quick to remove himself from the horror—of not only losing his father but also being overlooked as pharaoh—he forgot all about her.

What if she had not heard the news, arrived at the feast, and he wasn't there.

Would Peronikh ever see her again?

Chapter 9

Merkhet was as merry as merry can be. His father had never permitted him more than one drink before.

He was pharaoh now, and his goblet was replenished every time he emptied it. Sometimes before. Yet the banquet drew nearer to its inevitable close, made apparent by one guest attempting to fill his cup at several different flagons without so much as collecting a few meagre drops of the red wine he sought. The embers of the braziers, surrounding the celebration, dwindled. As did the guests. Merkhet was wandering around the banquet, soaking up what remained of the festivities and wondering where his brother was, when he bumped into someone near the serving tables.

'Sorry, didn't see you there. Not sure how I could

have missed you—' he said, looking up, '—in that ravishing white dress.'

She turned around, and an awful guilt rose within him. A relish of some sort had spilt down her outfit. She looked mad. 'Desert girl?' Merkhet asked, as if he couldn't be sure. But there was no mistaking *those* eyes. 'I'm so sorry. What are you doing here?'

She said nothing. Just like in the desert. She appeared to be trembling. Same as in the desert. 'Are you alright?' Merkhet asked. 'Are you cold?' He handed her his shawl. 'Sorry about the dress.'

Her acceptance of his apology and her thank you came as a simple, swift nod, and then she spoke. 'I wanted to see you. After the …'

He found it difficult to concentrate on her words, distracted by her dazzling blue eyes and the glimmering silver locket swinging around her chest.

'I'm devastated by your loss, Merkhet. He was a remarkable man, an incredible pharaoh.'

A fiery, no, an icy sensation surged through him, numbing him completely. His father was gone. The joy of the banquet was a fleeting illusion. It wasn't real. He opened his mouth to speak, but nothing came out. He froze. Just like in the desert, and the chill intensified.

'It was so brave of you to save me from the hyenas last week.'

'I'm not sure I did,' Merkhet mumbled.

She waved his words away. 'Please, it would honour me greatly if you would accept this,' she said, presenting him with a necklace.

As she placed its chain into his palms, her soft, warm hands brushed against his. The freeze melted away. Merkhet lifted the golden pendant of the sun god, Aten, over his head and then lowered it until the pendant fell against his chest. 'Thank you, Llora. That is incredibly kind of you.'

'How do you know my name?'

Merkhet smiled, tried to at least. But only one side of his face was cooperating, so he stopped the strained expression before it would look too odd. 'It's carved into your locket,' he said, pointing at the scrawl of her name.

She reached for it, holding it out in front of her. 'So it is!' she exclaimed, a condescending tone creeping into her otherwise sweet voice.

'You weren't wearing it in the desert, were you?' Great conversation, Merkhet, you utter fool.

'No, I don't believe I was,' she said, laughing it off.

Merkhet wanted to join in her laughter but missed his chance. Then he had no idea what to say. He stared at her, willing Horus or any of the gods to inspire him. Llora saved him instead, and not for the first time, he recalled. Maybe she was a goddess.

'The royal palace is so beautiful, Merkhet. The way it glows—'

'I could show you, if you like? Maybe one of the maids can fetch you a new dress, too.'

'Actually? That would be amazing!'

Merkhet waved aside the guards at the gate, and they began to climb the steep trail leading to the palace. 'Ptah's Point they call it, the dune the palace was built on.'

'We're so high up,' she said, panting a little.

'Some believe the dune will never lose its shape, will never fall victim to the will of the winds. The palace could very well remain a beacon on the hill until the gods no longer wish it so.'

As they reached the top of the slope, her face gleamed as she absorbed the beauty and magnificence of the complex.

After some servants retrieved Llora a new dress, which she wrapped around her arm, he escorted her through the palace. The glimmer of the Golden Throne lit up the hieroglyphic scenes painted on the walls; the dormant feline, Beebee, who opened one gleaming yellow eye as you passed her; and the gigantic war table where some of Egypt's greatest recent conquests were planned. Adjacent to the throne room were the royal chambers, and beyond them, the stone terrace. None of the usual delights were visible. The surrounding desert and the Nile River, both lost to the darkness. All that remained were the shrieks and chirps of the nocturnal wildlife that inhabited the area.

'That was wonderful. It was very kind of you to show me.'

'The sun will rise before long,' he started. 'I should have you escorted back to the villages, Llora.'

'Is that possible? At this late hour?'

Merkhet paused. 'Just this once.' He smiled again, hoping his face was not so contorted this time.

'Thank you,' she murmured.

The royal chariot was readied, and when it arrived, Abacca and Tendrence were tethered to it. The guard controlling the reins, let go of them. He and his partner moved to the passenger carriage. Merkhet clambered onto the front deck, where he offered his hand to Llora. She accepted his assistance and joined him. He grabbed the reins and gave them a gentle tug.

They were off, rolling effortlessly through Thebes, guided by the bright stars of the cosmos. Almost gliding along the Nile's banks, where the blend of hardened dirt and sand met, he pointed out some of his favourite constellations. She gasped in wonder at the Flying Chariot and the Scurrying Scarab. Maybe his knowledge of astronomy would impress Llora, even if his charioteering didn't.

All too quickly though, her village came into view, and his gut churned. He didn't want this evening to end. Not yet. Not ever. But unable to find a reason to heed his selfish desires, Merkhet eased the horses to a halt outside the village gates.

Llora tried to return his shawl.

'No, keep it. Please.'

'Are you sure?'

He nodded.

'Thank you,' she said, her eyes shimmering under the night sky's Sleepy Sphinx. 'Can I ask you something?'

'Yes, anything.'

'I have a friend in trouble.'

'What has happened?'

'He is required at the Judgements when they resume, and I—'

'Please,' Merkhet said, 'say no more. I do not wish your friend any harm, but I cannot go against the will of the gods. Ma'at embodies everything we do, and we must respect its laws.'

'I understand,' she said, a meek smile appearing on her face.

Merkhet worried about that smile. It unnerved him. 'Sorry, again, about the dress.'

Had he doomed their connection before it had a chance to grow? Of course he had. Why would she be interested in him anyway?

She leaned over to him, planting a kiss on his cheek. Instantly, his mind was set at ease. She bounced out of the chariot and ambled into her village.

The Aten pendant rested beneath his robe, against his bare chest. It had a slight chill to it, and yet he had never been warmer. He pulled it out, clasping it tight in his hands for the short return journey to the palace.

When the chariot arrived, Merkhet walked past the remnants of the banquet and trudged up the slope to his quarters in the palace. His mother would remain in the royal chambers for now. He did not have the heart to displace her so soon after their tragic loss. The sun was starting to rise, and the elation from successfully completing his first engagement as pharaoh, began to fade with the night shadows.

Overwhelmed by exhaustion, he had earned a long sleep. As he went to lay down, his mother greeted him. Her hair was tied back in a messy clump, long black strands of it floating at their own accord. Never had her hair rested out of place before. His mother was hurting, even more than he was.

'Son,' Merep said. 'You have done well today. Your father would be so proud.'

'I wish he was here.'

'I would traverse the Nile back and forth for

eternity to make it so. But death cannot be reversed.'

Merkhet sighed. If only it could, then his father could continue leading Egypt.

'You know that I am here to help you, right? As I did your—' Merep choked on her final word, the puffy shadows beneath her eyes appearing to throb.

'Yes, Mother, your counsel will be valued more than any other.'

'I see you met someone tonight,' she said, a faint grin emerging above the pain. 'Can you tell your mother anything?'

'What do you mean? Oh, her. No. I don't know.'

She giggled. 'Do not blush, Merkhet. But please be careful. You will receive much attention as pharaoh. Not all of it will be safe or wanted.'

'She wouldn't—'

'I'm not saying she would. But I'm allowed to worry.'

Merkhet nodded, stifling a yawn.

'Soon you must decide what role Peronikh will assume. Perhaps he would make an excellent Diplomatic Ambassador with that tireless mouth of his.'

'I wanted to speak with him tonight, but he did not attend.'

'He is hurting, no doubt, like we all are. Rest now, my son.' She kissed him on the forehead and snuffed out the flame lighting his quarters.

'Goodnight, Mother.'

Merkhet laid on his bed, stiff and exhausted, his mind groggy with fatigue and the beer's subsiding effects. He tried to consider Peronikh as a Diplomatic Ambassador. But he couldn't send his brother away and condemn him to a life of travel, the very role Merkhet had dreamed of assuming since he first read his grandfather's texts.

Could he?

Chapter 10

Peronikh received a deliberate smirk from one of the royal guards as he passed through the palace gates. It was none other than the same one, who had delighted in reporting to him and Merkhet that they must meet with their father after their unscheduled hunt. What was the man's problem? Had he propositioned the High Priest to embarrass him?

The morning sun beat down upon Peronikh's shoulders as he stormed up the sand dune, trying to suppress his rising fury. Unleashing it in a torrent of abuse would not serve him well. But he had not heard anything in the month since his father passed away and his brother ascended the Golden Throne. Not a single thing. Peronikh had the right to be angry, anyone would be.

The gods were wrong to intervene if Merkhet could not even provide him a courteous confirmation of the role he would assume. A mere indication would suffice, but no, nothing. It was infuriating and just another of the many reasons he detested living in the harem village with his mother. He was out of sight. Always the last to receive news.

His brother no longer attended royal classes, so Peronikh's previous daily contact with him were no longer possible. All prior attempts to connect with Merkhet, in the wake of the banquet, were denied, too. But not today.

No, today, Peronikh would stop feeling sorry for himself and demand clarity about his future. Or else wither away in the sweet embrace of the nip.

The toxic substance had worked wonders for him recently, helping him meld away the loss of his father, the uncertainty surrounding his role in Thebes, and the constant thoughts of Llora, the desert girl. But it was time for him to take command of his own fate, not wait for it to reveal itself to him.

The guards posted in the courtyard, at the entrance to the inner sanctum, were unmoving, barring his way in. 'I need to speak with Pharaoh Merkhet.' Still, they did not move. 'Now!' Peronikh demanded.

'He is busy.'

'I am his brother. I must—'

'Sorry, no interruptions,' the guard said, even though his face held no sympathy.

'Then at least tell me where he is.'

'We are not privy to his whereabouts.'

'You are the royal guards. How can you perform your duty if you don't know where he is?' Silence.

Typical. 'When can I speak with him, then?'

'When he is not busy.'

Peronikh retreated. How dare they treat him like that. His father would not have tolerated such blatant disrespect and insolence.

'My prince, my prince,' a timid voice called out.

Peronikh turned to face a small servant boy, likely from the kitchen, rushing down the sandy slope to meet him. 'Can I help you?'

'I may have some news, my prince.'

Peronikh stared at him, not in the mood for any further time-wasting.

'About your brother,' the boy prompted.

'Go on.'

The servant kept his silence, eyeing the jewellery on Peronikh's fingers. Deciding on his least favourite trinket, the prince studied his hands. Peronikh handed him an emerald ring and couldn't help shaking his head. Unbelievable. Extorted by a servant—could his day get any worse?

'The viziers,' the small boy said. 'Throne room. Most days.'

'What do they discuss?'

'I know not, my prince. Not allowed inside. See them come, see them go.'

'Anything else?'

'One more thing,' the boy said, pausing to glance over his shoulder. 'Training. Army barracks. Must hurry back now.'

'Wait, what training?'

'Big captain. In red. Must hurry.'

'Who? Taharva?' Peronikh asked himself, for the sneaky servant had already scampered back inside the palace.

His brother had always resisted combat training. Now he was embracing it?

Peronikh would have to investigate for himself.

Following the servant boy's lead, Peronikh found himself outside the army barracks later that afternoon. The boy proved his worth, and Peronikh made a silent vow not to punish him for his brazen acquisition. Especially when, over the last month, everyone else had sought to impede him at every chance. If not for the boy, where would he be now? It wasn't even a question. He would be back in his hut, devoid of all hope of justice, administering another dose of the pleasant poison.

The barracks were teeming. Soldiers in their crisp white linen scurried between training sessions, beads of sweat glistening on their skin. Egypt could never be too certain that the Hittites wouldn't dare confront them again, even with a pharaoh now appointed. They were a bloodthirsty people and unable to be swayed with reasoning. The clattering of swords and shields followed Peronikh along the main avenue of the compound. The sound and sight of these preparations hurt a great deal. It should have been him overseeing them.

Merkhet and Taharva were training in an enclosure at the far end of the barracks. A small arena, built for close-combat duels. Hemmed in with linen veils affixed to mudbrick pillars. Peronikh snuck up to the open-air enclave, careful to lift his sandals with each step. One inattentive shuffle and he would be discovered prying on a private combat session. But he had to understand what they were training for. He needed clarity, answers.

Finally, the gods showered him in a sprinkle of fortune—he was well within earshot of them as he crouched behind a pillar, hidden from view.

'Are you ready, Scrollworm?' Taharva asked.

'You can bet Ra's sunrise on that,' his brother said.

Merkhet's voice. Something had changed. He no longer sounded meek and unsure of himself, as if his shadow might trip him up at any moment. Peronikh stole a glance between the veils. Risky, but it had to be done. He had to blink several times. It couldn't be.

His brother's crownless head had been shaved. All except for a little thicket of black that sprouted from the back of his head. The thicket was tied up in a ponytail, but that wasn't the biggest shock of all. Merkhet was not wearing anything to cover his top half. No knee-length shirt. No gown or robe, just a necklace swinging about his front.

Peronikh could scarce remember such an occasion. Even on sweltering summer days, his brother was always fully clothed, and he never wore jewellery beyond the customary royal regalia.

Merkhet's slouch had straightened, if not disappeared entirely, and maybe he had even grown a couple of inches and trimmed up a little, too. Peronikh couldn't be certain about all the changes, but for the first time his brother impressed him. A hint of confidence had crept into his otherwise placid, shy temperament. Since the injustice of the High Priest's intervention, Merkhet had endeavoured to transform himself.

Yet he, Peronikh, was still the same, no closer to achieving anything.

Edging out farther to watch, he was barely concealed by the pillar. The Nubian charged at his brother. They exchanged a couple of blows, a tangle of spear and sword. The bronze-on-steel made a sweet lullaby as the weapons glided off one another. Merkhet stepped back, studying his opponent. He then pounced towards him suddenly, but Taharva dodged the attack with alacrity and ease.

'Have you thought more on what I said?' the giant Nubian asked, circling Merkhet as he twirled a spear about in his massive hands.

'I haven't forgiven myself. If that is what you're asking?'

'It is.'

'The guilt still gnaws at me. Some nights I wake from the most horrid dreams, clammy and drenched in cold sweat.'

'Release this blame.'

'I'm trying.'

'Good, and what of the desert girl? Any more secret meetings?'

Peronikh gasped—loud to enough to be heard. He dived to the ground and coarse sand kissed his lips and nose. Was the captain talking about Llora?

'Did you hear that?'

'Hear what, Scrollworm? What's got you so edgy?'

Peronikh's pulse pounded in his ear as he wiped

his face clear. Close. Too close. He would need to be more cautious.

'Nothing,' his brother said.

'Tell me, or when my spear rests against your gullet, you'll wish you had.'

'Bring it, old man.'

Whom was that training in the enclosure? It could not be his brother. If it was, he had the mettle to make an excellent leader. Peronikh wriggled back across, looking in again.

'Pharaoh or not, you will pay for that cheek,' Taharva said.

The Nubian rushed at his much smaller adversary, lunging spear-first with tremendous speed. Merkhet swerved out of the weapon's arc, and then he relaxed. Peronikh couldn't blame him, but it was a mistake. Taharva noticed the lapse in concentration and feigned to the right before propelling his weapon towards Merkhet's unguarded neck. He did not inflict the fatal blow, stopping his spear less than an inch beneath his brother's chin.

'We have reached your first lesson for today. You must never become complacent in battle. Now, spill it,' Taharva said, not lowering his weapon.

'Spill what?' Merkhet asked, his wide eyes watching the spear.

'Whatever is bothering you.'

'What if it's me?'

'Explain.'

'The Cursed Pharaoh. The citizens still whisper of it.'

'Let them whisper. Only cowards whisper.'

'The harvest is over, the floods are overdue.'

'By mere weeks, boy. The gods and nature do not owe us their reasoning, and why would they bother connecting with you during the walk if you were cursed?'

'You're right,' Merkhet said through gritted teeth. 'You should be one of my viziers.'

'I'm afraid I would have to decline such a position if it were to arise,' Taharva said, finally bringing down his spear.

'Still, this isn't fair. None of this. I didn't want to be pharaoh. That was decided for me, and now it consumes all of my time.'

'You can either embrace it and make your father proud—or you can allow the injustice to *consume* you—and Egypt needs you too much for that to happen.'

Merkhet sighed. 'I just want to concentrate all of my energy into my training, into father's funerary preparations.'

'You cannot avoid your duties forever. Run along now, Scrollworm. Come tomorrow, bring Horakhty with you.'

Their feet stopped scuffing in the sand, and their weapons no longer clattered together. The training, of which Peronikh heard little and saw less, was now over. He sprinted away from the barracks. A risky endeavour, spying on his brother like that, but he had gleaned valuable, valuable information.

Merkhet did not want to be pharaoh!

His brother may have found a freshly discovered tenacity in combat, to complement his physical improvements, but he had not completely transformed. He still lacked conviction and self-belief. A true leader couldn't afford to let doubt creep in and render him captive.

Peronikh smiled. He wanted the glory of the Golden Throne more than anyone. All wrongs could be forgiven once he graced the most powerful seat in the world. If his brother had no desire for it, Peronikh didn't see a reason why he shouldn't relieve the poor pharaoh.

Then a pair of the sweetest blue eyes floated through his mind, around and around, refusing to leave, and his elation faded.

Llora …

Where was she? What did Merkhet know of her?

Chapter 11

Merkhet awoke in his private chambers, despair gnawing away at him. His sweaty back stuck to the reed bed. What if it wasn't enough? What if he had failed his father in life, and now also in death?

He wanted to believe Taharva, wishing with everything, that he wasn't at fault. But Merkhet hesitated in bringing down the hyena. No one else.

Limbs twitching, he crossed his arms over his thumping chest. Calmness settled in, and it was enough to steady his rapid, shallow breaths. Yet *another* nightmare. The vivid nightly dreams of his father's heart being devoured, left Merkhet tense and foreboding. Could the gods be so cruel, as to deliver him an early verdict of the Weighing of the Heart ceremony? They could—but surely it was just his nerves getting the better of him.

Just shy of seventy days, seventy *long* days, Merkhet had spent in the Valley of the Kings. Toiling day and night, obsessing over every artefact that would furnish the tomb and accompany his father into the Afterlife. Despite all that, maybe Merkhet's unrelenting dreams were a desperate warning, to alert him to some critical, forgotten funerary preparation.

The Aten pendant dug into the soft tissue of his throat. Merkhet never removed Llora's gift, not even to sleep. He often woke with the necklace jutting into him, as it did now.

He adjusted it, thinking of her. Llora. What a blessing she was. Her mystery and beauty were unrivalled. Merkhet couldn't care less what some of the probing officials had to say about her presence. What did it matter that she came from the villages? From the delta marshes to the southern plains, they were all Egyptians, and his affection for her continued to blossom. Merkhet just couldn't bear to not see her.

Ever since the coronation feast, that was getting difficult. His insatiable workload to oversee his father's remaining funerary preparations and strict combat training with Taharva were just the beginning. The demands for his attention were mounting by the day. Merkhet's attempts to delay them would only become feebler after his father's burial. Sure, at least he didn't have the torture of the frequent hunts anymore. But it wasn't like he was spending all day, Llora by his side, basking in the sun's rays. Merkhet wouldn't mind so much if it were.

A peculiar queasiness, equal amounts of relief and nervousness, gripped him as he changed into his elegant black burial robes. The day had arrived, much quicker than he would have liked.

Today, he would say goodbye to his father, and tomorrow …

Well, who knew what tomorrow held for them? The graffiti on the city walls taunted him, circling round his thoughts. Without the imminent arrival of the life-giving flood, his people would wither and starve. The prophecy of the Cursed Pharaoh was becoming more of a reality than anything else.

Smoothing the creases of his robe, Merkhet exhaled, long and heavy. Passing through the open dining hall, he halted in the throne room. He half expected to hear his father's infectious laughter bouncing off the hieroglyphs. But it never did, and the throne was still empty.

Merkhet rushed for his mother. He could hear her in the adjacent chambers. Even though he could not see what she was doing, Merep's constant rustling made him smile. The joy was fleeting though, hampered by the prospect of the daunting day ahead. It encroached upon him like an unwelcome visitor at supper, happy to overstay its welcome and sour the mood.

He knocked at the entrance to her chambers.

'Merkhet, is that you? We must leave soon. The procession will begin shortly.'

'Yes, Mother. I am ready,' he called back to her.

Merep wandered into view, lifting the sides of her dress up from the ground. Her hair was still straggly, but it appeared to have some of its usual shine back. Perhaps some of the royal servants had pinned her down to wash it. 'What's the matter?' she asked.

'Nothing. Just want everything to go to plan

today.'

'Everything will be fine. You will be strong for me, won't you?'

'I will.'

'Then tell me, what is really the matter? I gave birth to you. I can tell when something troubles you.'

'It's silly.'

'I will hear it anyway,' Merep said.

'I've got this nagging feeling, like I've forgotten something and I'm going to—'

'Prevent your father from reaching the Afterlife? You're right, that is silly. Let's see,' she said, pausing to think. Her eyes tilted up, and for just a moment his exuberant and compassionate mother stood before him once again. 'Are the Book of the Dead scrolls written? Your father will need them to guide him through the trials that await.'

'Yes, Raina finished them. The priests have assured me the papyrus scrolls are inside the sarcophagus.'

'Excellent, and a great choice of scribe, too. She is as meticulous as she is pretty. How about the embalmers?'

'You already know they have finished preserving his body. We watched them administer the natron salts and wrap him up.'

'Yes, I do. But I wish to set your mind at ease. Were the labourers and artisans able to finalise the decorations?

'After I scolded the artisans for their inferior production of ushabti dolls, the canopic jars and everything else went according to schedule.'

'How did you punish them?'

'Double-time and reduced food allowances for a

week. They shouldn't have jeopardised father's relaxation in the Afterlife. He will need those ushabti to serve him.'

'You were right to do so. The greatest crime of all would be labouring one's way through immortality.' Her eyes watered, as if she might cry, yet her broad smile never faltered.

'Mother?'

'Don't you see, my son? You may not have been a couple of months ago, but now you are ready to lead Egypt.'

Maybe his mother was right. Maybe he could command his country and make his father proud.

First, they must bid farewell to Egypt's fierce warrior and tireless builder. At long last, the commoners' daily offerings and prayers outside the temples, and even the priests within the sacred inner sanctums, would cease.

The Valley of the Kings—the burial ground for all of Egypt's past, present, and future pharaohs—beckoned them.

An abrupt, silent chariot journey carried Merkhet and his mother to the temple district.

The burial procession had already gathered—thousands of solemn-faced blurs—all wishing to farewell the pharaoh. Merkhet scanned for Llora, but he would never spot her, not among the throngs of mourners. She'd promised him she would attend, and he believed her.

He and his mother carved their way through the masses, and citizens delivered heartfelt messages as they passed by.

'We share your pain. Egypt still mourns,' one lady whispered.

'He will make it to the Afterlife, do not mistake it,' a coarse voice assured them.

'A noble leader. Such a tragedy,' said a young man, not much older than himself.

They made it to the head of the burial procession when an acute twinge stabbed at his belly. Merkhet saw his father's open sarcophagus approaching and had to avert his gaze. He would not cry, not today. Instead, he looked around, studying the faces around him.

Peronikh was nearby, skirting on the edge of the royal gathering. His face was withdrawn, gaunt around the cheeks and eyes. Merkhet struggled to cope with the grief at times himself, but his brother was faring even worse. They needed to talk—and soon—if Peronikh's dishevelled appearance and recent distance were anything to judge by.

Taharva, his friend, mentor, and Chief of the Royal Guard; the viziers, Prahmun and Lufu; the High Priest of Amun and a score of his closest initiates; and a whole congregation of Egyptian nobles were also in attendance. So were the other variants of Egyptian life: the lowly harvesters living on the outskirts of Thebes, the well-respected artisans, and even the beggars that littered Thebes' alleys. The procession attracted them all.

Of those present, Merkhet had not spoken with many of them outside the administration and nobility, and one less had spoken to him. For among the procession were countless scribes, of which he had requested one in particular: Raina. He watched her with fascination, the talented yet mute scribe was armed with bundles of papyri and ready to record the day's sombre events.

The High Priest conversed in a low tone with his mother, but not long after their arrival, the burial convoy commenced. Thousands marched in unison towards the Valley of the Kings, a journey of several miles.

His father's lavish sarcophagus led the way, rested upon the sturdy shoulders of six soldiers. No greater honour could be bestowed upon an Egyptian soldier than to be selected as a coffin bearer of a beloved pharaoh. However, the esteemed role was not without its challenges. Given that, for the prominent procession members, the journey included crossing the Nile.

Under Merkhet's scrupulous supervision, the finest craftsmen and artists had toiled over the coffin's construction. He was not disappointed—the golden sarcophagus boasted a three-dimensional representation of his father in his prime, wearing the Double Crown and holding the crook and flail. Hieroglyphic prayers were painted in black along the sides.

Amun initiates surrounded the casket, carrying an assortment of canopic jars, which contained his father's organs. The jars, and the sarcophagus itself, formed a small sample of the countless treasures that would become the contents of Pharaoh Nekhet's eternal tomb.

The procession approached the Nile, after cutting between two deserted irrigation farms, where a fleet of small rafts awaited them. The river's flow was subdued, still awaiting the annual flood. The vessels would guarantee their safe passage across the Nile, for the placid river had many horrors lurking in its now shallow depths.

The soldiers bearing the open sarcophagus were the first to brave the journey. They placed the coffin in a raft of its own, then heaved their weight against it. The raft began to sail across the breadth of the river, gliding smoothly with the blessing of Hapi, the god of the Nile.

The sarcophagus bearers boarded rafts of their own, three to each, and used wooden paddles to propel themselves. A float of crocodiles hovered just above the river's surface, betrayed by their unblinking, bright yellow eyes. The scaly beasts surveyed the rafts through thin slits. Irked by the crocodiles' presence,

Merkhet peered again at the raft carrying his father, now approaching the final third of its crossing. But its momentum had slowed, the vessel almost at a complete halt.

Something was wrong. Water swirled all around the open sarcophagus. The casket bearers did not react, somehow unaware of the mounting urgency. At any moment, the coffin would dip below the green river and sink. Possibly forever.

'Mother,' Merkhet said, pointing at the raft.

Merep let out a high-pitched squeal, but it seemed distant, unimportant. Horrible memories of the desert surfaced, rising to the fore. Merkhet had failed to help Llora, failed to save his father. Now, his gruelling training with Taharva counted for nothing. Because nothing had changed. He was still the same useless child as he was before, just confronted with different scenery. The procession waited with bated breath, none more so than himself, as the raft continued to succumb to the will of the Nile and bring his nightmarish premonition to life.

Uncharacteristic decisiveness surged through Merkhet, and he spoke in an even, controlled tone, 'Taharva, my father needs you.'

The dependable captain heeded the plea, stripping off his burial robes and diving into the chaos of the shallows. His initial heroics—or maybe it was his mother's continued shrieks—inspired the transfixed casket bearers into action, too. They left the safety of their buoyant rafts, plunging into the river, while the Nubian powered through the water. It lapped around his ebony shoulders but did not slow him. He barked commands at the soldiers, and they responded, narrowing in on the partially submerged sarcophagus.

Merkhet edged closer to the river, but a hand tugged on the hem of his robe, stopping him. He dared a quick glance and was not surprised to see his mother. Helpless, he watched as his father's hopes of reaching the Afterlife were sinking right in front of him.

Taharva beat the soldiers to the drowning raft and launched himself beneath it. He re-emerged with one side of it hoisted an inch above the water level. The soldiers reached him, easing the coffin from the flooded raft. They firmed their grip and began to tread towards the riverbank, the raft compromised and forgotten.

His mother let out a nervous squeal to his right. Merkhet scanned the river—the crocodiles had disappeared. The carnivorous beasts would not miss an opportunity to feast. They never did. He anxiously clamped down on his lip, ignoring the strange taste of blood washing over his tongue.

The soldiers, shorter than Taharva, bobbed up and down under the strain of the coffin. The water crept past their shoulders, and when they approached the far bank of the Nile, the Nubian pulled away from them to survey the calm river. The stillness broke in a flurry of splashes and a soldier was dragged writhing into the murky water, relinquishing his position on the casket. The burden was passed on to the remaining soldiers, several of them disappearing into the murkiness.

A red patch rippled through the river, and a leg, severed above the knee, drifted away in the mild current. Merkhet could not hear any of the commotion as Peronikh waded into the Nile. His heart fluttered, skipping several beats, and then it burst into overload, deafening all else. His brother had to rescue the sarcophagus and their father's chance of reaching the Afterlife. He just had to. Merkhet could not have executed months of preparation for nothing.

Taharva hurled himself at the almost fully submerged raft, his immense strength on show as he ripped a wooden plank from the sinking vessel. Then the Nubian guard breached the gap and reached the soldiers. He secured himself as a barrier between them and the swarming crocodiles.

Swimming with frenzied strokes, Peronikh was closing in on the captain, who fended off one beast with the water-logged plank. But still, they besieged Taharva, jaws snapping at him and his paltry weapon. Worse than that, the coffin bearers had yet to recover.

Merkhet couldn't look any longer, but he never turned away. What would happen when their exhaustion overwhelmed their adrenalin?

His brother made it to the sarcophagus and wedged himself under it. The coffin bearers were able to steady with his help. They advanced towards the bank, heaving the sarcophagus to safety and clambering onto land.

Merkhet wanted to collapse in relief, but he remembered Taharva. The crocodiles, crazed by their taste of flesh, were encircling him. How many more times could he swing the plank to prevent their fatal advance? His arcing motions—to keep the beasts at bay—were narrowing with each twirl. They were mere feet away from him, the plank limp in Taharva's arms, when panicked splashing gained the crocodile's attention.

Some procession members had forced a small drove of donkeys into the river. Hapi's reptile servants accepted the sacrificial offering, meeting it at once, and tearing the flesh from the startled donkeys. Taharva relished the reprieve, swimming to the river's edge. Peronikh offered a hand and Taharva grabbed it, hoisting himself to sanctuary on the far side of the Nile.

The immediate danger had passed, and Merkhet was anxious to inspect the coffin. If water seeped through its exterior or sloshed into the open casket ...

He needed to remain patient while the remaining rafts were re-examined for their integrity. When the viziers on the far bank were satisfied, the rest of the procession that would make the crossing hesitantly formed a queue. Merkhet and Merep were among the first escorted to the other side of the river. When their feet touched the banks, they rushed to the sarcophagus. By the good graces of Hapi, somehow it was wholly intact. His father, too.

Merkhet gazed skyward, blessing the gods—all of them in their infinite mystique and power—that the flood season had not arrived on time.

The rafts floated back and forth across the river while the masses sang their glowing praises of Taharva and Peronikh.

Merkhet searched for his brother. So caught up in perfecting the funerary preparations, they had not spoken in quite some time. He wanted to thank Peronikh for his patience and heroics, maybe even discuss with him his aspirations.

But his brother was nowhere to be seen.

Eager to distance the procession from the near travesty of the river crossing, the initiates increased the tempo of the march. They broke out into an upbeat hymn and burned incense to commemorate the life of the departing pharaoh.

Merkhet's arms tingled, the hairs standing tall, as the sonorous tone of their mingled singing bounced off the cliffs ahead of them. The rhythmic drumming of a hundred feet complemented the chorus' sweet symphony, and what remained of the congregation joined in a few voices at a time.

Led by the High Priest, they slid between two

limestone cliff faces and into the Valley of the Kings. Awe and mystery exuded from every crevice of the valley. Encased by rocky cliffs, it was the perfect terrain for the construction of royal tombs. One day, Merkhet would be buried here, too. The thought unnerved him, and tiny bumps formed all over his body.

What remained of the once bountiful procession, poured through the valley, congregating outside his father's tomb. For two years the construction workers laboured to carve out the tomb's rock face, an intricate affair to stabilise the tunnels and the various rooms that comprised it. The work had officially finished last week, but still, Merkhet was concerned, checking and triple-checking every last detail in anticipation of the burial.

The tomb was open, awaiting the delivery of Nekhet's sarcophagus and personal treasures. At the decree of the High Priest, the soldiers descended the steps and entered the tomb. Merkhet and Merep were permitted access to oversee the final preparations. Peronikh, wherever he was, did not join them. Holding his mother's hand, they shuffled in behind the soldiers.

The stairs led down to a passage, where oil candles burnt low, illuminating great hieroglyphic scenes. The walls depicted his father's military triumphs, where the cowering Hittites and the passive Nubians looked up to the colossal, godly figure of Nekhet. Through the dim, bare antechamber, they skipped the annex to the left, where the miscellaneous goods were already stored. An assortment of pottery, oils, and wines mostly.

To the right, at the far end of the antechamber, two life-sized granite statues of his father guarded the opening into the burial chamber and the adjacent treasury room. The statues were eerie, the sculptors having solidified Nekhet's piercing stare for an eternity.

The casket-bearing soldiers passed between the statues and carefully lifted the sarcophagus up onto a raised stone slab. They slid it into position with a gentle thud before leaving the tomb, no doubt thankful to have completed their duty. The remaining treasures, including Thekla, were brought inside and placed around the treasury according to the judgement of the High Priest.

Merkhet and his mother were silent, standing in the burial room as they watched the initiates distribute canopic jars throughout the treasury as well as the two hundred-odd ushabti figures around the sarcophagus itself.

'My gracious queen, everything is in order,' said the High Priest.

'What about the Book of the Dead? How about the final prayer for a successful journey to the Afterlife?'

'The book is already contained within the sarcophagus. I am about to recite the final prayers and perform the Opening of the Mouth ceremony.'

Merep straightened. 'So, he will be able to defend himself at the Weighing of the Hearts?'

'My queen,' he said. 'Nekhet's soul will not need defending. His righteous deeds will speak on his behalf.'

'Will it also allow him to eat and drink in the Afterlife?' Merkhet asked.

'Yes, Your Worship. After the prayers and ceremony, the tomb will be sealed. Your father's corpse will remain undisturbed for eternity.'

Merep nodded. She had no more tears left to shed, deserting her in the same way as her speech. The High Priest returned an awkward smile, and Merep left the tomb. He then recited the prayer that would ensure Nekhet would reach the Fields of Paradise. After, the pharaoh's mouth was opened, so that he could eat and drink there, too.

The horrors of Merkhet's persistent nightmare were vanquished from his memory. The priest departed the burial chamber with a curt bow. Merkhet glanced around behind him—needing to be certain that he was alone. He tied the near-invisible length of flax between the two statues, protecting his father's sarcophagus from any wretched tomb robbers.

'Rest well, Father. One day we will reunite in the Afterlife.'

Satisfied with his final tribute, another defence to preserve the remains of his father, Merkhet reappeared from the tomb's depths. He gave the signal to the High Priest, who in turn, relayed it on to his initiates. Merkhet just caught a glimpse of the two halves of the stone door clamping shut from atop the stairs.

With the tomb of the Tireless Warrior-Builder sealed, it was decided.

No more delaying.

Merkhet must assume the full pharaonic duties, not just the ones that appealed to him.

Chapter 12

Peronikh leaned in, eager for the day's final Judgement to begin. Still weary from the burial the day before, they had dragged on far longer than he would have liked. Not wanting to be spotted in the crowd, he huddled among the back row of sweat-glistened spectators.

His neck itched, a sure sign that he was due to return to the harem village and ease the night away with his trusty arachnid companion. Growing itchier by the second, Peronikh's neck also threatened to seize up as he craned to get a better view. Not of the accused—shaking and swaying on the spot—but of his brother, the Fourth Pharaoh of the Eighteenth Dynasty. How was he faring in his new life, the one he did not wish for?

Raina hung behind Merkhet, where her keen senses absorbed the unfolding events, and her swift strokes recorded them on a papyrus scroll. Despite having no interest in the impending Judgement or its outcome, Peronikh did not want to miss a thing.

At the centre of the spectator-bound ellipse, Merkhet stood in the desert sand. A golden necklace rested against his bare chest, but Peronikh could not see it in detail from his distant vantage point. If the stifling conditions were bothering his brother, he did not show it. Merkhet had abandoned the Double Crown earlier in the proceedings, even before the first Judgement commenced, almost as if it were a burden. Now his growing ponytail was free, skimming the back of his neck. It was not quite the same calibre as their father's, which grew the length of his spine, but it was promising.

Merkhet grasped his wooden crook. In his other hand, the maatebes, an identical pair of cubes used by the pharaoh to deliver the gods' judgement. All eyes were drawn to him, like scavengers to a fresh carcass. Egyptians were supposed to worship his brother as a god—walking, living, and ruling among them.

But did they respect a *god* who couldn't even oversee a burial without a near catastrophe? What about one who couldn't deliver the annual flood? Even the crowd's hushed whispers were enough to silence the slow gurgle of the nearby Nile.

Merkhet raised his crook and the murmurs faded. 'Laseb,' he said, 'you are accused of trading stolen goods with many pilfered possessions found at your hut. You may stand before the noble people of Thebes but it is the gods who will decide your fate.'

The pharaoh—if he was worthy of being bestowed that courtesy—launched the maatebes upwards. Peronikh tracked their ascent as they flipped and tumbled through the air. Cascading into each other at their peak, they plummeted into the sand. Few cheered but most gasped.

Facing up were two suns: not guilty. Laseb's glee could have almost extended the length of the Nile. He bounced from one foot to the other.

'The gods are always watching, always judging us, and today, they have declared your innocence, Laseb. As their will courses through me, I grant you your freedom. Release his binds at once.'

Peronikh cursed under his breath. The man was guilty. There could be no disputing the damning evidence. How could his brother fail to intervene?

Merkhet signalled to the chief executioner to commence his bidding. The chief executioner responded, visibly disappointed as he walked past the pile of rocks that would have inflicted his punishment. The crowd wanted blood. They always wanted blood. They yearned for it in their chants of growing unrest.

The very same chants, that had a definite undertone of discontent, peaked as Laseb stretched his arms for the sun. A free man. A lucky man. He owed his life to the weakness of the pharaoh. Merkhet had failed in his duty—the gods were always testing. If Peronikh was perched beneath the Double Crown, he would have overturned the Judgement, just as certainly as Ra's daily birthing of the sun.

As the blood-crazed, disgruntled spectators dispersed to resume their affairs, Peronikh caught a glimpse of smooth glowing skin. He lurched forward, ready to rush at Llora and her charming knots of long black hair. But he stopped at once. Her arm slipped around Merkhet's waist, and they were laughing as they strolled towards the royal chariot.

In his blinding rage, everything became clear. After months of turmoil and uncertainty, clarity struck Peronikh harder than the Gongs of Sorrow ever could. He understood what he must do. He had to right the harsh injustice imposed upon him by the High Priest. The citizens' thundering disapproval of the Judgement's outcome said everything.

The gods obviously supported Peronikh, refusing to unleash the life-giving flood. The Egyptians would starve and civil war would erupt if something didn't change the current—and precarious—balance of order.

The graffiti was justified. His brother's—his *half-brother's*—rule was cursed.

Merkhet could not remain pharaoh.

Adrenalin still pumped through Peronikh, weakening the nip's cravings, as the royal chariot and spectators were clearing the vicinity.

Prahmun approached him, and the prince met his arrival with apprehension. Was someone finally about to give him some indication of the role he would assume, or would this somehow be reversed into a chastising for saving his father's sarcophagus?

'My prince, it is good to see you. Other than witnessing your heroics at the burial, I can scarcely place our last encounter.'

'I have been busy,' Peronikh said.

'I understand,' the vizier said. 'It cannot be easy to lose one's father.'

'Not easy? What would you know?'

'I lost a son once.'

Peronikh did not know what to say. Thankfully, he was saved from the awkwardness. The royal chariot had circled around, and Merkhet was advancing towards them. A pair of legs—*Llora's*—glistened behind him, brighter even than the golden chariot she sat in. Looking beyond his brother, Peronikh couldn't see her face. She was hidden from view, maybe concealing herself, as she cradled the Double Crown. It should be him returning to the royal palace with Llora at his side and the crown upon his head. Not Merkhet.

How did they even strike up a conversation, let alone progress to sharing chariot rides? His brother had been afraid of his own shadow for most of his life.

Merkhet stopped next to them, his stupid ponytail swaying behind him. 'Just the two people I need to see.'

'Is that so, Your Worship?' Prahmun asked him.

'Yes, particularly, my brother.'

Now? Now, Merkhet was ready to speak? After three long months, or near enough. This is how his brother would treat him, even after all the effort Peronikh had exerted in trying to prepare the piddling fool for his Pharaonic Trial?

The vizier bowed before Merkhet. 'I will give you a moment, then.'

'Thank you.'

Prahmun shuffled away. Peronikh waited for his brother to speak and was kept waiting. Merkhet wrapped his arms around him instead. Peronikh didn't retreat but didn't reciprocate his brother's tight embrace, either.

'Sorry this has taken so long,' Merkhet said. 'I should have come sooner, but I was hurting and busy. Always so much to do.'

Peronikh grunted and pressed his brother away.

Merkhet did not assume that as rejection because he continued talking. 'Thank you for saving Father,' he said. 'I froze, and you were there to act. The crown should be your burden.'

It should. Peronikh could not disagree with his brother on that. 'It was instinct. He deserves to reach the Afterlife.'

Merkhet clapped him on the shoulder. 'Thank you, Peron, for all you do and your patience. I can't imagine it has been easy awaiting your assignment.'

'It has not.'

'The truth is, after much contemplation, I could not come to a firm decision.'

'Why didn't you ask me? We could have worked together.'

'You weren't at my banquet for a reason. I wanted to give you space, time, to accept the mysterious workings of the gods. I enjoy them no more than you do.'

Peronikh grunted. 'Brother, seems more like the time and space were for yourself to comfort Llora. So, what will it be, then?'

Merkhet gave him a puzzled look.

'Well, what decision have you made? Firm or not—

you have made one, right?'

'I have.' Merkhet summoned Prahmun back over. 'You will train under the viziers, learn their role. In time you will become one of my advisers.'

A vizier?! What glory was there in advising the pharaoh when Peronikh should be Egypt's supreme commander himself?

'I'll allow you and Prahmun to discuss the finer details. Much to attend to.' His brother smiled, retreating to the chariot. It rolled away at once, with his hand resting on Llora's.

Peronikh reached clarity. No confusion or mixed feelings. However the pharaoh tried to explain his inattentiveness, did not matter.

Too little, too late, *brother*.

'There is a reason I have requested you as my understudy,' Prahmun said, handing him a silver feather necklace—the Amulet of Ma'at.

Peronikh sighed as he lifted the pendant over his head. 'Must I prompt you? I believe I've already waited long enough.'

'I share your doubts.'

Peronikh raised his eyebrows. 'What are you saying? Speak straight.'

'Your brother is not worthy of the Double Crown.'

'Anyone can see that,' Peronikh said. 'His indecision is rife. In his handling of me, when the sarcophagus began to submerge, and even just now at the Judgements. The man was guilty and Merkhet just let him go!' He paused, his enthusiasm souring. 'But the gods have made their decision.'

'Maybe not—'

'What is it?'

'It would be unwise to meddle with the intricate balance of Ma'at.'

'Tell me what you know. Egypt must come before my brother. Egypt must come before all.'

'Maybe you are right. I received an anonymous letter. I was going to ignore it, but—'

'Tell me,' Peronikh said, already listening with great intent. Whatever the vizier was about to divulge could be critical in his quest to secure the support of the entire administration.

'Have you seen that necklace he wears?'

'I have but in no great detail. What is it?'

'It is a dedication to Aten.'

'What relevance does the cult sun god hold?'

Prahmun shrugged. 'Maybe none, but the letter did reveal that the necklace was stolen.'

'Stolen? Why would he wear such a thing?'

'I know not, my prince.'

'I suppose it doesn't matter. My brother is a walking symbol of desecration to our sacred laws. He is a disgrace.'

'Maybe so.'

Idle chat would amount to nothing if Peronikh couldn't determine exactly what the vizier was angling at. He needed to be more aggressive, more direct in his questioning. 'Where is the annual flood? Egypt needs a pharaoh that can provide for its people.'

'It does, and you are cast from a different mould. I know it better than anyone. How is your mother?'

Peronikh gaped, stumbling to find words. His mother—what did the vizier know of her, want with her?

Prahmun persisted. 'Samena, is she well?'

'She is.'

'I'm glad. We do not see each other as often as I would like, as she would like.'

'Sorry?'

'We were together once,' Prahmun said, 'her and I.'

'When?'

'Many seasons ago, before you were born and before Nekhet stole her from me.'

'Stole my mother, what do you mean?'

'Never mind that,' the vizier said. 'It's a tale for another time.'

'Well, what would you ask of her now? What are you asking of me?'

Prahmun stared through Peronikh, his eyes fierce and determined and full of longing. 'A chance to explore what was. Only the pharaoh can grant her freedom from the eternal binds of the harem. Merkhet would never release her.'

Peronikh nodded, understanding what the vizier proposed. 'What now, then?'

'I'm not certain it is connected. However, a spate of jewellery thefts has been reported at the markets. Necklaces, amulets, rings.'

'It has to be linked,' Peronikh said.

'Then we must inform Lufu of our doubts about the state of the throne.'

'Should we not investigate the allegation first?'

'We cannot be seen to be concealing this. We must include my counterpart, or else he may assume we are scheming.'

'How do we proceed?'

'Follow me,' Prahmun said, 'I have an idea.'

Peronikh would need to contain himself when they

spoke with Lufu, for his excitement was palpable, growing inside him.

He couldn't—no—Egypt couldn't afford any complications to arise.

Chapter 13

Peronikh arrived with Prahmun in the administration precinct, a short walk from where the Judgements were held. They walked along the smooth sandstone portico and entered the main building. The viziers operated from there, as it was where all the important government records were stored. Lufu would be expecting his counterpart but not Peronikh, who hoped their visit would catch the shrewd vizier off-guard, gnawing through his rationale and resolve.

'Alright,' Prahmun said, his voice barely audible, 'if Lufu throws anything unexpected at us, use some initiative, will you?'

'I'll handle it.'

'Why are you sweating? Your neck is red and

angry.'

'I'm always like this,' Peronikh lied, dabbing at the perspiration lining his brow. Scratching unawares again. He really needed to control the nip's urges before someone might get the idea to check between his toes. That would be trouble. 'Let's do this,' he said.

The vizier nodded, and they strolled into the restricted administration workspace, after a brief examination of their silver feather amulets to the guards posted at its entrance. The room, adjacent to the entrance foyer, had a dull interior, designed with ample bench space and without any consideration for aesthetic appeal. Although, perhaps not ample enough because there were records scattered everywhere. Mounds and mounds of them. Was this what his life would be now, subjected to endless piles of paperwork? Peronikh groaned internally. What a disaster.

Lufu was ruffling through a particular set of papyri records and raised his head to greet them. 'Good afternoon. I was just looking for you,' he announced to Prahmun, before returning to his important document search.

'Lufu, I will be glad to assist however I can. But first, we must bring something to your attention.'

'We?' he asked, having not noticed Peronikh. 'If it is about those damn farmers again, I might lose my mind. We cannot force the flood to arrive. It will come when it comes.'

'No, you will be spared the torture of the farmers' woes today. Peronikh will be joining us as my assistant, learning from us during this crucial transition period.'

'Fantastic. Aha! There it is,' Lufu said, finally

taking a moment to rest from his ruffling. 'Now, what is the matter?'

'Crime has risen in the wake of Pharaoh Nekhet's death,' Prahmun said.

'At the markets in particular,' Peronikh added.

'Yes,' Prahmun said. 'It is rather concerning, and the market owners are outraged. Some are even threatening to abandon their stalls and head north for Memphis.'

'That is unacceptable. My dear associates, how do you intend to resolve this matter?'

'We were uncertain on how to proceed. We wanted to inform you and reach a unified decision.'

'I appreciate that. Well, it is obvious, isn't it? We must investigate the matter at once and apprehend the culprits.'

'Of course,' Prahmun said. 'Should Peronikh and I take charge on that? You look terribly busy.'

'Please. I am swamped. Merkhet has commissioned the records for the Nilometers as far back as we have them. He is worried about the flood's absence, as we all are.'

'We will rid Thebes' alleys of its petty criminals. You know we will, Lufu,' the vizier said.

Peronikh nodded in affirmation. They would rid Thebes of its weak, ineffective pharaoh, too.

Peronikh stirred from a long, restful nip-induced sleep.

Refreshed and determined for another productive day, he filled a copper bowl to the brim with oats, added water, and then stirred it over the dying embers of the harem's morning fire. A pot of honey lay nearby, he drizzled a generous ladle of the golden nectar over his bowl and gave it one final whisk. Simple, delicious, and filling.

Nourished, Peronikh ambled to the markets, where he had agreed to meet Prahmun. No doubt he was late, the sun was already high overhead and the ground sizzled beneath his sandals. In one of the lanes near where he had bumped into Llora, he spotted the vizier.

Prahmun approached a jewellery stall, amid others selling candles, corn, and ornaments. The market owner seemed dejected. For an otherwise stoutly man, the glum expression did not suit him. Peronikh was near blinded, by a glimmering reflection from behind the jeweller, as he drew closer. Hundreds of necklaces dangled from the roof of the stall, swaying at the behest of a soft breeze.

'Good morning, friend,' Prahmun greeted the man.

'In need of a new necklace, friend? Ye've come to the right place then.'

'Not exactly, but maybe there is something I can help you with.'

'Ye have me ears but not for long. Got a stall to run, see,' the merchant said, pointing at it.

'I have reason to believe that someone is wearing a necklace, which was stolen from you. Have you had any issues with theft lately?'

'Odd necklace has gone missin', but no worse here than elsewhere. How can ye help?'

'I'd like to apprehend the culprits and eradicate theft in Thebes—for good,' Prahmun told him.

'Won't get no objections from me,' the market owner said, his mood perking. 'What ye need?'

'Is there anything distinctive about your designs?'

'Etch my signature marks inna them.'

'What are those?'

'Scarab over the ankh.'

'Excellent,' Prahmun said, noticing the appearance of his apprentice. '*We* will continue to investigate. Just one final thing.'

'I'm still listening,' the merchant said, his curt tone a helpful reminder that he had a business to run.

'We may require your testimony. Would that be acceptable?'

'If ye can do your part, gladly do mine,' the merchant said.

'You honour your family and country. Thank you for your time. We will be in touch.'

The man bowed before them, and Peronikh almost bounded down the lane he was that giddy. The pure joy was reminiscent of the day when he was given Tendrence. He was another step closer to righting the wrong, and before catastrophe struck their beloved Egypt. The gods would be obliged to release the floods once he had achieved justice.

'You know what this means, don't you?' Peronikh said.

'Of course I do, boy. I told you I had an idea. And that didn't stop with ensuring Lufu was the one to send us on this quest of retribution.'

'You knew he would do that?'

'No. But I didn't ascend to the rank of vizier by

doubting myself,' he said, grinning.

'We need evidence now.'

'Yes, my understudy, you're learning!' An emphatic smirk trickled across the vizier's face before an expression of seriousness replaced it. 'Conduct a similar line of enquiry at the other stalls and present to me in the administration precinct.'

Armed with the various signatures of the craftsmen and having already reported his findings to Prahmun, Peronikh was eager to inspect his brother's necklace.

If they could verify their suspicions about the necklace's origins, it could be the deciding factor in securing Lufu's support and staging an upheaval of the throne. Peronikh licked his lips, as if he were savouring the taste of some juicy delight. He could not wait. The grandeur of the royal palace was just a fleeting stroll from the busy administration precinct.

Constructed atop a mammoth sand dune, the palace overlooked the Nile from its terrace. Its entrance was located on the side farthest from the river. They followed the dune around, passed by the guards stationed at the gateway with a terse nod, and clambered up the steep sandy slope.

With each step his feet seemed to sink. The sand swarmed around them, requiring more and more effort to set free. His laboured paces and the terrible cramp in his stomach told him one thing: Llora might be inside.

What would he say to her if she was? That he forgave her, that she should forget all about Merkhet and be with him instead?

By the time he and Prahmun faced the inner chambers, the knot at the bottom of his waist had tightened so much, he was almost keeled over. Laughter came from somewhere within the chambers, and Peronikh's oats gurgled in his stomach. It must have made an alarming *whoosh* because the vizier gave him a perplexed glance. But Prahmun's concern was cursory, for he walked through the chambers and out onto the terrace. Peronikh straggled in behind him.

Llora and Merkhet were entangled, arm-in-arm, on the terrace as they were perched over the Nile. Her head rested on his shoulder.

'I fortified it myself. Anyone would be mad to try and rob my father's tomb,' Merkhet said.

Llora giggled, nestling in even closer to his brother, and Peronikh's violent urge to belch reached a new height. He feared the worst: losing the battle and cloaking the stone-tiled terrace in his breakfast.

Prahmun startled Merkhet and Llora from their affectionate cuddle. 'Sorry, I trust I am not intruding, Your Worship, but I require your audience in an urgent matter. Would now be acceptable?'

Merkhet whirled around to face Prahmun. 'Of course. Llora, please excuse us a moment.'

His brother paused, eyes never leaving Llora as she stood to part way for their discussion. Peronikh's stomach settled as soon as she and Merkhet were separated. She walked past Peronikh, as elegant as ever, on her way back into the palace. But she averted her gaze, not even giving him a quick glance. He crumbled inside, a new, unfamiliar sensation overcoming him. His eyes tensed, his eyelashes twitched, and Peronikh summoned every ounce of his willpower to cull the urge welling from deep within him.

He struggled against it, like an insect in a blustery gust. Peronikh could not—would not—cry in front of his brother.

'Welcome,' Merkhet said, acknowledging Peronikh with a nod. 'What can I help you both with?'

Months of nothingness, then one short, pitiful conversation, and still all Peronikh received was a curt welcome and a stiff nod? His brother used to embody compassion and consideration of others. Not anymore.

'She will make an elegant Great Royal Wife one day, don't you think?' asked Prahmun.

'I'm certain she will,' Merkhet said. 'Now, what is this pressing matter?'

Peronikh's fury surged, suffocating his momentary hollowness. What—just because Merkhet had found a shape that wasn't pudgy and managed to grow a ponytail in the same fashion as their father—he deserved a girl as majestic as Llora? His brother's newfound, sly arrogance was insufferable.

'Right, yes. I wanted to inform you that we are investigating a flurry of robberies reported at the markets and look forward to presenting the apprehended criminals before you at the Judgements. Also, to congratulate you on your initiative for restoring the Temple of Aten. It is a brilliant way to commence your reign. It had fallen into a rather forlorn state.'

'Thank you both for your dedication. Yes, I am

committed to being more than a pharaoh that just maintains Ma'at. My father was a great commander, but there were areas of our great Egypt that he neglected. Too many of our people go hungry each day, parts of our exalted city lay in ruins, and more needs to be done in quelling the rise of foreign powers. With the help of Lufu and yourselves, we can rectify this and much more.'

'I—sorry, we,' Prahmun said, extending an arm to Peronikh, 'look forward to advising and assisting you on all such matters. Here, have a read of this.' He withdrew a scroll from his cloak and handed it to Merkhet. 'It is a schedule for the upcoming Judgements. Tell me though, what is this stunning pendant you wear?' he asked, pointing at a necklace dangling against the pharaoh's chest.

'It was a gift from Llora, a dedication to Aten.'

'Amazing. Peronikh, come take a closer look at this.'

Peronikh stepped forward, inhaling deeply as he did. He reined in his bubbling emotions and reached for the pendant. Its spiked sun rays were cool and smooth despite the day's heat. He turned it over in his hand and had to restrain himself from erupting with joy. The scarab and ankh were there, the markings of the first jeweller he and Prahmun approached. By the great grace of Isis, they were there.

All the tension and uncertainty, that had terrorised him recently, evaporated. Lighter and clearer, he released the necklace.

'What a marvellous trinket,' Peronikh said. 'Expert craftsmanship. I may even know the jeweller who made this.'

'In that case, please extend them my gratitude for their meticulous work.'

'I will. It is good to see you, Merk. But if you will excuse us, we must restore order to our hovels and alleys.'

As Peronikh bowed to his brother and departed the royal palace with Prahmun, the thefts didn't even cross his mind.

No, the imbalance of order far exceeded those dull crimes. The gods were deserting their country—chaos and devastation were imminent. They had abandoned Merkhet and only Peronikh could restore Ma'at now.

He, the Forgotten Prince, was ready—as he had always been—to command Egypt.

Chapter 14

Every time Merkhet started to feel some remote semblance of comfort and familiarity in his role as pharaoh, another unanticipated complication would arise.

He was always swiftly reminded that it was a tiresome and thankless duty he performed. The worst of which was when he delivered his first death sentence at the Judgements. Anyone with a keen eye would have noticed his whole body trembling and a voice so quivery, it could have held a dozen arrows. Nevertheless, Merkhet gave the command. Such was his work.

He stared out over the valley of Thebes, smothered by the agony of his rule. Merkhet frequented the terrace often since inheriting the Golden Throne, if for nothing else than to watch the Nile. The river tortured him though, the weakest he could ever remember it.

Why wouldn't it show some sign of life? *Something, anything.* Praying for the arrival of the flood was his least favourite daily ritual. Each day the prayers went unanswered, Merkhet's exterior began to mirror that of the Nile's, lifeless and wilting. Even presiding over the Judgements was less painful than this habitual torment.

The delay of the life-giving flood could mean only one thing: he had angered the gods. They must have wanted Peronikh to succeed Nekhet, but then why did they acknowledge him during the Walking of the Walls? Their essence enveloped him on that day, empowering him. Yet in his short reign, he'd somehow managed to not only lose their favour but also incur their wrath.

'Your Worship,' came a voice from behind him. Lufu.

Merkhet turned to face the senior vizier. 'What is it?'

'I come bearing grave tidings.'

'Out with it.'

'The Hittites, Your Worship, they are in Egypt and have annihilated some fishing villages in the marshes north of Memphis. Two hundred dead.'

'How were they able to cross the borders?' Merkhet demanded.

'We do not know yet. Usually, I would be there to investigate, but it is important that I'm here with you at this time.'

Merkhet could sense there was more to be told than this single atrocity. The vizier's face was unmoving. The Amulet of Ma'at lay still against his chest. 'What aren't you saying, Lufu?'

'I have retrieved the Nilometer records you requested.'

'And?' the pharaoh prompted him.

'The river is now at its lowest ever recorded level.'

Merkhet cursed aloud, the vizier flinching. 'Coordinate with the administration in Memphis, locate the Hittites and contain their advances. As for the inundation, there is nothing we can do.'

After Lufu left, all that remained were Merkhet's deeply ingrained and haunting fears. Failing his father. Disgracing their family legacy. Egypt torn asunder by famine, war, and disease. Faceless bodies begging him for food, water, and protection from the marauding Hittites.

Perspiration poured out of Merkhet's glands, and his heart beat so hard it might burst out of his chest. He crumbled to one knee, expecting he would patter the stone floor in sick. The irony of the lengthy harvest season taunted Merkhet like an evasive gazelle. There was nothing left to be harvested. The inundation was well overdue from seasons' past, and the Nilometer readings confirmed the direness of the situation.

Merkhet clambered to his feet, using clenched knuckles to propel himself up. He took three quick breaths and convinced himself that the sickness had passed. Inside the palace, he saw Taharva, standing outside the throne room.

'Ready the chariot, please,' Merkhet said.

The Nubian, not always in the mood for a verbal exchange, nodded and left him. Within seconds of Merkhet giving in to the throne's allure, Taharva summoned him with a gesture. At the bottom of the palace complex, the chariot awaited them, ready for an immediate departure. Two royal guards were already positioned on the baseboard when Merkhet hopped aboard.

Taharva climbed in beside him. 'Where are we headed, then?'

'The villages.'

At once, the royal guards grabbed a firmer grip on the reins, and the mystical beasts—Abacca and Tendrence—responded, pulling the chariot forward. They were heading towards their destination, and the Nubian, unlike moments earlier, appeared ready to talk. He was grinning, somewhat sheepishly, making sure that the pharaoh was aware of him.

'What?' Merkhet demanded of him.

'Missing her already, are you? When should we send word of the wedding to the nobles around the country?'

'Shut it, will you?' Merkhet was missing his newfound pillar of stability, Llora. They had spent much time together, especially since his father's burial. Her skin, her smile, they glowed and dazzled when all else wanted to engulf him in darkness. She had only left a couple of days prior and already he needed to see her.

Somehow, Taharva's grin stretched even wider, before a sense of seriousness returned to it. 'I've not seen her of late.'

'I urged her to stay with her family for a short while. They mean everything to her, and I don't want to stand in the way of that.'

'Have you met them?'

'Not yet,' Merkhet said.

'Good luck, Scrollworm,' the Nubian said with a cheeky smirk and then returned to silence.

Some of the nervous energy surrounding Merkhet's pharaohship dissolved, replaced by a new wave of unimaginable horrors. Meeting Llora's mother and brother. The mere thought left him clammy, and he succumbed to the drain of his duties, slumping over in the chariot's rear. He removed the uncomfortable and heavy Double Crown of Egypt, his *father's* crown, and placed it beside him.

When the chariot arrived outside her hut, Llora was arched over one of the village garden beds. Her legs glistened magnificently in the sunlight as she watered the plants, and in an instant, he was revitalised. Merkhet marvelled at her beauty. No matter what angle you gazed upon her, there was something new to admire. Llora glanced in his direction, and the watering pot fell from her grasp. Landing in the sand with a soft thud, the remaining water pooled beside it.

He disembarked the chariot, and she rushed over to embrace him. The warmth of her skin collided against his, and Merkhet was beyond content.

Taharva hung back with the guards, minding the horses and the chariot, while he and Llora retreated inside her hut. No one else seemed to be home. Merkhet followed her into her room, where she prodded him in the chest. 'I wasn't expecting you!'

'I wanted to see you,' he said.

'Likewise,' Llora said. 'But the pharaoh should not come here. Not to the peasant villages.'

'Why should he not? The villagers are the heart and soul of Egypt. The very fabric of our existence.'

Llora's eyes sparkled with appreciation, despite the tired lines beneath them. She smiled and glided over to her bed mat. Merkhet crouched down, joining her on the reed matting. She nestled closer to him.

'You should not have come,' she said, as if that settled the matter. 'But I am so glad you have.'

'Missed me, have you?'

'Yes, and ...' Llora averted her gaze for a moment.

'Where is your family?' Merkhet asked. 'I was hoping to meet your mother and brother. Tiaa, right? And Wuntu?'

Her lips parted to speak, as if she might say something profound. All Llora said was: 'You can't. They're away.'

'Does this have anything to do with the ragged lines under your eyes?'

'I'm sorry, I can't talk about my family now.'

'If I can help, you must let me know.' Before she could respond, Merkhet's stomach released an almighty, thunderous rumble, as if Geb had shaken the earth's core after a long slumber.

Llora giggled. 'Is my handsome pharaoh hungry?'

'What gave it away?' he said with a smirk.

She slapped him on the chest, and the playful hit echoed in the small mud hut, even though it didn't hurt. But then Llora's mood changed so sudden and without warning. Her gaze fell away from him, downward. 'We have a problem.'

Whatever it was, he had to help her. 'What is it?' Merkhet asked, softening his tone.

'We have no bread.'

'Then we will get some.'

'We can't. Yesterday we were told that the grain

supplies are empty.'

'Empty? Our stocks are depleted. But empty? That cannot be.'

'It wasn't just my family that were turned away. The rest of the villagers were too. Our people are starving, Merkhet.'

The words prised their way into his skull, lingering there. How could his people be starving some two months into his reign? Gods. Goddesses. Father. *Someone*, help! 'We will resolve this, together,' he said, clutching her hand tight. 'Take some villagers with you to the administration precinct. Collect as much food as you can and distribute it to as many hungry citizens as possible. Can you do that?'

Llora nodded, and Merkhet wondered if this girl had any flaws? Pretty. Smart. Passionate.

'Don't worry,' he said, 'I will provide for our people.' But would he — could he — provide for them? For a time, his confidence had swelled when he was training with Taharva and preparing his father's tomb. Now ...

'I know you will. You are Pharaoh Merkhet, kindest and bravest of them all. There's one other thing I have been meaning to ask.'

'Yes, my sweet?'

'You seem troubled ever since the vizier and Peronikh came to talk to you. What have they burdened you with?'

'Just some thefts at the markets. Nothing they can't handle. They were more interested in my necklace than anything else.'

'They were?' Llora looked at him, hesitance and conflict in her eyes. 'Maybe they have noticed, too.'

'Noticed what?'

'How it strains you.'

'But you gifted this necklace to me? I even sleep with it on.'

'I know,' she said, 'and there is nothing wrong with wanting to make your father proud. But—but to carry those expectations around with you all day is not healthy. I don't want my gift to be a constant reminder of his passing.'

'It is a celebration of his life, not a reminder of his death.'

'Please, Merkhet. I see how heavy it is around your neck. It would be best if you don't wear it anymore.'

She insisted, not only with her convincing words but with her beautiful watering eyes, too. Merkhet faltered for a moment but surrendered under the will of her wet, crestfallen gaze. He lifted the necklace over his head and placed it in her gentle hands, along with his Eye of Horus insignia. Her insistence confused him. Even though he had grown rather fond of the pendant, he allowed it to pass, kissing her on the cheek.

'Take my seal and present it to gather whatever food you can. Go to the royal palace if you must. I will investigate our depleted food stocks for myself.'

Merkhet caressed her cheek, then strode out of the hut to board the royal chariot. His deepest fears flashed before him again, except this time he was able to banish them with ease.

Egypt needed him.

Masses of Egyptians were turned away, unfed and uncertain, and Merkhet was none the wiser of their plight. What use was a leader who did not know the troubles of his people?

He understood the situation would intensify the longer the inundation resisted their calls. But dire, already? Merkhet could not fathom how this could be. Prahmun and Lufu had some serious explaining to do. He descended from the chariot, his pace a determined trot.

Inside the administration building, the viziers were ruffling and sifting through scrolls. Merkhet could only hope they were attending to his royal decree.

Peronikh was not present, and that was for the best. Merkhet did not wish to scorn his brother so soon, not after finally giving him purpose. It was unfortunate that in his own scramble to adjust to all the changes, he'd forgotten about Peronikh, leaving him in the dark since their father's death.

'Your Worship, I was not expecting you so soon after my visit to the palace this morning,' Lufu said.

'What a pleasant surprise,' Prahmun added.

'This is not an amicable visit. I need answers, and you better have them.'

His stern voice must have shocked them, for they stopped what they were doing and were drawn into his unrelenting stare. Even as they stooped low, bowing, they locked eyes with him.

'Of course, Your Worship. What is it?' Lufu asked, rising from his deep bend.

'I have trusted you to carry on supplying the food

to the citizens of Egypt on my behalf, but perhaps I've been blind in doing so.'

'Not blind, just neglectful,' Prahmun said.

'Excuse me?'

'How long—'

'Prahmun,' Lufu cautioned, holding out his arm.

The younger vizier waved it away. 'No, he needs to hear this. How long were we meant to tolerate your avoidance of responsibility? Now you have the hide to come in here, accusing us of incompetence?'

'I was preparing my father's tomb for his journey to the Afterlife.'

'Any of a hundred administration officials could have performed that duty.'

'Enough,' Lufu said, a hint of venom in his voice.

'I am here now,' Merkhet said. 'Tell me, and tell me true. What is the current state of our food stores?'

'They are running low,' the senior vizier said.

'Running low? Or exhausted?'

'Running low,' they confirmed.

'For Aten's bright rays, we're still in the harvest season! The food supplies should be at their peak—how is this possible?'

'My dear pharaoh, the harvest was insufficient this year,' Lufu said.

'Insufficient or not, do we still have grain for bread?'

'We do,' Prahmun said.

'Then explain to me, why our tireless villagers were denied their state allowance?'

'With the flood's absence, we've decided to take some precautions.'

'You've decided, have you? Without bothering to

consult me?'

Prahmun looked away, appearing mildly uncomfortable. 'Of course not. We didn't want to bother you. When the flood arrives, it will be irrelevant.'

'Starving citizens are far from irrelevant. I could be mistaken, but I believe that my role as pharaoh is to maintain Ma'at. Is that—or is that not—my primary function?'

'It is so, Your Worship,' the viziers responded.

'If my people aren't eating, then I am failing my duties. I will not take any chances with the delicate balance of Ma'at. Feed everyone. Reduce the allowances if you must, but everybody eats. You hear me?'

'At once, Your Worship.'

'Organise a small battalion, not too many soldiers, given the Hittite escalation. Have them search the northern provinces of Nubia for additional food supplies. Scour the unchartered lands if need be. It is clearly going to be a tough year.'

The viziers nodded in agreement, possibly afraid to speak any further.

Satisfied, at least for the moment. Yet an undeniable urge nagged at Merkhet. He could not describe where it stemmed from, but it could not be ignored.

He needed to connect with the gods and truly attune his mind and soul with theirs.

Crossing through Luxor, Merkhet strode along the avenue of sphinxes, towards Karnak.

Paved in stone, it connected the two temple districts. The lion-bodied sphinxes faced inward with their human heads, looming at him from both sides. He must have passed hundreds of them, maybe over a thousand, for they stretched an age. Raised up on platforms, they all stared him down from their pedestals. Unmoving in centuries and unwilling to release their sharp gaze, they convinced him: his pharaohship was cursed.

As the avenue ended, two giant obelisks towered over him. Eighty feet of red granite stone, at least, and covered in hieroglyphic scenes. Their narrative of the gods dominated the landscape for all to see. Slipping between them, his fingertips brushed across their surface, sinking into the symbolic engravings. He was in the Precinct of Amun, where it was eerily quiet. Much unlike its usual flurry of movement—the morning prayers, offerings, and rituals were not visible.

Through the temple's garden, he shuffled into the Hypostyle Hall. Hundreds of columns, all inscribed with Amun's power. The passage to the inner sanctum lay before him. Its gentle waft of spices was thick and pleasant, but he didn't breach it. If there was no one at the temple, something was wrong. The serenity turned haunting. Merkhet would not find peace here—where was everyone?

The Temple of Aten was a busier scene than he had anticipated. As one of his first major decrees as pharaoh, he commanded that it be restored from its forlorn state. Admittedly, Llora's affinity for the temple and his own attachment to the necklace, the one he no longer wore, may have influenced his decision.

Yet he had not anticipated that he would be confronted by a wall of Amun initiates surrounding the temple's perimeter. The priests were silent, still. Unnervingly so. The labourers and construction workers appeared relieved at the sight of the pharaoh, bowing before him. They guarded their frustrations with the priests loosely, mocking the statue-like initiates with rude hand gestures and exaggerated imitations of their stillness.

Merkhet approached the flustered construction overseer. The man had less hair than the last time Merkhet had spoken with him, maybe a week ago, and an unpleasant stench enveloped him, reeking of defeat.

'What is happening here?'

'Your Worship, it is a joy to behold you,' the overseer said, bowing. 'The Amun priests are protesting. We have been unable to work since yesterday.'

'They have been like this all through the night, too?'

The overseer nodded, his face glum with resignation. Merkhet was stunned—his father had warned him numerous times to be wary of the Amun Priesthood. But this was madness.

'What are they protesting against?'

'I'm not much of a gambler, but I would stake my wife that they are most upset with your decree to restore the temple.'

'Those greedy swine. My father exhausted vast resources to extend the Temple of Amun. Sweet Isis and her children's tears, their entire precinct was expanded just two harvest ago.'

'I know. I have tried to talk to the High Priest and end this farce. He is adamant that he will speak only with you. I sent to the royal palace hours ago to inform you. A message was left with the viziers.'

His advisers had failed him again. Who exactly was on Merkhet's side? But he could not dwell on that, and instead eyed the wall of initiates.

The High Priest featured at the centre of the protest, positioned near the temple entrance. His pure white robe, wrapped in a leopard skin shawl, contrasted those of the initiates, clad in all black. Merkhet marched towards the High Priest, who was unflinching.

'High Priest, what is the meaning of this? We have Hittites to expel from our lands, I do not have time for this.'

'Who is asking?'

Merkhet stopped himself from unleashing his words in a furious stammer. Inhaling deeply, he spoke. 'It is Pharaoh Merkhet, the fourth of the Eighteenth Dynasty.'

'Your Worship, I am sorry. I did not recognise you without your crown.'

Merkhet rubbed the back of his neck. His crown was in the chariot. He did not have his seal, either. It was with Llora. How could he be so foolish, as to give this fanatic any opportunity for a snide remark. The man had already hindered his life enough with his interference at the Walking of the Walls.

'The Amun Priesthood resents your blind commitment to the lesser god, Aten.'

'It is not for you or your folly band of priests to judge my actions. Your job is to appease Amun, and in doing so, help me maintain Ma'at. Move aside, end this nonsense.'

The High Priest seemed to weigh up the directive, calculating the outcomes. 'Very well,' he said. 'We will leave peacefully, but bear in mind, the patron god of Thebes, is no longer in your favour. Your thoughtless actions have displeased the God of the Winds, the King of the Gods, our humble hidden one.'

The vexing priest did not bother to conceal his wicked smile as he stepped away from the wall of initiates. It was almost if the High Priest was thrilled that Merkhet was pharaoh, and not somebody else. The score of priests followed their leader, shadowing his departure. One behind the other, they were herded back to the Temple of Amun.

Merkhet did not need to instruct the workers to return to their duties, they did it of their own accord. He pressed through them and between the obelisks at the temple's entrance, where he reached the luscious, temperate garden. It was the only part of the complex that had not fallen to ruin, despite the lack of care. Vibrant flowers, not native to Egypt, of all colours and fragrances blossomed there.

Kneeling among their unkempt and scattered beauty, their smells reminded him of easier times, where his concerns were fewer and far more trivial. Merkhet pleaded noiselessly to his father and the gods. Aten, Amun, Horus. Whoever would listen.

He was trying his best but required guidance. Needed their help before he drowned in his own inadequacy. Would they give him the chance to prove his legitimacy to the throne? Whether the gods heeded him or not, a wave of relief swept over him, and he left the temple, radiating with renewed positivity.

The lingering doubts of being the Cursed Pharaoh were dispelled, along with his concerns about the High Priest. It didn't matter who was supporting him. The floods would come.

They would—and they would cleanse and heal all the lands.

Chapter 15

Peronikh scratched and scratched at his neck. The skin was raw and puffy and ready to bleed.

But this had nothing to do with the nip. What else could he do? After Prahmun cautioned him that engaging Lufu again so soon would not work in their favour, Peronikh accepted the vizier's counsel was justified. Although he wasn't thrilled to admit it, if Lufu suspected their intentions, he would blindly oppose them and be convinced of nothing. If they were to succeed in restoring order to the throne, they needed Lufu on their side.

So, Peronikh mustered all his strength and resolve to delay the impending unveil of their startling discovery: the Cursed Pharaoh wore a stolen necklace.

Ten—possibly more—painful days went by.

Peronikh feared if they suppressed their revelation any longer, he would burst into flames. The day had finally arrived though. Prahmun, always punctual, was already waiting for him. Resting against a stone pillar under the portico of the central administration building, he rose to his feet. 'We alert him to the Aten necklaces that were stolen, that the designer engraved them. Nothing else. Am I clear?'

Nodding, Peronikh trailed the vizier inside. They found Lufu bent over an enormous scroll. Unfurled, it had small stones placed over the corners to keep it that way. Lufu was muttering inaudibly to himself as he inspected the document.

'Lufu,' Prahmun said, 'we come bearing news of our investigation.'

'Must I beg for the outcome?' the vizier asked, not shifting his focus from the scroll.

'We understand that necklaces paying homage to Aten were targeted by the thieves.'

'What is the great unveil? Have you apprehended the culprits?'

Lufu's tone was harsh and irritable, unlike any other time Peronikh had dealt with him. Whatever was on that scroll, it could not be good.

'Soon,' Peronikh said. 'We can identify the stolen goods.'

'How?'

Prahmun shot him a devastating glare, as if to say guard your tongue—or risk losing it. Lufu, still preoccupied, did not notice.

Heat flushed to his face, and Peronikh persisted despite the warning. 'The jeweller engraves his work. Any Aten pendant bearing ...'

Lufu finally looked up. His intense bloodshot stare made the hairs on Peronikh's arms rise. 'Bearing what, my boy? Can you not see how busy I am?'

'They are, err—'

'Likely stolen,' Prahmun said.

'Likely? How do you propose we separate the thefts from the trades? Do we just go about detaining everyone with an engraved necklace? Well, maybe that is not such an absurd idea. It could ease the burden on our depleted grain stores.'

Peronikh was careless, so excited to advance his plans that he failed to consider all the options. Even though he was severely sleep-deprived, the vizier was right. Merkhet received a gift, likely stolen, but what of it? Circumstantial and nothing more. Almost useless. Even worse, recently his brother had opted not to wear the necklace for whatever reason.

'What have you done to address those issues, Prahmun?' Lufu asked. 'Pharaoh has made his disappointment in our performance clear.'

'What can we do? I just don't know what to make of anything anymore. When Nekhet was pharaoh, everything was so easy, so simple.'

'I know not, either. All last night I studied prayers and rituals, searching the ancient texts for answers.'

'The answers?' Peronikh asked.

'To the crisis that confronts us, dear boy. The floods, they are well and truly overdue. The Hittites become more emboldened by the day.'

'Are the gods displeased with us? Angry with the pharaoh? He does seem to have an unusual fascination with Aten,' Prahmun said.

'Perhaps we have angered them,' Lufu said.

'Or maybe he is too young to lead Egypt,' Peronikh said.

Lufu sighed, his exhaustion apparent. 'We've had younger. The gods are testing our resolve, but we cannot be so hasty to forget the message delivered to the High Priest. They insisted that Merkhet be crowned, and we must support his rule.'

'Perhaps you are right,' Prahmun said. 'We will leave it for the gods to decide. Pray the floods arrive soon.'

'Pray, indeed,' the senior vizier said. 'May the gods have mercy on us all.'

Prahmun gave a furtive glare in Peronikh's direction. 'Good day, Lufu.'

Peronikh did not understand what the vizier was trying to achieve, but he would not pray. It infuriated him that Prahmun even pretended to be free of prejudice. A pointless endeavour. Egypt would be better off if everyone spoke their mind without the fear of divine reprimand. The thoughts were already formed—was everyone so gullible to believe that the gods cared for the distinction?

No matter what the viziers said, not even the inundation could save his brother's tenure now. Weakness upon the Golden Throne could not be tolerated. Would not be permitted. Soon, Peronikh would have Lufu's support, and that of the entire administration, even if it required him to persuade them individually.

He would do that for his Egypt, and no setback could prevent him.

Peronikh was not kept in suspense long. He had barely cleared off the portico when the meaning behind Prahmun's glare became apparent.

The vizier dragged him by the wrist. Around a corner they went, into the shadows between administration buildings. 'What was that?' Prahmun demanded, his voice edging towards a hiss.

'I lost my thoughts,' Peronikh said, shrugging. 'It happens.'

'I told you to keep it simple. Do you not understand the damage this may have caused your own ambitions?'

Prahmun was right, and Peronikh held his silence. He could have—may have—done serious harm to his plans. With any luck Lufu would be too preoccupied to dwell on the matter further.

'We are trying to convince Lufu of Merkhet's incompetence, not illustrate yours.'

Peronikh did not get a chance to speak.

'It stops right now. The nip. Before you undo all our hard work. You've had ample chance to grieve and sulk.'

The prince was left reeling in the approaching darkness.

How did the vizier know? How long had he known?

Chapter 16

Merkhet woke but kept his eyes shut, afraid of what new atrocities the day would hold for him.

For every minor victory he enjoyed, something was lurking nearby in the shadows to steal it away from him. Moments after the gods accepted him, someone questioned his claim to the throne and labelled him as cursed. He was able to navigate the coronation banquet without much difficulty other than a bit of a stutter. He even met Llora there.

But then the constant nightmares of his father, being denied his entitlement to the Afterlife, overshadowed the funeral preparations and almost materialised at the burial procession itself. The Judgements were torturous. The Hittites were relentless. Interpreting the gods' will, and without fail, the crowd would always groan if their bloodlust was not satiated.

The nastiest surprise came from the viziers themselves. They were meant to support him, to ease the burden of ruling. But they did not trust their pharaoh to involve him in the considerations of the country's dwindling food stocks. At least Merkhet reinvigorated a little faith in himself when he was able to banish the High Priest from his wrongful protest at the Aten Temple.

Yet it didn't matter how much he believed in himself. Unless he could deliver the flood, the people's disquiet would keep resonating at the Judgements and temples, and they would continue to be sent away with hollow, rumbling stomachs.

Merkhet sat up in his bed. A raucous flowing, faintly reminiscent, echoed in his chambers. He rubbed his eyes, trying to establish its source. He couldn't quite remember how he recognised the persistent gushing.

Somehow, inexplicably, he knew he should. But then, after a few more forced blinks, it dawned on him. He scrambled out of bed quicker than the dreadful summer evening when a scorpion tried to cuddle him in his sleep. Through the palace, Merkhet went into the throne room, where he rapped on the entranceway to the royal chambers. No response. Merkhet burst through there in a flash, out onto the terrace.

The stone floor was already baking, even though the sun still had that orange glow, the kind you see at first light, surrounding it. But his feet didn't seem to mind. They were elsewhere, splashing in the cool rapids of the inundation! Oh, the sweet, sweet annual flood had finally arrived.

At long last, the gods heeded his desperate pleas. The life-giving silt, he had yearned so desperately for, would sweep through the lands.

The brown-green river rushed by him, relentless. Maybe not with the ferocity that Merkhet had become accustomed to from past seasons, but it was something to rejoice. The water churned through the lands, snaking its way towards the northern delta. The pharaoh beamed, as the pent-up anxiety that had built up over the course of his short but tumultuous reign was released.

He was not the Cursed Pharaoh after all.

For the next week, Merkhet perched himself on the terrace to embrace the wondrous view. The music of the Nile was anything but smooth, but its roaring notes were harmonious to his ears.

Each day he had to pinch his cheeks—had they really come, the floods that would save his people? Exposed to the elements—sun and wind—he watched the river swell to life. It soothed him, and his soul fluttered with peace.

The rare afternoons when Llora joined him on the terrace, their hands intertwined, and he never wanted to let go. They would sit there for hours until their sun-drenched skin begged them for mercy. Even then, they were just as likely to stay longer. To Merkhet's surprise, she even conceded to his exuberant pleas and returned the necklace to him, which he adorned at once.

Just shy of one month had passed since the burial of his father, Pharaoh Nekhet, the Tireless Warrior-Builder. The bittersweetness of that day still lurked within him, sometimes resurfacing. Those moments reminded him of how much he struggled to establish himself as pharaoh—a position his father had manoeuvred so effortlessly. New challenges were thrust in Merkhet's direction every day, problems that he could never pre-empt.

Aligning the viziers with his vision, accepting the cruel reality of balancing Ma'at, dealing with the nuisance that was the Amun Priesthood, and the uncertain favour of the gods themselves. Beneath all that, Merkhet still contended with the enduring necessity to make his father proud, of which there was so much uncertainty.

He tried to prepare himself for the difficult periods that were still yet to come. Every decision, every non-decision was under scathing scrutiny. If the inundation was insufficient, the citizens and the administration would heap the blame on him until he drowned underneath it. Some of them were fond of casting the blame in any direction but their own, and they always assumed safety in numbers.

Merkhet vowed to eradicate the toxic officials that plagued his administration. It sickened him how they all came crawling to the fore now that his father had passed. He would happily do away with all of them, and Egypt would be the better for it.

The Nile's banks were bulging, having already swallowed significant portions of the red desert. Merkhet dared to believe that even though the river's swollen currents had begun to settle, they would be blessed with ample planting and harvesting conditions. Only the Nilometer reading could confirm—or destroy—his optimism. But if the levels were insufficient and the Nubian rains that swept through the cataracts had receded early, strife and uncertainty would vanquish them. If famine didn't.

Trundling down the palace slope, as Merkhet had done most days of his life, he headed to the Judgements. An unfamiliar whistling noise penetrated his entirety. The sound reached a deafening pitch and was getting closer. He spun around, pivoting on the spot, searching for the howl. His eyesight had to be betraying him. It couldn't be possible.

'Dear mother of Bastet!' he cried as a murky brown cloud blanketed the desert sky beyond the royal palace.

The inexplicable cloud whirred at terrifying pace, heading straight for Thebes. Merkhet was rendered captive, watching it carve a path of destruction. Hurtling closer and closer, he tried to start his startled legs, but they were rooted to the spot. Soon, it would not matter. He would be swallowed whole by the angry cloud.

He punched himself on the thigh, and his legs begrudgingly responded. He was away and bounded the short distance inside. Fighting against the heavy palace door, now reinforced by the vicious winds, a waft of red cloud squeezed its way through the gap. Merkhet wheezed, shoving all his weight and strength behind a final lunge. The door obeyed him this time, slamming shut.

Panting, he collapsed in the throne room. He attempted to soothe a frightened Beebee as the palace's foundations shook. Its structure appeared to be holding firm, but how would the rest of the city fare if the winds carried on their path? Merkhet willed them to dissipate, but he had no control over this sandstorm. Set—the god of the desert and storms continued to relay his anger to the Egyptians. His anger at the pharaoh. Why else would a sandstorm of such ferocity assault Thebes?

The braziers rattled, threatening to tip out of their holders, as the winds refused to relent for hours. But their devastating howl was not the worst of it. As loud as the sandstorm was, Merkhet could hear only one thing.

The words of the High Priest taunted him. *Your thoughtless actions have displeased the God of the Winds.* Not just the haunting rhetoric—but also the priest's smug face as he delivered it—was emblazoned in Merkhet's mind.

Before he could assert Egypt as a dominant and diplomatic force, Merkhet would need to calm the gods and restore order to the lands.

Chapter 17

Merkhet squared up against Taharva, sword in hand. Their sparring sessions were his brief yet much needed daily reprieve from leadership.

No burdening thoughts of responsibility or duty encroached upon him during these sacred encounters, and somehow, the physical exhaustion gave him the clarity to focus on the demands of ruling. He pranced around the giant Nubian, nimble and confident in his developing reflexes. Taharva lowered his spear just as Merkhet was about to lunge and strike.

'What is it?'

Taharva groaned, insisting Merkhet turn around. When he did, he faced an entourage, which had gathered behind them. The viziers, his brother, and a whole host of soldiers. Something was wrong. They knew better than to interrupt his morning ritual.

'What has happened now?' Merkhet asked, the words catching a little. 'I was not expecting your presence here at the barracks. We still need to assess the damage from the sandstorm.'

'You are right, we do need to do that,' Prahmun said.

'We are almost finished training. Since when have the viziers needed a military escort around Thebes?'

'Oh, this is no escort. Well, it is, but not for us. We will be inspecting the city later today, but you will not be joining us.'

Merkhet struggled to believe what he was hearing. 'Have your wits deserted you, Prahmun?

'Do you forget whom you are addressing?' Taharva asked him, with more of a growl than speech. The sunlight glinted off his bronze spear but that did not deter the vizier from pursuing his contemptuous tone.

'I am perfectly aware of your title, Your Worship,' Prahmun said, stooping in a mock curtsy. 'But it is irrelevant now.

'Horus help us. What are you talking about?' Merkhet asked.

'The administration has lost faith in your ability to lead Egypt,' Lufu said.

'We have no time for such folly.'

'This is no folly, boy. The readings of the Nilometers do not lie.'

'A pharaoh that fails to maintain Ma'at is an unworthy one,' Prahmun declared.

'This isn't funny, Prahmun. The poor inundation will have to wait. We have another sensitive matter to address. We must convene the administration at once. We need to devise a plan to help those affected by the sandstorm.'

'We will be addressing that and anything else that may arise, but as I have stated, you are unfit to rule the Egyptian Empire. You have brought great shame upon the Pharaonic Institution, and the gods have sent clear signs of their mistrust in your reign.'

A murmur of agreement from the soldiers echoed Prahmun's sentiments.

Losing his patience, Merkhet raised his voice. 'You've done nothing but sit by idly as you claim to be my most trusted adviser.'

'Merkhet—formally the Fourth Pharaoh of the Eighteenth Dynasty—you are to be exiled from Egypt immediately,' Prahmun said coolly.

'How dare you! Your insolence will be punished. What are you hoping to achieve?'

'I hope to ensure the continued prosperity of Egypt, which you have demonstrated yourself incapable. Now, seize the former-pharaoh!'

The soldiers hesitated. They were wary of Taharva and the pointed-spear that he gripped at his side.

'I am pharaoh, chosen by the gods as Nekhet's successor. We cannot entertain such nonsense notions.'

'Guards, seize him at once!'

'Any such decision must be taken to the Judgements,' Merkhet said, pleading, not with the viziers and guards but the very gods themselves.

'No,' Peronikh said, stepping from behind the shadows of the viziers. 'I don't think so. A Judgement is unnecessary for thieves.'

'What are you talking about, brother? You need to

see a physician. You look unwell.'

'That necklace you wear so proudly is stolen,' Peronikh said, ignoring any concern shown for his health.

'Not possible,' Merkhet said. 'It was a gift.'

'What a shame, brother. A necklace bearing the exact same markings as yours was reported stolen.'

'This is madness. All precious crafted metals bear markings. How can you know one stolen from one traded?'

'It has the scarab overlaying the ankh. The evidence is undeniable.'

Merkhet didn't check the necklace. He didn't need to. It matched, but that didn't mean anything. What was happening? Of all the challenges and perils facing Egypt, they were now fighting each other.

'Seize him!' Peronikh commanded.

'No, stand down. I beg you,' Merkhet said, holding the Eye of Horus seal for everyone to see. 'Egypt needs a unified front, now more than ever. You cannot forget the daring Hittites plundering our lands.'

The soldiers turned to Lufu, seeking his essential confirmation. They would not intervene against Merkhet's orders without the direct approval of both viziers. The senior vizier's expression was neutral, his eyes dazzling with conflict and indecision. Then he delivered a slow, begrudging nod of affirmation, and chaos flared up within the training arena.

Merkhet was quick to extend his arm and keep the soldiers away with the steady poise of his sword. He looked at Taharva, but the Nubian was incapacitated, standing motionless with the blankest of expressions upon his face.

It was in Taharva's rare failure to act that the soldiers were able to swarm the pharaoh. They knocked the sword from his grasp. Merkhet flailed at them in a flurry of kicks and punches. But they secured him and began dragging him away. His shouts echoed all around the enclosure as he cursed the viziers for their ineptitude.

The last voice Merkhet heard in the barracks was Peronikh's. 'Let the captain go. If he wishes to accompany Merkhet in exile, he is free to do so.'

Exile? His brother had to be mistaken. Division and disharmony would only further harm Egypt. He could not provide for his people if he was sent away. There had to be a mistake. The most harrowing thought came to Merkhet as his feet fell behind him, making a trail in the sand.

Why did the gods intervene in some matters and not others?

Chapter 18

Peronikh was hurried to the administration precinct, where he was being fitted into the ceremonial white robe for the second and final time. All within an hour of Merkhet being forcibly removed from the barracks and exiled from Egypt forever.

The servant girls patted away the creases on his front. Peronikh distracted himself from their pleasant caresses with an unexpected realisation. The royal palace was now his home. He enjoyed visiting the palace—but to live there? Everything he ever wanted was soon to be his. The Golden Throne, the Double Crown, the war table, the view from the terrace, and everything else that came with pharaohship. All his.

The gods supported his rule and had from the very

outset. Yet he still itched and sweat at every waking hour and sometimes resting ones, too. An unfortunate consequence of abandoning the nip, nothing more, and that was a fair price to pay to reclaim his birthright.

The Walking of the Walls ceremony commenced with little fuss. No announcements from the viziers. No gathered sea of citizens. Peronikh exited the city walls and traced their course. Not even a few gates into his reflective journey, Merkhet's horrified expression as he was escorted from his homeland—began to haunt Peronikh's consciousness. Would his brother ever understand?

Maybe not at first, but in time, Merkhet would. He understood better than any that their country must always come first. One day Peronikh would tell him just how sorry he was, but right now he couldn't afford to be dragged down by the weakness of his emotions. Egypt needed healing.

Even though he was certain of his actions, that they were justified and right, each step was twice as difficult as the preceding one. The sun burned thrice as harsh and the warm gusts were some of the most stubborn he had ever come across. At least the farmers that flocked to the riverside could distract him from his torturous walk. The flood waters had receded and in they swooped to plant the seeds in the fertile mud left behind. Egypt's immediate hunger crisis would not be solved just yet, but the future was looking brighter.

After what seemed longer than the eternal Afterlife, Peronikh re-emerged through the city walls, unchanged. He examined his hands, turning them over, searching for a sign. The gods did not reach out to him, as Merkhet claimed they had for him. Was Egypt's plight destined to get worse, before it would get better?

Pondering this bitter thought, amongst many others, Peronikh was escorted to the royal palace in the royal chariot. His newest luxury made short work of the journey *home*, where many civil servants were roaming the plateau outside the gates, preparing for the evening's banquet.

His mother was awaiting his arrival inside the dining hall.

'Mother,' Peronikh said. 'It is so good to see you!'

Samena embraced him lovingly in outstretched arms. As he pulled away, she gave him an affectionate peck on the forehead. 'How has this come to be, my son? I'm not sure I understand.'

'Another time, please? I'm tired, let's just enjoy the feast tonight.'

She did not argue, and Peronikh was incredibly grateful. He did not want to lie to his mother.

'Oh,' he said. 'I have a surprise for you as well.'

'What is it, Peron?'

'My first act as pharaoh will be to relinquish your vows to father. The first life is too short to spend it in servitude of those already in the Afterlife.'

'Are you sure?'

'Certain. You will move from the harem village to the palace with me.'

His mother looked equally ready to cry just as she might smile. She nodded, and their conversation flowed better than it had in years. Hours later they strolled down to the feast, where Peronikh's cheerfulness was quickly stripped.

Set up in the exact same place, it was a stark contrast to the reports he had heard of the jovial banquet held for his brother. A sour mood lingered in the air, infecting everyone, as if it were contagious. Fewer people attended, and he couldn't blame them. The Egyptians needed a return to normality, not festivities. Observing all the glum faces around him was depressing. Even Raina, who always bore a neutral expression, was unenthused to be documenting the evening's events.

Peronikh was an unwilling participant in the feast's proceedings, a foreigner at the very heart of it all. He didn't touch the food or drink. None of the simple grain and fruit offerings really appealed to him. Why wasn't he jubilant? This was what he had dreamed of since he was a young boy. It was what he deserved.

Then the understanding of his unrest, his unease walloped him. The dreams of this day always featured a queen at his side. Llora's raw, natural beauty was worthy of such recognition at the pinnacle of their society, but where was she?

Prahmun probably delivered a speech similar to the one at Merkhet's coronation feast, but Peronikh couldn't say for sure, not having attended himself. He received the crown and his royal insignia from the vizier. Peronikh tucked the scarab beetle seal inside his robe and sat the crown on his head. From the moment it rested on his scalp, an acute, constant buzz penetrated his existence, boring into his every thought and drowning out his surroundings.

A locust plague had swept across the northern villages of Thebes in the hours before the banquet, and that wasn't the worst of it. Merep scowled at him throughout the proceedings. Somehow, she knew.

Blotched tears were smeared across her face, but behind that, was anger. Maybe even hatred, and she was unrelenting. Her gaze made Peronikh's skin itch so much that he was relieved when the guests stopped their reluctant dancing.

The musicians were dismissed, and Peronikh took his leave. Rest did not come easy though, and not because it was his first night sleeping in an unfamiliar room.

Merkhet's horrified disbelief. Merep's cold glare. Those glum, inconsolable faces from the feast stuck with him all night, even though Peronikh was right to act when he did. Egypt would have perished if he didn't.

Everything would be better now. He just needed Llora by his side.

Chapter 19

Llora looked at the empty space beside her. The space *he* sometimes sat—but not in over three weeks.

As her stomach rumbled, she remembered Merkhet's gentle features and broke out into a fleeting, goofy smile. It wasn't the same as seeing him though. Somewhat akin to comparing ripe fruit with its over-ripe cousin—enjoyable until you remembered the true sweetness that existed. He was gone. Exiled from Egypt, and she didn't even get to say goodbye.

Llora was lumped on the humble comforts of her reed mat, a place she often found herself when things were awful. What would she have even said to Merkhet—sorry? How could she explain everything that happened? Her lust for theft and how it led to the unknown man orchestrating her every move, which spiralled into the disappearance of her brother and Merkhet's exile—hardly appropriate supper conversation.

Despite initially being forced upon Merkhet by the devious manipulation of that hooded-monster, she did develop a genuine connection with him. The courage he demonstrated to set aside the hurt from the loss of his father was remarkable. He ruled valiantly even when everything and everyone was against him.

In their short time together, his body matured to meet her own vain standards. Merkhet grew taller, slimmed around the waist, and a handsome adult face emerged. But he still managed to keep that adorable dimple on his chin.

Llora sighed—he was even able to solve the mystery of how everyone knew her name. Wearing a necklace bearing her name on it while on a stealing spree. She was a damn fool.

Merkhet was a true gentleman, but he wasn't Peronikh, and maybe no amount of sunshine would see his skin turn that dreamy olive shade. Merkhet was meek and gentle, and Llora would not change that of him. He wasn't his brother.

She would seek out Pharaoh Peronikh, just as soon as she had an answer for the question he was bound to ask.

Why? Why had she left him in the lurch? Why had she said nothing? To answer that truthfully would endanger her little brother, and Llora wasn't sure she could risk that. She wilted underneath a fresh wave of guilt. A sole victory against two staggering defeats.

Sheer divine will alone may have rescued Laseb at the Judgements, but Llora was claiming it as her win. She needed to, knowing that she could have done more—should have done more—to save Merkhet.

Maybe he would never have been exiled if she didn't return that wretched necklace to him. Maybe with a little time and the right information, he could have saved Wuntu from the grip of the conniving man.

Llora was adamant the hooded-man would never relent. But Merkhet was no longer pharaoh. Her duty was surely complete. The monster, whoever he was, would be obliged to return her brother, and she will have balanced the score.

Merkhet was gone, and all that remained was Llora's unwavering determination to bring Wuntu home and return his toy lion to him.

Llora was collecting water from the village well when it happened.

The vile man, the one who had stopped her from ever truly resting, appeared in her life again. As always, his face was hidden. He cornered her against the well and must have stalked her to do so, waiting patiently for the perfect moment, without a single person in the vicinity to save her. Like a scorpion strike, the most glaring detail struck her. Wuntu was not with him.

'Hello, my dear.'

'Where is my brother? I have held up my end of the bargain.'

'Not so hasty, young one. These things take time.'

'No, they don't! Return him now!'

'You are hardly in the position to bargain, you foolish girl. I need another favour before I can release young Wuntu.'

Llora glared at him, wishing her eyes could make him shatter into a hundred thousand fragments. 'You cannot be serious. What is it this time?'

'No need for the aggression. It is a nice and simple task. You even have experience at it.'

She said nothing. What could she say? This monster had done his utmost to strip her of everything. The only thing he was preserving was her life.

The wretched man sighed. 'I wish it were different,' he said. 'The pharaoh was not meant to be exiled. That was the last thing I wanted. Now it will be a while longer before you see your brother.'

Helplessness encased her. How long would Llora have to wait? How long would her mother be able to wait? The man would not answer such questions, but he may indulge her with others. 'What did you want— if not that?'

'Not so fast,' he said with a sneer. 'Plans may have changed, your duty has not.'

'How can I? He's gone.'

'Don't worry that pretty, little head of yours. What I ask won't be difficult.'

'What?' Her blunt responses were the only way she could curb her mounting anger. If she could just find a sharp object nearby and stab him with it until …

'I've seen the way he stares at you. Women are the

downfall of all weak men.'

'Who?' Llora asked.

'Peronikh. Reprise your role as the pharaoh's companion. Your role is more important now than ever.'

'I will not play your silly games any longer. You hear me?!'

'Please, what choice do you have? There are forces at work that you couldn't even begin to comprehend.'

Then he sauntered out of the peasant village while his infuriating rhetoric formed a thick impenetrable veil around her. Whoever he was, had dealt ultimatums at every turn, casting his smug superiority in her face with every condescending jest.

Llora would not tolerate his toxic and senseless scheming any longer. The terrifying consequences of her theft followed her everywhere. An invisible shadow, slowly suffocating her. The locusts' screech came pouring into her mind like it was an open gateway. Maybe she did deserve to answer for her crimes. But did any of that matter anymore?

The manipulative man was responsible for the chaos engulfing Egypt, not her. Least of all, Merkhet. Llora had to do something. She bared her teeth, determined to dismantle the wicked man's tirade.

For Wuntu. For Merkhet.

Chapter 20

Somewhere north-west of the Egyptian border, the sweet tormenting smell of distant, distant Llora strangled Merkhet. He sank to his knees, the truth collapsing him.

'No, you don't, Scrollworm. Up you get.'

He had failed to maintain the balance of order and protect his people. No wonder his country didn't want him.

Just when Merkhet had finally grown confident enough to stop mumbling in front of her and actually enjoy her radiating pleasantness, it was all stripped away from him. The country he vowed to serve above all, had no love for him, no place for him.

He would miss the hours, hands clasped together

in perfect silence, where all his worries would fade away with the setting sun. Fond memories of Llora would stay with him forever, even if she would not.

'We've not come this far for you to give up now,' Taharva said, stooping to lift Merkhet with ease.

They had come far. Taharva was always urging him on. At least Merkhet could thank his brother for that. The last thing he heard, before the jeers of the citizens took hold, was Peronikh instructing the guards to allow the Captain of the Royal Guard to pass. *If he wishes to accompany Merkhet in exile, he is free to do so.*

Merkhet was grateful because he didn't have anyone else. Not Llora or his mother. Nor his father, who he missed most of all. He yearned to be with them all. They were the four corners of his world and made all other maps obsolete.

Peronikh would have been previously except Merkhet couldn't shake the uneasiness of his brother commanding the guards to seize him. An order out of love for country or one of lust for the throne? The latter stirred dark sentiments. What part had his brother played in his exile?

Merkhet clapped Taharva on the back. 'You're right, friend. We must continue.'

Always the hardest, he made those first few steps. He wasn't humiliated through the alleys to just flounder in the desert and die. The murmurs of his countrymen and women following him as he was dragged through the markets and the temple districts by his ponytail. *The Cursed Pharaoh* they muttered in hushed tones, disgrace etched into their unfamiliar faces.

For the better part of a month, the soldiers—once

bound to his command—had prodded him and Taharva the entire way to the border. On arrival, they were tossed across the border and handed a water sack each. Banished forever. Never to return. Nor did Merkhet have any intention to. Not after the way he was disrespected.

No, he would survive for himself, for the memory and honour of his father.

With only a vague understanding of where they were, Merkhet wasn't certain they would survive though. The desert terrain was much the same as Egypt's, if not a little rockier. He and Taharva required inconceivable amounts of resolve to endure the searing days, outlast the freezing nights, and then motivate themselves to trudge on through the unfamiliar land.

The anger stemming from their predicament ebbed and flowed, slowly being replaced with misguided optimism. Somehow, everything would be fine.

But nothing was fine. Two days earlier, their water sacks had squeezed out their last drops with an emphatic gush of air. They couldn't even establish how many days had passed since they left Egypt.

Taharva recommended, and he agreed, that their best chance of survival was to carry on. Carry on, keep calm, and hope the gods would heed their calls for help. But the deities weren't listening—maybe they couldn't—maybe their reach stopped at the borders. Merkhet shook his head—stories were often told of how the gods influenced battles on foreign lands. Almost every pharaoh had a hieroglyphic relief detailing exactly that. His father was imbued with the agility and grace of Sekhmet and the cunning of Set against the Hyksos. He had said so himself.

When Merkhet became so thirsty he feared his tongue may escape the harsh imprisonment of his mouth and crawl across the desert floor in search of water, a sign appeared before him. Wedged in the sand, its markings were in a familiar language.

A Syrian scrawl, not too dissimilar to the Hittite's, indicated that drinking water could be found nearby. Never before did he recall the countless hours and days spent studying with such fondness. His heart plummeted. What if he was hallucinating?

He slapped himself on the face, once on each cheek. A dull pain stung them, lingering beyond its welcome. However, the sign was still there, and Merkhet would have jumped with joy if he wasn't so fatigued.

'What does it say, master linguist?'

Merkhet wanted to smile at hearing that, but he didn't—couldn't—for fear of fainting. 'Water. Close.'

'Let's not delay then,' Taharva said.

Next to the scrawl was an arrow pointing to the right, and they followed it. Merkhet didn't need his royal education to work that one out. His thirst was overwhelming, but his spirit lightened, and he almost glided in the direction of the arrow.

Merkhet's stomach was an empty pit, having only received the odd unsuspecting insect, lurking beneath the rocks, as sustenance. Their plight was real, but now they had a glimmer of hope to cling to, and Merkhet clung to it fiercely with everything he could muster.

The rekindled prospect of salvation was dimming fast. It had peaked at the sign and now it was all but gone.

Merkhet's surrendered to a vision of his mother

upon hearing his fate. Her blustering sobs as the details of his exile were recounted to her again and again, almost forced him to be sick.

Shaking the images away, Merkhet gripped the pendant of the Aten necklace, the one Llora had returned to him. Whenever he wanted to give up and melt into the scorching sand, it coursed a mystical power through him, renewing his will to survive. Maybe, just maybe, his fortunes would change and one day he could be reunited with his loved ones.

Something hovered in the distance. Something other than sand and rocks. His vision was blurry. Merkhet couldn't quite make it out though. Drawing closer, a single step at a time. Every one of his muscles were screaming now. If this was a false alarm, he was not sure he would be able to continue.

This was it—do or die.

The distant scenery came into focus. An opening. The mouth of a cave emerging from between the rock face. He powered on, his steps so clumsy he might crumple at any moment.

Taharva groaned in ecstasy when they reached the opening. Before the mouth of the shadowed cave front, lay a sparkling pool of water. The oasis appeared cold just by the way its surface shimmered in the sunlight. Merkhet, distracted by its beauty, stared at it while his companion dashed for the water. Another noise, one of pure pleasure, came when Taharva drank. He muttered something to his former Nubian gods, and then whirled around to Merkhet.

'Drink, Merk, drink. It's glorious.'

Merkhet moved towards his friend, towards the shimmering beauty. His dehydration was so severe that he shuddered as he bent for it. When his face dipped into the surface, a few precious drops soaked into the sand, but he gulped the cool water in great mouthfuls. It sang to his coarse mouth and throat as it passed down.

Forgetting all about Llora and his family, about Egypt, Merkhet's new life was decided. He would immerse himself in the oasis for the rest of eternity, frolicking in its pool of iridescent, life-giving liquid until his skin was saggy with age.

The cavern was cosy, having just enough room for two people to sprawl out. The sun angled through at first light, pelting them and ensuring they could not oversleep. But Merkhet didn't mind.

In just over a week they had crafted themselves a way to sustain, to exist. The constant hunger and thirst disappeared, and he enjoyed the monotony. No surprises here at the oasis. No one would arrive during a private training session and drag him through the alleys by his hair. The wonders of the waterhole, that was replenished each morning when they arose, wouldn't allow such an injustice to happen.

Large trees—all trunk and branch, with no leaves or foliage—grew from gaping cracks and holes in the surrounding rock face. From that they were able to snap off enough branches for firewood. Sharpened stones served as flint, and the fires strangled the night chill.

Merkhet couldn't believe their luck when wildlife regularly appeared, seeking the life-giving pool, as they had. The sand cats eyed he and Taharva warily as they slurped from the oasis. A mutual peace was forged between claw and their own sharpened tree spears. The mountain goats and gazelle were unafraid. They should have been. Meat and added warmth were a bountiful luxury after Taharva stumbled upon a forgotten blade, a dull and rusted sickle.

Merkhet sat by the cavern fire. The flames twisted and curled, sizzling when embers sparked into the air. The Aten necklace burned against his chest, but he did not remove it. If he denied that Llora crossed his mind half a dozen times an hour, every hour, he would be a liar. But something about the simplicity of what they had established, reminded him that life was to be enjoyed, not fretted and wished away. If the routine they followed bothered Taharva, he never mentioned it. Hailing from a traditional Nubian village himself, perhaps he too, was relishing the serene quiet.

As the embers smouldered and lost their heat, Merkhet bid his loyal friend and protector goodnight. Wrapping his goat skin around him, he drifted to sleep.

A shuffling noise made Merkhet propel himself upright. It was early, and in the gloom of dawn, a man stood outside the cavern. Merkhet blinked and his vision steadied.

The man was of a reasonable size, but nothing compared to Taharva. As pale as a full moon, the newcomer's complexion negated any intimidation factor he may have gained with his frame. The man must have spent all his time beneath shelter. His lavish accessories were astonishing. Covered in jewellery, his insatiable lust for rings, bracelets, and necklaces was palpable. Whatever shiny objects Merkhet could imagine, he wore them.

'My water,' the man cried in Hittite. 'You've tainted it! What have you southern savages done? My men will get you for this.' The apparent oasis guardian—released a hearty chuckle.

Taharva, now awake, laughed with him, as if to say *good luck with that*. Merkhet glanced around, unsure how to interpret the man's odd claim. The guttural foreign accent was unnerving, but the oasis guardian had no weapons and appeared harmless. Besides, where could his men be hiding?

'Deal with it,' Merkhet said, also in the Hittite tongue, and his brash assurance even surprised himself. He had nothing left to lose as he stepped out of from the cave's shelter. Nothing except for the fine oasis before him, and he was tired of living under the crippling shadow of fear. 'There's no one else out here. Our dirty southern skin will taint the water all we like.'

Taharva grunted in agreement, not able to speak Hittite. He followed Merkhet, who shook off his animal hide covering and edged out of the cavern.

The oasis guardian trembled at the knees and rage seized the whites of his eyes. 'SEIZE THEM! NOW!'

On the outskirts of the oasis, soldiers were pouring in from behind the rock face that concealed their cavern. Merkhet froze, horrified. An overwhelming urge, to dive into the divine oasis and pretend he was still dreaming, surfaced within him. Talking tough was fine, had even seemed easy, but now Merkhet was unable to move.

This would be how it would end—on constant rotation—trying to prevent the advancing soldiers from killing him. Or worse, detaining him. A brute grabbed him from front-on, pinning his shoulders at his side. Another soldier secured his arms from behind, and the first one released him, scampering over to Taharva. Merkhet wriggled and wriggled, but the man's defiant grip did not waver.

The remaining soldiers converged on Taharva. He repelled their attacks, somehow having already acquired one of their swords. Merkhet then lost sight of the Nubian, obscured by the approaching oasis guardian.

As the man's eerie, pale skin attracted a tinge of pink from the strengthening sunlight, Merkhet's courage returned. He would not surrender, no matter how dire the circumstances. If not for himself, he would fight for the loyal Nubian, whom was still at his side, even after everyone else shunned him.

A well-timed elbow cracked the ribs of his oppressor. Merkhet squirmed his way free of the now slackened grip and the guardian's outreaching arms, only to be tackled from the side. The hard ground ripped away layers of skin as they tumbled about in a frantic struggle. But he was soon outclassed by an experienced opponent.

'Well done,' the creepy guardian said to the soldier restraining Merkhet. 'You know the deal. I get the belongings, you take the prisoners.'

The oasis guardian started to lift the Aten necklace from him, and Merkhet was powerless to stop it from happening. But then the crazed man stopped, his greedy hands coming to a sudden halt.

A sharp prick in his stomach made Merkhet look down. A sword, entrenched in the oasis guardian's core, had sliced right the way through. Taharva stepped from behind the guardian, and his body fell to the ground in slow motion, blood spurting onto the sand as the weapon was withdrawn. But in his fall, the oasis guardian's weight dragged down on the necklace, snapping its chain. The pendant rested, unmoving in his hands. Merkhet tried to stretch for it, but still grappled from behind, had no chance of reclaiming it.

A group of five armed assailants bombarded Taharva. They circled around him, forcing him against the rock face. He was surrounded, but the Nubian would never back down. He slashed at one, nipping him along his front. Then Taharva received a slice of his own for his troubles. Searing pain smeared his face, yet the determination to break their ranks never dissipated.

The captain feigned with an overhead swipe, and then booted the closest soldier in the chest. The soldier recoiled, stumbling backwards. The Nubian did not wait for him to recover, lurching forward and striking the man with unrivalled savagery. The Hittite warrior attempted to catch his detached head, before falling to the ground in a headless heap.

Carving his way through their staggered formation and flurried attacks, Taharva rallied. The remaining soldiers steadied themselves and were ready to go another round. The captain fought valiantly, bringing about the quick demise of another two soldiers.

The final two started to coordinate their attacks. Charging them, they matched every one of his thrusts. Then the momentum began to swing. Taharva was tiring, and they forced him backwards, one lunge at a time. His barrage of assaults had failed thus far, and now he was struggling to block their onslaught. His sandal slipped on one of the many pools of blood—not yet fully soaked into the sand—and he sank to his knees.

The soldiers sensed an opportunity to finish off the hulking Nubian, breaking their cohesive formation. One of them advanced, lofting an axe above his head. He must have intended to split Taharva in two, but he was slow, arrogant.

Taharva sprang upward with terrifying speed. The incisive blade slid straight through the man and threatened to hoist him in the air as it penetrated the soft muscle between the rib cages. Taharva lifted himself to his feet and removed the weapon from the spluttering carcass. He charged at the last soldier. The Hittite made little effort to defend himself, and his lopped-off arm, still gripped his axe, crashed into the red-strewn sand.

Merkhet could not deliver the warning in time. A crunching blow struck his friend on the side of the head. Somehow, more soldiers had materialised. From where, he would never know.

Then blackness. Utter agony coursed through him. An intense pain burnt into the back of his skull, and Merkhet collapsed to the ground. Lying face down, semi-conscious, and eerily aware of the blood teeming from him.

Chapter 21

The gods wanted Peronikh to sit upon the Golden Throne.

They declared as much when they withheld the annual flood for so long—and then when it did arrive—it was wholly underwhelming. The worst in Egypt's history. A savage sandstorm descended upon Thebes while Merkhet ruled and the Hittites were threatening to invade. None of that was happening now.

Yet in the weeks after his brother's exile, the citizens moaned. Oh, how they complained. Chaos was lurking in every alley and hovel of the city, waiting for them. With unsafe streets what could they do but hide away in their mud-huts, avoiding the markets and temples? Even the sun had a dull gloom they said.

Grating and unjustified, Peronikh couldn't fathom why their grievances were ever uttered. Nothing was wrong with Thebes, not now that he was commanding it. Still, what point was there boasting a city of one hundred gates if none of them were frequented?

Peronikh sat on the throne, where he was shrouded in darkness. He had insisted the royal guards remove Horakhty. Staring at Merkhet's bow—with the Eye of Horus staring right back at him—was too unnerving.

Unsure of how he could appease his unsettled compatriots, Peronikh rapped his fingers on the cold, smooth surface, searching for the solution. Visions of being pharaoh swirled through his mind—the *before* visions—where he was always doused in golden light, infused with the strength of the gods themselves as he dismantled their enemies, limb from limb.

None of that was a reality. The stark dimness of the throne room was sobering. If he wasn't so busy, he would be wallowing in the grip of a cherished love. The one he had ignored since Prahmun called his ambition into question. But the nip's call was growing louder by the moment. Soon its clamouring and relentless beckoning would be undeniable.

'Your Worship,' a guard said, startling him. 'A girl has presented herself at the gates. She wishes to speak with you.'

'Who is she?'

'It is Llora, the girl who used to entertain your brother.'

Peronikh's heart thumped quicker. What could she want now, after all this time spent pretending he didn't exist? His initial reaction was to reject her, especially the way the guard associated her with Merkhet, but those words never left his mouth. 'Bring her in.'

'At once, Your Worship.' The guard bowed before him and departed.

What could Llora want? If she came grovelling to him, he would send her away quicker than the farmer who tried to blame him for the abysmal floods suffered under his brother's reign. Peronikh had seen her two times since that fortuitous moment when he bumped into her at the markets. Briefly at the Judgements and most recently on the terrace.

Each occasion was more painful than the last, and it was no secret why. She appeared happy—genuinely happy—in the presence of his brother. Things had changed, but a strange bout of nervous energy still overcame him when she emerged in the doorway.

'Hello,' she said.

'What brings you here?' The words were as harsh as his tone, but he couldn't take them back.

She stared back at him, her blue eyes dazzling in the gloom. 'I went to the coronation banquet to see you. And you were not there.'

'My pharaohship was stripped from me.'

'Not for long.'

Peronikh bit down on his initial retort. 'Why did you come here tonight, Llora? To stir trouble?'

'No. Why weren't you at the banquet? I went for you.'

'I couldn't face to be there. I was mortally embarrassed to be ousted in favour of my incompetent brother.'

'Mortally? When did you become such a coward? The young man who saved me in the desert was brave, heroic.'

'I am that same young man.'

'Prove it,' she said. 'Hear me out.'

He did, and if Peronikh wasn't conflicted in the short wait for her arrival, he was now.

She had come back to him. Peronikh was wary initially, but he could not deny Llora's eyes. Big and blue and full of remorse.

She was as honest as she could be, telling of her family's struggles with starvation, and at the time of Merkhet's banquet she desperately needed his help. She regretted it because an awkward distance had crept between them. But her family meant everything to her, and she would always put their needs ahead of her own.

If her eyes and gently spoken words hadn't already mended his wounded pride, her lips certainly did. Their divine lusciousness reminded him of a sweet and juicy summer fruit, maybe pomegranate.

Llora's return was met with much scepticism. His mother, Samena, led the charge. Even Merep, before she escaped to live in the harem village, regarded the village girl with venomous disdain. The viziers especially questioned Llora's motives. But Peronikh did not care what any of them had to say. She was trustworthy.

'Why won't the gods commune with you?' she

asked. 'You are a decisive and worthy leader. The least you deserve is to be informed of how to restore order and balance to Egypt?'

Restore order—what did she mean? Had the impassioned village peasants polluted her mind, too? However, the words she did not say bothered Peronikh more than the ones she did. Llora did not refer to him to as the *rightful* pharaoh.

'Let's move to the terrace,' he said. 'I find it easier to think there.'

She followed him out there. The terrace's serenity was as vibrant as ever. The birds fluttered and chirped. The afternoon sun shone with purpose. Even the Nile was healthier than when Merkhet had slouched beneath the Double Crown.

Peronikh, captivated by Llora's stunning beauty, found it difficult to concentrate in her presence, no matter how drab or glorious the scenery. Adjusting the front of his loincloth, he was adamant that it would be much easier to focus if she didn't smell twice as pleasant as her kisses tasted.

'So, if we continue feeding everyone with the resources we have and double the ritual sacrifices to the gods—they should come around, right?' Llora was determined. It glimmered in her eyes and resonated in her sweet voice. He adored that about her. He went to speak but then he saw horror dawning on her face. 'The sun,' she said, pointing skyward. 'Peronikh, what's happening?'

Her voice had shifted from calm and pleasant to panicked in an instant. Peronikh followed her finger. It was far too early for sunset, but a dull tinge had surrounded the sun. He stood on the terrace, confused.

Llora clutched at his arm tight and dragged him into the dim throne room.

'The sun,' she repeated.

'What about it?'

'You saw it, didn't you?'

'I suppose it did get a little darker.'

'A little darker? The sun just vanished before our eyes.'

'It's always dark in here,' Peronikh said. 'Here, I will give us some light.'

Beebee's gleaming eyes and the Golden Throne were all that was visible as Peronikh fumbled for flint, to spark the smouldering braziers back to life. The flickering flames produced enough intermittent light for Llora to release her talon nails from digging into his arm.

'You didn't see it, did you?' she asked, as she sat on the smooth stone floor.

He joined her, linking his arm in hers. 'See what?'

'This isn't funny, Peronikh. We just watched the sun nearly get swallowed whole by a shadow.'

'Never mind that now,' Peronikh said. 'Come here.'

She nestled in closer to him. The warmth of her ripe body pressed firmly against his. He pulled Llora in tighter, burying her face in his chest. She didn't seem to mind, and the gentle way he caressed her cheeks kept her there. She swivelled to face him, and their eyes locked together. Her whites, hopeful and endearing, reflected at him. Too much to resist, Peronikh leaned in, shutting his eyes at the last second, and planted his lips onto hers.

As their tongues intertwined, a flaming sensation,

unlike any other, spread across him. Llora traced the outline of his arm muscles with a soft finger, and he slipped his hand down the back of her dress, tickling her back.

The kissing became more passionate, more lustful, and Peronikh surrendered himself to the moment.

Chapter 22

Llora could not part ways with her ruined dress, still lying on the ground in tatters. It sparked a memory.

She was back in the desert, back with the hyenas and the royal family. Scared for her life, the brilliant, blinding gleam of Pharaoh Nekhet's golden war hammer dispelled the beasts' snarls and snaps, reinvigorating her with hope.

From that recollection, surfaced an idea. It was bold and fraught with risk and could even endanger her brother's life. But if the vile man had no intention of returning Wuntu, why should Llora let that deter her? Her plans were never anything other than stupid and reckless.

Something was up with Peronikh, and there was

plenty wrong with Egypt. She had to act.

What Llora required was muscle, and it could always be purchased for the right price. Anything could. So, she went searching for men, the kind known to accept strange job contracts for the promise of boundless riches. She liked to call them bruisers or brutes, and lucky for her, these men were known to linger in the peasant villages.

First, Llora approached Laseb for assistance, with a pleading tale of how she was able to persuade the pharaoh to grant him mercy. Her old friend did not shift though. Assuring her he was now a man of honour and integrity, he quickly sent her away.

Impressionable men were proving difficult to track down among the sandstorm-ravaged village ruins. Llora found a bruiser gathered around a sombre campfire with his family, all silent, all staring into the flames. Calling him aside, she dangled the enticement of unimaginable treasures before him. He resisted at first.

They all did, and rightly so. What she proposed to them was utter madness. What she proposed to them betrayed the very foundation of their society, but when the gods were already destroying their beloved city, now was hardly the time for rational and precedented action. So, she persisted, pleading with them until her voice became coarse and gravelly. Chaos already engulfed Egypt—what further harm could befall them?

One at a time, Llora persuaded them. Each was sure to negotiate their terms of payment. Whatever they could carry, they could keep—and she had no qualms in meeting their demands. She just hoped her plan would work.

Llora and her brutes were quickly in the midst of the Valley of the Kings, passing between its discreet opening in the cliffs.

The journey was easy without the sweltering sun, and the usual night patrols were nowhere to be seen around the city's alleys. Crossing the Nile didn't pose them much trouble either. Abandoned rafts had awaited them and gentle strokes propelled them across the river. Finding the tomb would be another matter. Not many were privy to the knowledge of its location.

Llora and her bruisers marched through the valley in brooding silence. Before leaving the villages, she used the flames from a campfire to light an oil lantern and tucked the cannister inside the lining of her dress. Withdrawing it to guide their search, the lantern's orange-yellow flicker was invaluable.

They found plenty of tombs but none of them bore the right seal. If it wasn't for her flame, they would never have found any. Along the way, checking every crevice they stumbled upon, it dawned on Llora that maybe this mission was about much more than saving Egypt.

Theft was one of few acts that brought her joy, and in anticipation, her entire body went giddy with excitement.

'I've got something,' one of her brutes called.

'Yeah?' she called out.

'There's a hunting bow down here. That's the seal, isn't it?'

Descending the steps, Llora was staring at a grand hunting bow spread across both halves of the tomb's sealed doors. Nekhet's tomb.

She balked momentarily upon reaching it, as the severity of her planned atrocity set in. The band of bruisers had not spoken the entire way there, and they didn't seem inclined to start now, either. Guilt flooded over her. It didn't stem from the heinous act they were about to commit—Llora had come to grips with that—but she had left out a crucial detail when convincing them to accompany her. The tomb was protected, lined with traps.

Merkhet had boasted of its design in the days leading up to the funeral and even well after it. Not once did he reveal any of its finer details. Llora shuddered, and the darkness, her greatest ally, concealed her discomfort. Her deceit would stay with her until the time she was buried—if she were to be granted that privilege. She shuddered again.

'Alright,' she said, placing her oil lantern on the floor. 'If we push at the join from here, we should be able to bust it open.'

The brutes assembled around the seal, joining her. On her command, a mere grunt, they all gave a mighty push. The boulder didn't budge.

Llora cried out in frustration, wiping sweat from her brow. 'Let's try again, all together now.'

The men strained, herself included, leveraging their hefty frames against the door. It moved a touch—or did it? Pressing all their weight into it again, this time it definitely moved. They persevered, buoyed on by their progress, and their persistence was rewarded.

The seal shifted, creating an opening into the tomb. Llora tried to squirm her way through the gap. It was not quite large enough. A few more dedicated pushes from her hired brutes and the doors eased farther in, granting them access to the tomb. It would be a tight squeeze, but even the bulkiest of them would manage to fit his way in. Just.

Llora silently prayed that the gods did not deem her actions worthy of immediate vengeance. She collected her oil lantern from the floor, and its light illuminated the passageway into the tomb. The band of muscle lumbered in behind her. Leading them through the hallway, Llora heard their gasps of astonishment as they saw the magnificent hieroglyphic scenes painted upon the walls.

She clapped one of them on the back as he stared at the scene of Nekhet's triumph over the Nubians. 'Come on, we have to be quick.'

They pushed on into the antechamber, where Llora stopped suddenly, and the bruisers bumbled into her. Two identical statues of Nekhet confronted them, and Merkhet's goofy smile shrouded her thoughts.

Anyone would be mad to try and rob my father's tomb.

'What's the hold up?' one of them asked her. 'It's creepy down here, and you promised us riches.'

'If you value your limbs, you'll be patient,' Llora said, warning them. She waved the lantern in wide arcing motions, illuminating the dark corners of the tomb. After several measured arcs, a glint between the lower segments of the statues caught her attention. She bent down closer, inspecting the trap. A length of flax, near invisible. She smiled at the discovery. Merkhet, you devilish rogue!

'Whatever you do, do not trip on this wire,' she said, holding the lantern above it.

Llora accepted their silence as confirmation of understanding, and she hoisted her legs high over the flax. They copied her exaggerated movements, piling into the burial chamber. The flickering light revealed the impressive sarcophagus and an adjacent room that gleamed with riches.

The men were jiggling and rustling through the hordes of treasure before she could say *Horus forgive us.* Llora didn't mind that they were filling bags and bags to be slung on their shoulders. She was more than happy to uphold her end of the agreement. They could take whatever they wanted, as long as they were still able to transport Thekla to the royal palace.

The mighty golden war hammer glimmered, even in the tomb's gloom, as it leant against the far treasury wall. Llora was so thankful that she didn't have to pry open the sarcophagus to retrieve it. Some pharaohs were known to be buried with their weapons, and intruding on the Afterlife was where she drew the line. There was no redemption from that.

'Hurry up! The lot of you. We need to return now.'

The men groaned in reply.

'Don't forget the war hammer,' she reminded them.

Thekla was so dense that it required two of them to carry it. Even then, it was not a comfortable lift. They were careful to get their legs over the precarious trap. As they made their way through the tomb, their pockets and bags jingled to the merry tune of vast wealth. Then a crack as loud as thunder muted the jingling for a moment, and the entire tomb shook.

'What was that?' one of the men asked.

Llora tapped at the hieroglyphs. 'We need to leave. What are the other three doing?'

The not-so-greedy and compliant men shrugged, unknowing.

'Hurry up,' she called out. 'Don't think for a second we won't seal you in.'

'Alright, alright. There's no need to be like that.'

'Don't forget the—' But it was too late. She heard a sudden whoosh and gurgled screams. Trepidation filled her as she crept farther back into the tomb. In a single flicker of light, she saw the rusted and spiked gate that had plummeted from the ceiling, impaling their skulls and wedging their bodies to the ground. Llora gasped and averted the lantern from the gruesome scene. She could do nothing for them. They were already dead, and the tomb was shaking again.

The ground shuddered beneath her feet, the work of Geb. The God of the Earth was laughing, and his tremors made it difficult to gain traction. She bounced her way between the walls, using them to stabilise her scurried movement.

Panic engulfed her. What if the tomb collapsed on her? Up ahead, her bruisers were nowhere to be seen and had left behind the war hammer. Llora ignored the quaking rumbles and hunched over the weapon. Even in the dire situation and the pervading gloom, Thekla's alluring sparkle drew her in.

The metal was smooth and pleasant in her grip. She was losing her mind—had to be—for the weapon was lighter than a sheaf of papyrus when she lifted it from the ground and spun it in her hands. Llora made to leave the tomb with the war hammer. How easy it would be to complete her plan and present Peronikh with a weapon that was powerful enough to change their fortunes with the gods. But something nagged at her, stopped her. Guilt, maybe, or was it something else?

She was running out of time to debate. The tremors were intensifying, and yet all Llora could concentrate on was a hazy image of Merkhet. He was always harping on about placing Egypt first, above his own needs. What was she doing here, really? She could delude herself into believing that Thekla was a symbol that would give Peronikh the confidence to restore order.

But this wouldn't help him serve Egypt's needs. Llora was only here to serve herself and her needs. Calmness overcame her. She set down the weapon and hurried up the steps while she still could.

The brutes were gone. They had their treasure, so why wouldn't they leave her behind? She didn't condemn them. They could have easily sealed the door again, trapping her to a drawn-out, painful demise. But the bruisers did not, and now Llora could not move the stone mass by herself. Not even an outcry of anguish and all the force she could muster would restore the outward integrity of the tomb. Did it even matter anymore? Thebes was a darkened hollow of its former glorious self.

Llora made the downhill trek with gusto, eager to separate herself from the defiled tomb and her companions' corpses. At the bottom, she was confronted by the Nile once again. The vessels they had boarded to cross the river were gone.

Peering across the water, Llora thought she could just see their outline on the other side. Walking along the banks in search of another raft, everything ached and threatened to cramp. A quarter mile in, she was fortunate to stumble across a shoddy vessel. It would have to do.

A sense of relief spread through her tense muscles as she clambered back on land. Llora was surprised to see the two brutes, who had fled from the tomb, a little ahead of her. They were at a standstill. She couldn't work out why they had …

Then Llora saw why. A wall blocked their way forward. It was alive, moving. Her stomach churned, and even in the dim light, the men appeared to be shaking. The scarab beetle wall towered over them. Darker than darkness itself, the big black chittering shadow extended the width of a large temple, almost encompassing them entirely. The shadow was waiting for them to move.

Llora kept her distance. The bruisers made a sudden lunge forward at the beetle wall, the chinking of stolen spoils ringing out. They broke through it easy enough, but the wall seemed to chase them, sticking to their skin. One of them tripped and fell beneath an angry horde of scarabs. The other stopped to help his comrade.

Helpless, she watched on in horror as they were both swarmed. Oh, how their screams were horrifying, emanating from beneath the wall. Llora could do nothing for them. Self-preservation was the only course of action.

The scarabs buzzed with delight, returning to their formation. Her comrades were gone. She made a sideways step, and the wall followed her.

Llora was facing two undesirable options. Go through the living wall of certain death or head back across the river, where the gods' wrath might truly be waiting for her. She stood there quivering beneath the great shadow.

Time was too delicate to avoid Thebes forever. A bountiful inundation had eluded them, and their crop yield was already going to be limited. But without sunlight, there would be no crops to harvest at all.

She grimaced, bounding towards the wall with ferocious resolve.

Just before she reached it, Llora closed her eyes and leapt into the mass of black unknown.

Chapter 23

When Llora showed up at the royal palace panting, Peronikh's mind was already embroiled in turmoil.

Everyone in the preceding days had spoken in low tones, as if the world were ending. Their eyes accused him, as if it was somehow his fault. Although he couldn't quite understand the urgency or the severity as Llora described it, she had his attention. He could not deny those eyes, not in a million harvests.

'An earthquake?' he asked her.

'How did you not feel it? The whole city was shaking. I thought I could help. I should never have—'

'You've not done anything wrong. There was no great rumble in Thebes.'

'Things are getting worse,' she said. 'We must do something.'

The end of the world speech was coming again. How could everyone see it but him? Peronikh was laying low on the throne room floor with Llora. They were discussing the type of sacrifice that might appease the gods when someone came rushing in, muttering frantically.

Beebee hissed at the intruder, the same way she often did at Peronikh. He and the feisty feline had finally reached a mutual agreement after many tense encounters. If he didn't disturb her, she would not hiss at him.

The bustling figure did not acknowledge them at the base of the war table and offered no reaction to the agitated Beebee, either. At first, Peronikh didn't know who it was. However, the voice quickly surrendered its anonymity: Prahmun.

'It wasn't meant to be like this,' he said. 'Not like this at all. Just enough to unsettle the throne, but not this. Never this. Plagues, sandstorms, earthquakes. Even Ra has abandoned us. How has this come to be?'

Prahmun, in his erratic pacing, wandered through to the royal chambers, and must have gone out onto the terrace because he did not return.

'Notify the priests, we must prepare for the sacrifice at once,' Peronikh said quietly, handing Llora his royal seal.

She shuddered as she looked at the scarab beetle insignia in her palms.

'What's wrong?' he asked her.

Llora said nothing. He helped her up, and she hugged him, clinging on tight.

'Go now, Llora. Spread the word, give the people hope. I will deal with Prahmun.'

Once she left, Peronikh strode out to the terrace, where the vizier was whispering to himself.

'I even set the administration to resume their active duties. We truly supported Peronikh's rule, yet the gods are still not satisfied. He was to be our saviour. I was sure of it.'

'What do you speak of?'

'Your Worship,' Prahmun said absently.

'Enough of the courtesies. Tell me what you mutter about?'

'Merkhet was not worthy of the throne, yet still Ma'at has deserted us. Nothing has improved under your reign and now chaos consumes us all.'

'Explain what you mean. Now.'

'It's not your fault,' the vizier said. 'I was wrong to assist you.'

Peronikh could sense his cheeks flushing with rage. He released his mother from the vows binding her to Nekhet for this man, and he would repay him that courtesy dealing in mysteries and insults? 'Why were you wrong? Merkhet was failing and we needed to act.'

'I should never have tampered with the burial raft,' Prahmun said, his cold eyes drifting away from Peronikh.

'How could you! My father could have missed out on the Fields of Paradise. I could have lost limbs to the crocodiles.'

'My bitterness consumed me. I regret my actions, of course I do, but my worst deed was corrupting your mind. The gods can never accept you as their pharaoh.'

Peronikh could strangle him. He really could. The same anger he had developed for the wretched High

Priest began to surface. But a slither of restraint, he didn't know he had, stopped him.

'I passed the Pharaonic Trial. I am the only one the gods recognise as their living embodiment.'

'No, you aren't.'

Peronikh slammed his fist into his thigh. 'Explain yourself, or you'll need—'

'You really want me to strip you of this?'

'What do you mean?'

'I told you,' the vizier said, 'you are cast from a different mould.'

'What mould do you speak of?'

Prahmun told him, and Peronikh was torn at his very essence, the words shattering everything he ever knew.

'Leave. Now. Stay away from my mother,' he said, his hands shaking.

He meant it.

Chapter 24

'Taharva. Taharva, wake up,' Merkhet said, pleading with his friend. 'Wake up, will you?'

Darkness engulfed them, but Merkhet's eyes began to adjust to the gloom. He could just distinguish the outline of the cell that contained them.

Taharva lay on his back, and frustratingly, out of reach. A slight rise and fall of his chest, even if it was irregular, was a welcome sight. But his otherwise stillness was disconcerting. Merkhet wanted to shake him back to consciousness, but he couldn't. The Nubian was too far away. As Merkhet's restraints prevented him from reaching his loyal friend, helplessness cascaded around him.

How long since they were captured in the desert? Days, weeks, or had it been even longer? Merkhet had little understanding of the events since then. Only that they had travelled a vast distance, and all the while were bound at the limbs and at the mercy of their cruel captors. Merkhet's head ached and throbbed from all the beatings. Bruises and gashes littered his body. His neck was stiff, and it was missing something. What was it missing though?

Padding at the tender skin, Merkhet remembered his necklace was gone, stolen by that deluded oasis guardian. He and Taharva had been beaten, their slim worldly possessions taken.

The stone walls seeped with frostiness, maybe they were underground. Despite the chill, for the first time in ages, his forearm burned. Merkhet placed his cold hand over the scar, where the bowstring had struck him in the desert. It went numb, but not before the rest of his body did. Everything that happened since that moment was his fault. If he had just shot down that forsaken hyena before it bit his father, none of this would have happened. Not his exile. Not the sandstorm or insufficient floods, and certainly not his mistaken elevation to the Golden Throne.

Merkhet sighed, a great big waft of air gushing from his mouth. Why weren't Taharva's breaths doing the same? Was he breathing? He had to be. He just had to be.

The Egyptian's worries were laid to rest. A heaving groan and a stir. 'Thank Horus, you're alive,' Merkhet said.

A few sputtering coughs echoed in the prison chamber.

'Taharva, speak to me. Are you alright?'

'Yes, Scrollworm,' he said, his voice as feeble as an

elderly man.

'You had me worried for a while there, old boy. It's good to hear from you,' Merkhet said, grinning at Taharva, even though he probably couldn't see it yet.

'And you. Where are we?'

'Hattusha, I think. Can you feel the chill in the walls, the floor?'

'Chill? My feet are numb, and my chest is frozen,' the Nubian said, finishing with a hearty cough.

'Egypt is in turmoil. I can sense it.'

'Most likely. The chaos will only strengthen in your absence.'

'What would you have me do? You were there, you heard the viziers.'

'I heard them, but you are the rightful pharaoh. If your country comes calling, you will answer.'

'I was exiled for my failure to maintain Ma'at.'

Footsteps reverberated from the corridor outside their chamber, growing nearer with every *clack* on the stone floor.

'I know,' Taharva said, his voice dropping to the barest of whispers. 'I don't understand what happened—or why. But you must guard your tongue here. For the sake of the gods, do not speak their language again, Scrollworm.'

Merkhet was unable to respond. Their cell door creaked open.

The first of the two guards commanded them to get up, but neither of the prisoners moved. Merkhet feigned ignorance at the direction. Taharva, however, could not speak the guttural mountain tongue and remained silent. His and the captain's bindings were released from the hooks mounted on the cell walls but were still tied around their wrists. Lifted to their feet, they were shoved into the corridor, an endless, torch-illuminated walkway that sloped up and up and up.

The icy air abated as they climbed, and Merkhet sensed a slight warmth spread across his chest when the corridor finally flattened out and unfurled in several different directions. The guards prodded him left, then right, and multiple more turns that he could not track. Then he and Taharva were escorted through a massive wooden door, the side entrance into a grand chamber, where a man sat upon a throne.

The Hittite king stood when they entered, a thick white robe in contrast to the standard black of his people. Merkhet and Taharva were encouraged to shuffle farther inside, with prods in the back, until they were only feet away from the Hittite leader, a man who resonated power from his prominent size and stern exterior.

'My valued guests,' he said, bowing before them. 'Welcome to Hattusha. I am Silantus, King of the Hittites. I trust that the dungeons are comfortable and not too cold during winter.' The king's smirk stretched across his face until it was buried within his dark beard. 'No, not much for talking, hey? That is rather interesting. My sources tell me you have quite the mouth, young one.'

Silantus' eyes bore upon Merkhet, making him uncomfortable, but not nearly as much as the sensation that Taharva was doing the same from beside him. Merkhet would need to keep quiet, as his protector advised. Nothing good would come—could come—from open and honest dialogue with the king. His rush of energy, bordering on arrogance, in the prelude to their capture at the oasis was already working against them. What else did Silantus know about them?

The Hittite leader's patience was not enduring. 'Very well,' he said. 'Bring forth the big one.'

It wasn't until now—in the grand chamber, where the Hittites likely held their state court sessions—that the full extent of Taharva's injuries became visible. The Nubian was pushed closer to the king. Nasty purple lumps littered his barren scalp, reflecting the roar of the great fire behind the throne. One of his eyes was so swollen he could not open it.

Dread swirled around Merkhet's stomach. What was the king going to do to his friend?

'We are the savages you are taught us to be, that much is true,' Silantus said, switching to Egyptian. 'But what you may not know about the Hittites is that we are fair above all else. If you answer my questions truthfully, young one, no more harm will befall your friend here.'

The dread thickened, sitting heavy and unrelenting. What did the Hittites want to know about him?

'Can you speak our language?'

Taharva had insisted that they reveal nothing, and Merkhet would not let his protector down. He did not speak. The Hittite king gestured to his guards, and they stepped forward in an immediate response. One held Taharva from behind while the other punched him in the face. The thud sickened Merkhet, and he tried to show no reaction, but his face was likely a contorted grimace.

'I'll ask again. Can you speak Hittite?'

'No, I cannot. Neither of us can,' Merkhet said.

'Interesting. I shall have your captors murdered for their inaccuracies, then?'

Merkhet did not flinch. He could not afford to show weakness.

'Where in Egypt are you from? The big one doesn't look like he is from Egypt at all.'

'He is not. Near Thebes, a small fishing village.'

'What business does he have in a small fishing village?' the king asked, gesturing to Taharva. 'What business do you conduct there? Given you are one of maybe ten people, in the whole of Egypt, who can speak fluent Hittite.'

Merkhet scoured his mind for a witty response, something that would save his loyal friend from further punishment. Nothing came. If the king didn't know who they were already, he had a fairly good idea.

Word of the exiled pharaoh, matching his own description, must have escaped Egypt by now. Merkhet made a feeble attempt to hide his long hair behind him. When he did speak, it needed to be with certainty and conviction. He couldn't stutter, but he had stalled for too long.

Silantus didn't even issue the guard with another signal. He didn't need to. His liege, overcome with impatience, just began wailing on Taharva, who was unable to defend himself. Punch after punch crashed into his face and body, blood splattering the ground around him. The guard, himself, winced, as if he were inflicting just as much pain to his own hands as he was the Nubian's.

'Stop it. Please! What do you want to know?'

'Who are you?'

'Jepsu,' Merkhet said, the desperation reeking in

his voice.

The Hittite king must have sensed it too because he leaned forward in rapt attentiveness.

'I swear to you,' Merkhet pleaded, 'I cannot speak your language.'

More blows were dealt, and Taharva lost his posture for the first time. A bend in his knees, a hunch in his back. But the spluttering was the worst of it. Wheezing for breath, through mouthfuls of blood.

'Remove them,' the king said. 'I have heard enough lies today.'

A thick trail of crimson, dripping from his many wounds, was smeared on the stone floor as Taharva was dragged out of the chamber. Gurgling on and spitting out blobs of the dark liquid—how many hours could he have left?

Merkhet shivered, despite the warmth radiating within the hall. From the death of his father, to his miserable time as pharaoh, to being exiled from his beloved home. It could get no worse.

Now everything was stripped from him.

His home, his family, his girl, and now his friend. All gone, lost to him forever.

Chapter 25

Peronikh's bitterness and wallowing spanned much longer than it should have.

He shunned Llora's attempts to reach him. Hiding away in the harem village, Peronikh turned to his other greatest comfort. The nip. Its sweet embrace welcomed him back, as if he had never left it behind. A part of him wished he hadn't.

Llora did not question his whereabouts, just hugged him tight as he returned to the palace. When she broke away, her light blue eyes, the big beautiful sapphires they were, glistened with wetness. Peronikh's eyes started to water, too, as he whispered his devastating news.

'A sacrifice will not be enough, will it?' she asked.

'To appease the gods, I mean.'

He didn't know what to say. He wanted to believe a massive sacrifice could set everything right. At the Judgements, when Merkhet failed to sentence the thief to death, Peronikh became certain that he was destined to be pharaoh and could provide stability to their country. Now …

'What will we do?' Llora persisted.

'I don't know.'

'You cannot give up now. Egypt still needs you. I need you.'

'How can I resolve this? I'm not the—'

'We could rescue Merkhet. Maybe the gods are distressed at his treatment? He had nothing in his heart other than the wellbeing of Egypt.'

'No,' Peronikh said.

'Tell me any other way, and I will not stop helping you until it is done.'

Llora was right. She was always right. Peronikh could not deny that he would have sulked eternally and never acted without her guidance. His mother's sobs echoed through the palace, reminding him that he had a role to perform. All Egyptians did, always. Peronikh's role was clear: return Merkhet to his homeland.

'We will rescue him,' Peronikh said, almost choking on his words. 'But I need you to escort our mothers to safety. Can you do that for me? For them?'

She nodded. 'Where will we go?'

'Anywhere but here. Make for Nubia. Go as far south as you can.'

'Must it be now?'

'Yes,' he said. 'The royal guards will escort me to

the army barracks, then they will accompany you.'

As Peronikh descended the palace slopes, fires lit up the city's great expanse.

Reports were delivered to him of angry citizens, buoyed on by the belief that the gods had abandoned them. But Peronikh had not taken them seriously. He should have though.

The administration precinct was ablaze, or the ruins of what was left of it—maybe there were some earthly movements from below after all. Maybe the sun had dimmed a little because before the fires flared up across the city, it was shrouded in shadows. Peronikh could see the alleys were empty now. He could see the markets and farms were deserted, and the country's food stores were dwindling lower by the day. Soon Egypt would starve, and plagues and natural disasters were waiting for them everywhere, unsuspecting.

Peronikh headed for the army barracks to assemble as many soldiers as he could. Urgency was critical. Retrieve Merkhet or be buried in Thebes, beneath the will of the gods and the outraged, famished Thebans. He clung to the distant hope that the gods might alleviate their rampage upon witnessing them begin to atone. Peronikh and his escort skirted the burning administration precinct. Llora held his hand as they moved, with the royal guards surrounding them in a protective circle.

The barracks were just as chaotic as the rest of the city. Peronikh watched the soldiers scurrying in every direction, possibly seeking shelter from the chaos. They were lacking direction though, and rather affronting, not even one of them acknowledged his arrival.

'Where is your commander?' Peronikh questioned a soldier passing by him.

'Who knows anything anymore. I—,' the man began, correcting his tone as he saw the Double Crown. 'I am sorry, Your Worship.' Halting his movements suddenly, he stooped over in a low bow. 'I'm not sure. People are frantic and lost.'

'I know how we can repel this madness.'

'What do you need?' the soldier asked.

'Gather every able body we have. Man, woman, donkey.'

The man nodded, now dutiful in his conduct. He was quick to act, bounding towards the nearest battle horn. He raised the horn to his lips and blew into it. The deep thrum echoed through the army barracks and beyond.

'Llora, you must go,' he said. But Peronikh did not release her hand. Instead, he spun her round and planted his lips on hers.

Drawing himself away was harder than refusing the nip. They could easily hop on Tendrence, ride off into the darkness, and take their chance with the elements and gods. But he knew they could not. Llora must have known it too, for she wept silent tears. Peronikh went to wipe them, but she swiped his hand away.

'Save our Egypt,' she said. 'Hurry, you must.'

Then she was gone. Hidden behind a veil of red,

she was whisked away by the royal guards. But he could not dwell on the departure of Llora, for the horn had worked. The straggled and dishevelled Egyptian army assembled before Peronikh. He scanned the crowd, there had to be five thousand of them at least.

Impassioned Thebans, men and women not even in the army, gathered before him, and he was losing his nerve. Would they follow him? He didn't have a plan and had no knowledge of Merkhet's whereabouts or condition.

Peronikh emptied his burdened conscience. 'Can you see the chaos that spreads unopposed, consuming our beloved city?'

The soldiers exchanged disgruntled murmurs, growing increasingly restless.

'There is only one way,' Peronikh said, raising his voice. 'Merkhet was exiled in haste, and we must retrieve him to restore the balance of order.'

Buoyed on by the startling revelations, they began to hiss and shout. He had to win them over, as best he could, before they turned on him.

'Egyptians have always looked after each other, but we turned our back on one of our own. I turned my back on—' He stared beyond them, the words caught. 'That is why the gods are angry.'

More contemptible hissing surged out of the crowd.

'I can't promise that our quest will be easy or that we will escape unscathed. I can't even promise that we will succeed. What I can promise each of you: I will be the first one into combat. Follow me on this journey, not for me but for your country, and I vow not one of you will come to regret it.'

Peronikh allowed that to wash over the soldiers for a second. His words were just that. He hoped that they the appreciated hearing the unabridged truth for the first time in a long while.

'Who is with me?' he asked tentatively.

'To the very end!' the soldiers bellowed in chorus, every single one of them raising their weapons high. 'For Egypt!'

'Gather supplies and prepare our fleet. We sail north!'

'Do we assemble the chariots?' a nervous voice asked, chiming in above the rabble and clink.

'No, the terrain will be far too treacherous for the chariots.'

At that, the soldiers set about preparing for an imminent departure. They readied mules and horses to transport their supplies aboard the fleet. They packed food and pouches of water, loading them onto the animals. The soldier, the one who raised the alarm, stood beside Peronikh, awaiting orders.

'Soldier, take this crown to the palace.' Peronikh handed the Double Crown to him, along with the scarab seal, his royal insignia. 'Return with the War Crown.'

'At once, Your Worship,' the soldier said, departing.

Peronikh oversaw their preparations to leave, commanding his troops to new levels of efficiency. They sharpened their weapons and primed themselves for the uncertain journey ahead. He worked them hard, assisting where possible until the blue War Crown sat on his head and the army was ready to depart. At least, as ready as they would ever be.

Empowered, Peronikh led the army away from the barracks. A determined army of five thousand men and women stomped their way to the river. Their docked fleet, in excess of one hundred river galleys, would carry them northward. If the wind and currents permitted, they would save precious time.

Peronikh slept little and ate less in the days the army sailed to the Nile's delta region in northern Egypt.

The eternal darkness messed with his body too much. Instead of rest, Peronikh grabbed an oar at every opportunity, joining the soldiers as they rowed endlessly, propelling the wooden vessels—crafted from Egyptian acacia—ever northward. Fishermen and their families gathered along the banks of Abydos and Asyut, offering the passing galleys the odd catch they could spare. Their sullen silence and hospitable charity were definite pleas for help.

Progress was difficult, not just because the bedraggled citizens stole their focus. The river had lost all the urgency the inundation had gifted it, and the winds blew south with a vigour never before encountered. The Nile slowed more and more the closer they got to the delta. Its already weak currents were further divided among the fanning channels, and the soldiers were forced into overdrive, in a bid to maintain their momentum. But it was still much quicker than the alternative: transporting an army of five thousand on foot through the desert heat.

In a little under two weeks, they were nearing the end of the river and the point where the journey would continue on land. Peronikh's arms were screaming for a break. He was struggling to match the output of his fellow soldiers when the galley's sail burst into flames.

Panic and terror spread among the crew quicker than the fire did along the sail. Peronikh panned around in the enveloping darkness but couldn't see their attackers. Behind him, more galleys were adrift with fire. He barked orders, but they were lost in the confusion of the onslaught. As the inferno spread from sail to deck, it began to illuminate the delta around them. Four chariots were lined up along the eastern riverbank. Their occupants continued launching fiery arrows into the sky, and more Egyptian vessels fell victim to their ambusher's flawless aim.

Peronikh abandoned the flaming ruins of his boat, joining many of his comrades as they plunged into the Nile. Bobbing to stay afloat, an unexpected gulp of water made him splutter and delay his command. Spitting the liquid from his mouth, he yelled, 'Archers, loose!'

The archers responded, nocking their arrows and releasing them in a flurry. But the chariots had already rolled out of range and the arrows thumped into soft mud. Some Egyptian soldiers, already climbing the riverbanks, were ready to give chase.

'Leave them!' Peronikh shouted. 'Rescue your comrades, secure whatever supplies you can.'

Furious, he paddled ashore. Their fleet had not just been compromised; it had been decimated. Galley after galley sank beneath the surface, and his optimism was shattered. His grumpiness weighed him down far more than his soaking garments. He paid no heed to the drips falling from him, observing the salvage operation in stewing silence. Who had attacked them? The chariots appeared to be of Hittite design. However, it was dark. He couldn't be certain.

A frantic cough from the river caught his attention. A fringe bobbed just above the surface, but whoever it was, was clearly struggling to stay afloat. Peronikh jumped back in, hoisting the drowning figure the last few feet to the bank. He climbed out after the limp figure, panting a little from the sudden exertion.

The long mop of hair coughed some more, voiding their lungs of unwanted river water. Wet strands of hair were swept aside, revealing a gentle face. Peronikh was surprised to see Raina. She opened her mouth as if to say *thank you*, but nothing came out. He had not expected her to tag along on this harrowing journey.

'Record in excruciating detail the fearless leader that rescued you from the Nile. Leave out the rest.'

The scribe appeared ready to return a smile but settled with a neutral expression, her default.

The ambush was a significant setback. The only saving grace in the face of such a calamity was that no lives were lost. However, a sizable chunk of their treasured food and water stocks sunk beneath the surface, spoiled and irretrievable. They would settle at the bottom of the murky riverbed.

Also, despairingly out of reach were their warm garments, packed in preparation for the winter chill they were heading towards.

Peronikh helped soldiers herd the mules from the river, unwilling to speak of the shameful ambush.

Peronikh paved the way, surging forward.

The army followed on his heels as they crossed the border, stepping forth into unfamiliar northern lands. The eternal darkness was now behind them and glowing sunshine lay ahead. He surrendered himself to the peculiarity of the moment. Fresh wind blew across his face, and the pure air serenaded its way down into his lung passages, filling him with boundless energy. It was almost as if he was breathing again for the first time.

He was ready for the next step of their quest to find Merkhet, whatever that may be. Peronikh wanted a clear sign, something he would not usually seek from the gods. He thought his eyes had betrayed him when he saw smoke plumes rising on the horizon of the setting sun. Sure enough, everyone else saw it too.

As they crept closer under the fading twilight, Peronikh's excitement pulsed in his fingertips. Whoever created the fire, posed little or no threat, not against the might and magnitude of their army. Besides, there was no visible activity at the camp, other than the low-burning fire.

The army were approaching the flames fast. Peronikh turned sharply on his heels, motioning for the soldiers to stop. They did—coming to a grinding halt— as quietly as could be expected of an army that size.

Peronikh pointed out a handful of soldiers, ten in total. 'You are all with me. The rest of you stay put, stay silent.'

His message was passed along the ranks, spreading quick and quiet, like a tantalising court rumour. Treading lightly to avoid detection, Peronikh moved towards the camp and signalled for the others to disperse themselves.

When they were no more than ten feet away, Peronikh could just see the dormant bodies of four bearded men sleeping snugly in a shallow cave. He could even hear the crackling of the flames. An oasis, contained by stone, shimmered at the mouth of the cave. With more than double their numbers in the immediate vicinity, he held no reservations for pouncing on the slumbering men. When each of the sleepers had a sword or two hovering just above the soft tissue of their throats, Peronikh gave a hearty clap.

The bearded men awoke, startled by the noise. A couple of them came perilously close to exacting their own grim demise. The pointed blade, pressing against their throats, convinced them to lay back down.

'What is the meaning of this intrusion?' one of them asked in Hittite. He had the bushiest beard and his querulous tone undoubtedly exposed him as their leader.

Peronikh spoke softly in their language, verging on inaudible, 'Just wondering if you have any chariots with you?'

'No chariots here,' the same man said.

'Well, how about a friend of ours, perhaps you've seen him?'

'Hard to say. Care to elaborate?'

Peronikh shaped to hit the man but restrained himself. 'A young Egyptian boy.'

'That narrows it down,' the man said.

Restraining himself again, Peronikh vowed it would be the last time. How would Pharaoh Nekhet have proceeded?

Peronikh recalled one of his favourite lessons with the Tireless Warrior-Builder: the art of extraction. He could picture the words leaving the pharaoh's lips.

The trick to obtaining information is to target what they hold dearest. A scribe values their hand above all else. They can find new writing implements if they must but cannot replace a hand so readily.

What did this brazen soldier value most?

'Cut out his impudent tongue,' Peronikh commanded, in Egyptian this time.

The soldier—standing over the Hittite leader with the flippant tongue—lowered his sword threateningly.

'Alright, alright. I shouldn't have said that, but we know nothing. I swear to you!'

'What are you doing out here?' Peronikh demanded of him, reverting to the man's native language. 'Where are you from?'

'We're explorers.'

'Explorers, you say? Let me check your bags and see.' Peronikh rummaged through their supplies. 'Where are your maps? All I see are food and weapons. You must be a mighty brave band of explorers.'

'We have …' The man fidgeted. 'Fantastic memories, maps are not necessary.'

Peronikh grinned at the grimace that appeared on the man's face. He had messed up, and he knew it. A slip of the tongue. Who would've thought that this man's mouth would ever land him into trouble?

'Speak the truth now,' Peronikh said, 'and you may just be alive come tomorrow's sunrise. Where are you from?'

The thick bearded man paused, collecting his thoughts. 'Hattusha. We're scouting the regions for expansion.'

'Have you seen any Egyptians in your travels?'

'Yes, yes,' he pleaded. 'The boy you spoke of. He is our captive. So is the big one. Took out a whole heap of us that giant before we bludgeoned him.'

'I'm not surprised. Quite the warrior is our Taharva. Where are you holding them?'

'Hattusha, our capital.'

'How far are we from there?'

'One-month march, if the weather is favourable. But why bother? The city is impregnable. You will never see your friends again.'

'Don't you Hittites learn from your mistakes? You're always underestimating the will and might of the Egyptians.'

'I guess we don't, but we have answered all your questions. Will you leave us now?'

'You have answered all my questions—'

'Truthfully, too! What do you say?'

'Kill them,' Peronikh said, switching back to Egyptian. 'Strip these marauders of their clothes and trinkets. Fill all our water skins in the oasis. We set course for Hattusha at once.'

Chapter 26

After the agony of the events in the great hall, the stone's chill had embodied Merkhet. Even the twice daily broth, delivered at dawn and dusk, could not warm him up. Not after what he had witnessed. Had caused.

Taharva was mercilessly beaten because Merkhet refused to give up his own identity. At least that's what his friend would have believed in the last moments of his life, but really, Merkhet just didn't deliver the information quick enough.

Then it was too late for it to make any difference. The words sat unspoken and hollow in his throat, just like the ready-drawn bowstring that could have saved his father in the desert all those months ago.

The pain of that loss had not subsided, only

strengthened with time. It tormented him night after night, in his waking moments as well as his resting ones. Merkhet would give anything to return to those simpler days. When he was free from burdened thoughts, and his only duty was to attend royal classes.

Teaming up with Peronikh and their reliable steeds, they formed a formidable charioteering duo. Merkhet controlled the reins, and his brother smothered every target as they left their peers behind, choking on great wafts of sand. Or the hours spent with his father hunched over the war table, Merkhet barely level with the world map strewn across its contoured surface, and the pharaoh would educate him on his favourite subject: foreign affairs.

Although those memories brought a tear to his eye, none of it was right. Not anymore. Now that Merkhet understood Egypt and its delicate balance, he could not ignore it. Could never ignore it.

No matter how betrayed and hurt he may be, Merkhet would always rise for Egypt when his country needed him. Because that's what his father did, and his grandfather before him, and what any Egyptian worthy of the gods' favour would do.

Chapter 27

Peronikh pushed onward, ignoring his near frozen extremities.

The Egyptians' warmer garments had sunk, along with their flaming galleys and their hopes, to the bottom of the Nile. The cold pierced his skin, forming chill bumps all over it, but nowhere suffered worse than his feet. The sandals he wore offered no protection from the freeze, numbing him to the core. They had to be close now. He twisted Merkhet's necklace in his hand, just one of the many spoils from their slaughter at the campfire.

The falling snowflakes settled on the twisted green leaves of the towering bark trees. He had relied upon the inkling that Hittite defences might be relaxed at the height of winter. His gut instinct was justified, coasting through the region without impediment. Peronikh carved his way through the forest's fringe, flinging the low-lying branches out of his way, and depositing clumps of white powder on the snowy ground. He abruptly reached a steep cliff face, thankful to not go careening off it.

From atop the cliffs, he could see their destination. It was obvious why the legacy of this immense city preceded it. Other soldiers joined his side, gazing down upon the magnificent stonewall metropolis— Hattusha—the Hittite's impregnable fortress.

Peronikh stood there in amazement. The Hittites fortress was built on the steepest of ravines, encased by the protection of the surrounding mountain ranges. Not that they needed the natural defences. The city's stone walls stretched on for miles and were thicker than any defence Egypt had to offer.

An outer wall enclosed the entire city, set across the sloping terrain. An inner wall, even thicker than the outer, created a central sanctum, where a castle dominated. Gateways into Hattusha were plentiful, decorating the colossal outer wall, with imposing watch towers overlooking their entrances.

Raina plopped down beside Peronikh, easing her scribal kit off her shoulder. In their haste to reach Hattusha, he had forgotten that she was with them. She was an elusive character but predictable all the same. Her obsession with writing controlled her. Even now, her beady eyes glistened with an understanding that he was incapable of comprehending. He longed to read the words she crafted but allowed her to work uninterrupted, instead, following her gaze to a structure he recognised.

A pyramid. How had he not spotted it earlier? Constructed at the highest point of the city, it was the closest feature from their current vantage point. There had to be at least a hundred steps leading to its apex. The fortress' outer wall ran across the top of the pyramid and an arched gateway was embedded into it. The pillars, erected either side of the entrance, were carved in the shape of sphinxes. Even from a distance, Peronikh found the presence of the sphinxes unnerving. Their eyes pierced through him as they gazed south—all the way into Egypt.

The Egyptians' silence extended into the minutes as they digested the enormity of their task. For a brief moment of purity, Peronikh had forgotten all about their quest, succumbing to the serene aesthetics of the wintry valley below them.

The magic was temporary. He started to see Hattusha as a massive, unconquerable hurdle rather than an architectural marvel. How would they breach the defences of a city forged out of the granite mountains themselves?

Peronikh retreated to the confines of the dense forest, and so began the establishment of their camp.

Several days passed, the camp near lifeless.

The weary troops rested, grateful for a break from the monotony of endless marching. They used the forest as cover, unnoticed by the Hittites. Peronikh—

and his council of battle commanders—had yet to devise a worthy strategy for rescuing the exiled pharaoh If he was even in there, or alive, that was.

They desperately needed a plan. For at least the last two weeks, they were forced to further ration their depleted food stocks to survive, and Peronikh had neglected to consider the carnage that likely awaited them upon return to Egypt. He shuddered. But it wasn't the frosty air, seeping through his tent, that got to him. What home would they be going to? He hoped Llora, his mother, and all the innocent Egyptians were safe from the gods' ceaseless rage.

Seated in his private tent, Peronikh was observing a period of quiet contemplation. A massive obstacle stood between him and salvaging Egypt. An impregnable fortress. How would someone else approach this problem? Force would not do. What would Merkhet do when faced with such a task? He would ramble on about establishing meetings and orchestrating a diplomatic outcome. Peronikh was questioning how that could ever possibly work when he was struck with a bold idea.

His excitement caused him to fumble as he reached for a papyrus scroll and an ink pen. He pursued the idea with vigour, not bothering to consult his commanders. He had grown weary of their constant admonishment. Nor would he allow them to undermine his efforts by enlisting the help of Raina. No, he persevered. So, when Peronikh stared at the message composed on the scroll, he was satisfied. The words had come freely and quickly, even though the stakes were never higher. He re-read the note to convince himself it was as clever as he deemed it to be.

Silantus — King of the Hittites,

I write to you with intentions to resolve this mounting tension between our great empires. Every day I hear whispers of your movements to conquer Egypt. We both boast incredibly powerful armies. Does it really matter which is the most powerful? Can we not come to some mutual understanding, or perhaps, even strike an alliance?

It is time we end this senseless conflict. We are willing to set aside our ambitions of expansion into the Hittite regions if you will grant us the same courtesy. I have prepared a peace treaty, which we can discuss at length until we agree on its terms.

Meet me at the ranges of Aladaglar as soon as you can. Do not delay.

Yours Sincerely,

Peronikh — Fifth Pharaoh of the Eighteenth Dynasty.

Maybe diplomacy was valuable after all. For his entire life, Peronikh had distanced himself from its teachings. Now, it could possibly save Egypt from an unnecessary conflict and complete eradication.

Peronikh summoned the commanders to his tent, so that he could divulge the plan. Once they were convened, he presented the scroll to them. One at a time, they perused it with great intent. Silence settled in the tent until all three of them had read it.

Exchanging confirmatory glances, 'It's brilliant!' they exclaimed in unison.

'We can meet them at Aladaglar and crush them for good this time!'

'No, no, no! You're all missing the point,' Peronikh

said. 'We will not wage a battle. The Hittites have demonstrated time and time again, they're savages bred for destruction and bloodlust. We are short of supplies and our strength wanes by the day. Not to mention fighting in unfamiliar lands and unfavourable conditions. We cannot afford any harm to come to our troops, not at this crucial time.'

'Well, if not a battle, what are you proposing?'

'With any luck, Silantus will share the same simple thinking you have just kindly demonstrated for me. He will leave with his army in anticipation of warfare. I'm sure of it.'

Peronikh halted a moment to see if anyone of them could align their thinking with his strategy. As he suspected, they were incapable. Not only would he have to lead the horses to the river, he would have to make them drink from it, too.

'Then we sneak into Hattusha and rescue Merkhet, at which point we can return to Egypt before it is too late …'

'How will we sneak inside that damned fortress?' they questioned him.

'Surely I must not be required to do all of the work?'

Peronikh enjoyed their sullen silence more than he should have. He presented the Hittite garments, the ones they had acquired from that mouthy band of *explorers* in the desert. Their faces lit up brightly with understanding, but Peronikh wasn't convinced that they had unravelled his master scheme in its entirety.

'We will trick them,' he said, 'into opening the gates with this disguise. When we breach the gates, they will be at our mercy.'

The commanders nodded in collective agreement, perhaps too afraid to notion otherwise. It didn't matter, Peronikh was adamant that he had summed up the situation appropriately. They would find Merkhet and Taharva alive.

'Organise a herald to deliver our peace treaty,' Peronikh said. 'Find the toughest and most stubborn soldier among our ranks. I will provide them with instructions tomorrow.'

'Of course, Your Worship. But first, I have a question, if I may be so bold?' one of them asked.

Maybe they weren't as dull as they all looked.

'Yes, out with it.'

'Why Aladaglar?'

'Aladaglar is a compromise. Ideally, we would send them north to the Black Sea, allowing us unopposed passage back south into Egypt. But they will never go for that. Why would we be north of Hattusha?'

'Again, excuse my reckless tongue, but what draws you to Aladaglar?'

'Fear not, you were summoned here to speak your mind,' Peronikh said. 'In their minds, it would be a logical place for us to travel. There is a chance we can skirt around the gorges of Aladaglar and avoid the Hittites altogether. Failing that, if we are forced to fight, we did recover there briefly before surging towards Hattusha. We know that terrain better than anywhere else in this forsaken hinterland.'

The discussions faded, and the gathered officials departed the tent. Peronikh, having had no prior opportunity to recuperate from their arduous journey, allowed his exhaustion to get the better of him.

Peronikh awoke to the dulcet tones of chirping forest birds, the most peaceful rousing he'd had since leaving Egypt.

The much-needed rest rejuvenated him more than he could have ever anticipated. His relieved muscles and joints granted him a new lease on life. He exited his tent, seeking the commanders. They were easily found nearby in the camp clearing—the main hub of activity.

'Morning,' Peronikh greeted them.

'Afternoon, Your Worship,' they said, correcting him.

Peronikh recoiled at the passing of time but quickly let it go. 'Have we prepared the herald? It is crucial our message is received today.'

'We have indeed. He is awaiting your final instruction.'

'Bring him forward at once.'

The herald stepped forth, unmistakable, dressed in a plain white robe. The herald hovered before Peronikh, taking a solitary knee.

'Rise,' Peronikh said to him. 'Deliver the scroll to the Hittite king. Soothe his fears when you are granted his counsel. Upon leaving the city, set your course due south for Aladaglar until the mountains can cover your tracks.'

'Do you have any questions about your role?'

'No, I am ready.'

'Very well.'

Peronikh placed the papyrus scroll into the herald's outstretched hand, hoping his own steely gaze would instil courage in him. The herald gracefully regained his feet and stooped into a deep bow. He then proceeded to clamber upon the magnificent, brown steed awaiting him at the edge of the clearing—Tendrence.

Peronikh's horse was not known for his reliability, but he was fearless in his maturity, and the best horse for this vital task. The herald guided Tendrence through the forest's thickets as man and steed disappeared.

As best he could, Peronikh indulged in his meagre breakfast. Nothing excited the taste buds quite like rock-hard bread. Their food supplies were running precariously low. The forest had not provided as much game as they would have hoped. Nevertheless, he was grateful for the sustenance. Especially so, given that on the latest stock count, they only had sufficient provisions for another few days.

With food lining his stomach, Peronikh headed to the cliff face and secured a prime position to watch the descent of the herald. After some time, he spotted him atop Tendrence. Draped in all white, he blended in with the surrounding landscape. He covered ground rapidly as more and more soldiers joined Peronikh. Their feet dangled over the cliff's edge. A nervous, excitable energy permeated the air. Everyone sat with bated breath, tracking the herald's approach to Hattusha. Everything came down to this.

The herald arrived at the base of the pyramid, coming to an abrupt halt a few feet from it. He sat on

Tendrence, motionless except for craning his neck in the direction of the watchtower. The gate slowly swung outward. Two Hittite guards ambled out of Hattusha, spears at their sides. They descended the steps to meet the herald, who dismounted Tendrence, presumably at their request. Suddenly, they grabbed him.

The onlookers, gathered around Peronikh, let out a collective, horrified gasp. Tendrence scampered away with lightning pace, startled by the Hittites' unprovoked brutality. Peronikh cringed. Who knew how far, or where, his beloved horse might stray.

The herald struggled, but he was no match for the guards' combined strength. They hauled him up the steps of the pyramid and inside Hattusha. The gates closed promptly behind them—and in a moment of tragedy—the Egyptians' already feeble hopes were all but crushed.

Peronikh stared in disbelief, fresh drops of snow falling from the darkening sky. No, no, no. It wasn't meant to happen like this. He was supposed to go through on his own accord. What realistic hope did they have of storming those massive walls now? Peronikh was shaken from his brooding by one of the battle commanders.

'Snap out of it, will you? The soldiers are looking at you to be our pillar of strength. All we can do is wait. No point fretting until we know what we're up against. He's resourceful, he's tough. That's why he was chosen for this duty.'

Peronikh nodded. 'You're right.'

The Egyptians waited and then waited some more. None more impatient than he. After a tormenting afternoon, the sun receded behind the mountain ranges for another day.

Under the uncertain nightfall, Peronikh found himself wedged somewhere between clinging to hope and bracing for failure.

Chapter 28

More than ten weeks without flow—Llora's body was well overdue to flush out her monthly toxins. Its absence could only mean one thing. Any other explanation was …

Inconceivable.

How hopelessly ironic. Nausea and queasiness often woke her, as it did that morning in the improving light. The sun had not returned, at least not as she once knew it. A small shining beam trickled from the sky, just enough to understand that it was day, not night. Whatever the fate of the quest to restore Merkhet upon the throne, a slither of belief blossomed in heart.

Then Llora remembered her distressing journey through the Valley of the Kings, shuddering. To think that if the scarab wall had eaten her alive, the disgusting bugs would have received a little unformed bounty for their troubles.

Chaos reigned all around her, around everyone that remained in the city. But she hardly noticed any of that anymore. The real struggles were lurking in her mind. Failing to protect Merkhet, she chose to save her own skin instead. Then she betrayed him further when she nestled up to Peronikh. Now she could never rest, even when she was asleep.

Some days Llora summoned the courage to peek out over Thebes from the palace's terrace. The shelter of her adopted home was all she had, ever since she organised for Samena and Tiaa to be escorted out of Thebes. Llora did not accompany them on their journey. She could not even bear the thought of being elsewhere when Peronikh returned.

Her mother was hesitant to leave with Samena and the cluster of royal guards, fretting that her son may come home in her absence. But Llora wouldn't allow Tiaa to stay, not when her own darkest suspicions were that they might never see Wuntu again. Thebes was just too dangerous, too volatile. She couldn't have her mother around, not when the unknown man might decide to extend his wrath beyond her brother at any moment.

Merep, a distraught shell of her bubbly self, sometimes ventured from the harem village to the palace on Llora's insistence. They shared the pain of Merkhet's exile, but Llora feared she would soon regret her own stubborn courtesy. Any day now the bump in her belly would form and the whole world—or what was left of it—would know her secret.

'Thank you for your kindness, Llora. I do not have much else to keep me going.'

'Merkhet would find comfort, knowing that we at least have each other.'

Merep smiled. 'You are right.'

Hours could pass like this. The conversations eerily similar on each occasion. Despite the sporadic company, a numbing loneliness settled in after the army departed, chilling Llora to the core. The sun could not warm her, not yet. No one she cared about was in Thebes. Yet she stayed. She should have left the ruined city behind her, although she had good reason to ignore her compelling desire to flee.

Llora rested her head in her palm and decided she would wait patiently for them to return. Whoever they might be, whenever that might be—it was the right thing to do.

Thebes, once an active city of glamorous trade, was now depressing and desolate. Anybody without the good sense to abandon the city was in hiding, tucked away from the gods' wrath. But Llora refused to be a prisoner any longer. Nothing would be achieved while she cowered inside the palace. She exited the royal complex, no longer as wondrous as it once was. The palace's outer walls were cracking, threatening to crumble in the next stern breeze.

Llora gritted her teeth, determined to atone for her sins and inaction. She vowed to help whoever she could while she waited for the army to return. Peronikh and Merkhet to return. She hoped that, given time, she would learn to soften her self-loathing. It could not be healthy for her, or the baby.

The city's alleys were void of life. Dry blood

soaked the sands, her sandals gripping in the stains. The administration precinct was a decimated wreck. The damage here was some of the most catastrophic of anywhere in Thebes. The once magnificent structures were reduced to scorched piles of burnt sandstone. If Egypt survived beyond the gods' wrath, the restoration period would extend for many years to come, possibly across many pharaohs at their current rate of ascension.

Llora heard a shuffle of feet, coming from the ruins of a nearby building. Her curiosity outweighed her caution, and she went to investigate. Perhaps someone was injured and in dire need of assistance. Drawing closer, she heard people speaking hurriedly.

Two distinct male voices. Both familiar. Llora was right—one of the people definitely required assistance—but she was not equipped to provide it. The unstable and vile mystery man. The other voice belonged to Prahmun. She was sure of it.

Llora crouched outside the ruins of the building, listening to their conversation.

'Have we taken it too far?' Prahmun asked.

'*We*? Your task was so simple.'

'I-I-' the vizier stammered. 'I did not envision chaos such as this could be possible. I am sorry.'

'You're sorry? Thebes is in ruins,' the unknown man said.

'I got carried away.'

'Your incompetence is truly astounding. All you needed to do was help destabilise the throne, not destroy the country. I had already done all the hard work, convincing the citizens of the Cursed Pharaoh.'

'That was you?'

'Who else, Prahmun? I even gave you that letter

about the stolen necklace. That certainly wasn't so you could meddle with the pharaohship.'

'But the gods were unhappy with Merkhet.'

'What are they now, then? Ecstatic, overjoyed?'

Prahmun did not respond.

'You should have left it to me to interpret the will of the gods, but never mind your failures now. The initiates are progressing quicker than expected, and in other developments, some soldiers have returned from Nubia with intermediary provisions. We are keeping the supplies safe.'

'Shouldn't the viziers distribute the food?'

'No, you have done more than enough damage. Just pray that the army can rectify this mess and restore Ma'at. Or who knows where my wrath will turn next. Maybe towards your beloved Samena.'

Llora squealed and had to hastily smother her gaping mouth to stifle it. How did this monster know of Samena? Did he know of her mother, too? He had already caused so much harm to Thebes and the people who called it home. Llora gulped hard, her throat struggling to accept that he appeared in no mood to relent his malicious ways.

'How do you—,' the vizier tried to ask.

'Never mind how I know of her, Prahmun. I even have the location of where the guards escorted her. Now leave me, I have important work to complete in Giza.'

Prahmun strode out of the ruins, and Llora exaggerated her crouch, ducking farther behind a mass of rubble. She waited a moment, wondering if the man of her nightmares would surface. He didn't. She entered the remains of the building and confronted him herself.

'You,' she said, her voice laced with venomous anger.

How the gods had mercifully spared him, this man who shrouded himself in the dark cloak, she would never understand. Even in the lightened gloom, he was recognisable only by his voice. Llora hoped the gods could see him for what he was. Only they were worthy of judging his depraved acts—and if the gods were worthy of her devotion—they must have something remarkable waiting for him.

'Llora, how wonderful it is to see you.'

'Who are the initiates? Are they in Giza?'

'A thief and an eavesdropper. A delightful if not surprising combination.'

'Is that what you're doing with my brother, feeding him with lies?'

'The initiates are not your concern.'

'When will you return Wuntu?' she asked, pleading with the man so callous his pupils were cold and translucent.

'Who's Wuntu?'

'MY BROTHER!'

'Oh, he does not go by that name anymore.'

'You can start to make things right,' Llora said. 'It's not too late. Release him from whatever prison you are holding him in.'

'He is in the dark, but he is not being held against his will. Why is it so hard for you to understand? Does that beautiful face hinder your mind? He is free to choose, as they all are, and he has chosen a life of greater meaning and servitude.'

'My brother would be able to see this mess and

decide on a better course. You disgust me. Even Set has more integrity than the likes of you.'

The man, who had caused Llora so much anguish and misery, removed his hood and smiled at her.

A gleeful, haunting smile on a face she recognised.

Chapter 29

Merkhet slumped in his cell. Why had the gods abandoned his rule? How could he explain the sensation that some momentum, some force, was gathering to summon him back home?

He couldn't. He had so many questions and no way of getting answers. Yet his silent contemplation was interrupted when King Silantus appeared, unannounced. Even in the cell's encroaching darkness, there was no mistaking his identity. A powerful aura surrounded him, radiating off him.

Merkhet was perplexed by the sheer generosity of the Hittite king in the time after their initial encounter. Not once did Silantus attempt to starve him, or so much as threaten to deny him a meal. Merkhet was eating as well as he ever had, was never bound or restrained, and was even provided with routine head shaves to sharpen his appearance. That did little to stifle his anger. It was directed at himself, just as much the king. Taharva was shown no mercy, and if there was a force gathering, Merkhet understood that as only one thing. Justice for the loyal Nubian, his friend and guardian.

'Good evening, young man,' Silantus said, greeting him in his usual boisterous manner. He always spoke in Egyptian, as fluent as a native, and his accent didn't betray him. 'How is my favourite prisoner?' the king asked. 'Looking awfully cramped in here.'

Merkhet said nothing and just looked up at the king as his face came right up to the cell. He saw a true leader, and in a weird way, the Egyptian wished he could be more like him. Assertive and dominant, in presence and action. Silantus would prove a challenge for the greatest of pharaohs. No wonder Nekhet the Tireless Warrior-Builder was never able to tear apart the Hittites.

'Today is your lucky day,' the king said.

Merkhet's heart pounded in anticipation of the news, but the king held his tongue a moment, just long enough for Merkhet to squirm.

'Jepsu,' Silantus said, pausing to wink. 'You're coming with me. We have a war to win.'

Merkhet, distracted by the king's antics and sudden acceptance of his false name, was slow to respond. 'A war? What war?'

'Yes, yes. Your people are up to something, and they will never catch me out.'

'My people are up to something?' Merkhet asked,

trying to weave feigned innocence into his voice.

'We can discuss the finer details later, but for now, you're coming with me.'

Silantus unlocked the cell door. It swung open, and Merkhet stepped out into the hall, the cell creaking shut behind him.

Outside the cell block, he was able to appreciate Hattusha for the first time, even the true depth of its icy bitterness. Unlike his entrance to the grand city, this time he was conscious, and every step through the walled metropolis was akin to a puncture wound through his feet.

The city was vastly different to the farms and temples and mudbrick huts that dominated Thebes. The exterior defences were unimaginable. So thick. So high. Perhaps the gods themselves would struggle to breach those walls.

Men tapped away at white-hot steel, tempering the metal to their will. Flames roared from pits, where women grilled meat and skewered vegetables. The people, all draped in black, manoeuvred through the streets with purpose. Deducing that the hustle and bustle likely related to the impending war that Silantus mentioned, Merkhet brimmed with curiosity. Had Egypt come to rescue him?

Conflicted about his homeland, he didn't understand whether he should be angry at his compatriots, or excited at the prospect of maybe going back there. Merkhet had always shown his people kindness, treated them as his own family, as his father had before him. Yet had they shown him, the Cursed Pharaoh, the same respect?

The Hittite king called out. 'Jepsu, will you quit

dawdling? We have an important battle to prepare for.' Silantus turned to face him. 'Ah, I see the problem. You will get some cover for your feet soon enough. Come along now.'

'Thank you,' Merkhet said, grimacing as he quickened his pace to match the powerful strides of the king.

'Much better.'

Merkhet assumed they were headed for the city's main gate. Their path cleared as Silantus approached. The honour-bound Hittites, eager to show the king how prompt they could move out of his way, almost made a competition of it. All around Merkhet, soldiers rushed to complete hurried preparations. He longed to know what sparked their urgency. He had not picked up the slightest hunch of a looming battle in the preceding days.

Something must have happened to set this in motion. He dedicated a silent prayer to his fellow Egyptians, pleading to the gods, deafened to his voice they may be, to protect their people from harm.

Silantus stopped in front of an illustrious chariot, stationed at the main gate. It had a cover to protect its passengers from the harsh Anatolian elements and an elongated baseboard to support more occupants. The design was spectacular, finer than any Merkhet had seen in Egypt. The wheels were fixed in the centre of the baseboard and that made sense. The chariot would have much better balance on rough terrain. It was the first time he'd had the opportunity to study the Hittite chariot in detail, and he couldn't wait to improve the Egyptian design.

Silantus wound rope around Merkhet's wrists. 'I'm

sorry to have to do this to you, but I'm sure you understand.'

The bind was firm enough, so no matter how much Merkhet discreetly wriggled his hands, he would be unable to slip free.

The king picked him up and heaved him into the back of the chariot. 'Right, I'll be back soon, and then we can chat. Promise. For now, make yourself cosy in this fantastic chariot of mine. You've probably not seen anything the likes of it in your quiet fishing village.' He glanced down at Merkhet's feet and added, 'Oh, and someone will be along to tend to those purple feet of yours. Wouldn't want you to lose a toe now, would we?'

Silantus sauntered off, conveying his importance with each immaculate stride. Merkhet required no further invitation to heed his advice, sinking into the back of the chariot. After months of sleeping on cold stone, he could have fallen asleep on that furry haven forever. Instead, he studied the stars in the sky. Brighter and bigger than Egypt's, somehow their glow made him yearn for his mother. For Llora. Only the gods understood the pain their absence caused him. But did they care?

Merkhet's eyes fluttered open. He had napped, and the sun would soon emerge, the faintest orange glow already beginning to sneak up on the horizon. His feet were no longer throbbing, someone having fitted them with a woollen material in his slumber. The glow brightened as Silantus returned, almost a direct response to his presence. He boarded the chariot with a stunning woman, no doubt his wife.

The Hittite king waved his arm out of the chariot,

and the gates grunted against mounds of frost and snow as they opened outward. The chariot lurched forward, pouring through the gates. Merkhet gazed around, thousands of soldiers accompanied them across the valley. Some of them tasked with the unpleasant and tedious job of clearing the snow from their path.

'Jepsu, this here is Queen Haliya. I'd say to keep your hands to yourself,' the king sneered with delight. 'But that isn't going to be a problem, is it?'

'No, I suppose it won't,' Merkhet said, looking down at the rope binding his wrists together.

'If we are supposing, I suppose you must be curious about why you are here? What is happening?'

'I suppose.'

Silantus laughed, nudging the queen with his elbow. 'Alright. First things first. You're here because I respect you. For months now, you have been our prisoner. Not once have you moaned or complained. I admire that. Especially for a boy of your age.'

Months, already? Merkhet didn't really know what to say, opting for silence. He did not want to overstate his burning curiosity to cut into the heart of the matter. Silantus didn't appear to notice Merkhet's passive approach, least of all take offence to it.

'It is more complicated than that though,' the Hittite king said. 'You're Egyptian. We're at war with your people. So, the sad truth is you may prove useful, should I find myself in a position to bargain or demonstrate my ruthlessness.'

'You don't have to justify yourself. I understand.'

Merkhet could see the relief wash over the king's face. If the Hittites weren't responsible for his father's death, it would be hard not to like them and their charismatic leader. But was it not Silantus who gave the command to slaughter Nekhet?

'So, this war, the one with the Egyptians,' Merkhet said. 'Tell me, what has led us to this moment?'

'Knew you would be interested in this,' the king offered with a smile. 'As the two great empires that we are, naturally, we clash. We both seek to expand the breadth of our soil in similar regions.'

'I am aware of our complex history. I mean, what exactly has sparked the threat of war so suddenly?'

Merkhet had an odd desire to divulge his true identity to attract more respect and bypass these unnecessary formalities, even though to do so would be a fatal mistake. Still, the temptation lingered.

'Right, right. Well, yesterday our gates were greeted with an Egyptian herald.'

'What did he say?'

'He didn't have a lot to say, really. Even after we beat snot and teeth out of him, which made me think that their intentions are true.'

'What intentions, Your Grace?'

'The herald presented a papyrus scroll from Pharaoh Peronikh.'

Merkhet's heart faltered, his hands becoming clammy at the mention of his brother. Hearing his name associated with the esteemed title of pharaoh did little to appease the confusion Merkhet harboured for his homeland. He knew all along that Peronikh would replace him on the throne, but it made it no easier to digest.

Maybe, Merkhet was better off staying in Hattusha. They treated him well enough. But his desire to achieve justice for Taharva and his father burned anew, warming him in the cold and testing climate.

'The scroll details that the Egyptians wish to meet at Aladaglar to agree to the terms of a peace treaty,' Silantus said. 'Needless to say, I'm wary. I have been around for too long to think any differently. If I am right, we are on course for war, not peace.'

Merkhet contemplated all the possible outcomes, whirling them round and round his mind. A genuine peace treaty, or an ambush? Horus above, which would it be? A treaty meant that Peronikh was hoping to have his brother and Taharva returned. A dangerous ploy if the Hittites were to figure out Merkhet's identity. Or the alternative, all-out war with depleted and weary soldiers. Either way, Merkhet was not brimming with optimism.

'I pray that it will be a short war, my dear,' the queen said. 'You know I hate being away from Hattusha for too long, especially in this dreary cold.'

She spoke in Hittite, and Merkhet, forgetting that he was not meant to understand her, was slow to adopt a puzzled expression. Luckily, neither the king nor queen noticed. Silantus regarded his wife with intrigue. It appeared as if he wished to scold her for making an insolent remark, but at the same time the prospect of doing so scared the life out of him.

Merkhet observed her raw power. She was a woman that commanded attention. Her beauty. Her assertive gaze. Her mere presence. She could not be faulted. Despite being younger than her king, Silantus and Haliya formed a formidable partnership.

The chariot rolled forward on the second day, drawn by the rhythmic canter of the horses. Deep discussions never ceased. Merkhet was so engrossed in them, it was only just dawning on him that the mountains encasing Hattusha were now far, far behind them. No more snow. The new terrain was flatter, the air not as cold, but still brisk enough for an Egyptian to be longing for home. The grass kept low to the ground, afraid that it might miss out on something important if it grew too high, and a light frost covered it.

Merkhet expected that they were approaching Aladaglar if they weren't already there. Apprehension and unanswerable questions compounded his worries. What state was the Egyptian army in? What had Peronikh done to feel so guilty that he must personally come and retrieve him? Merkhet shuddered, expelling the grievances from his mind. The rope binding his wrists began to rub, irritating his skin.

On the third day after leaving Hattusha, the chariot came to a stop. Silantus gave Merkhet a cheeky wink, confirming his suspicions. They had arrived. The Hittite king bounced out of the chariot and on to the ground of Aladaglar. He held his hand out for Haliya to steady herself as she disembarked, too.

After assisting his graceful queen, Silantus ushered the leering Merkhet out of the chariot. The young Egyptian's eyes had not strayed too far from the captivating Haliya for most of the journey. He was lucky. The king did not catch him.

Merkhet scoured the landscape, as far as his eyes would allow. Nothing. Nothing, except the Hittite forces in a large, empty field at the base of a winding ravine. 'What now?' he enquired.

'Now, we wait for the Egyptian *peace treaty* to

arrive,' Silantus said. 'It's not like they would be stupid enough to try and breach Hattusha. Besides, I have my lucky battle charm here with me.'

'You,' Haliya said, 'only claim victory because I make it so.'

Chapter 30

Each flicker of the campfire in the night nagged at Peronikh, like a hungry fisherman without any nibbles. No sign of the herald, but movement, so much movement behind those impregnable walls.

Finally, the sun popped up over the horizon, illuminating the lands below. The Hittite army poured out of the numerous city gates, passing between two of the mountains that encased Hattusha. The course of their direction was unmistakable. Aladaglar.

He gulped. That was the easy part. By the time the mild winter's sun was high overhead, the Hittites were measly specks in the distance, drawn to battle by the powerful allure of their insatiable bloodlust. The Egyptians gathered along the ragged cliff face to watch them depart. They huddled in tight-knit clusters, shivering around campfires as clumps of snow littered the forest floor, and whispered their well-wishes for the brave herald.

Peronikh ached with an unshakable guilt. The unfortunate disappearance of Tendrence and the fate of the herald, whatever that may be, weighed on him. The man, serving his country, hadn't deserved to be taken prisoner. At least it wasn't for nought. Silantus gobbled up their bait, as if he were feeding for the first time.

Now, they could rescue Merkhet and Taharva, and masses of soldiers retreated to the camp's hub to prepare.

Inside his tent, for quite possibly the twentieth time in the last day, Peronikh inspected the robes they had stripped from the Hittite soldiers in the desert. Most of the blood had washed out, but there were some small patches which did not.

If the next phase of their plan were to be successful, darkness would be their greatest ally. Their disguises would not hold up under glaring daylight. But maybe—and it was a dubious maybe—under the cover of nightfall, they could deceive the Hittites guarding the gate. To bolster their chances, Peronikh hand-picked the five *would-be* Hittites himself. They all marvellously adorned the free-flowing beard customary of the mountain dwellers.

Peronikh weighed up their odds. The plan was risky, but it just so happened to be the only one they had. If the Hittites saw through their guises, they were doomed. The walls of Hattusha would be impossible to scale undetected, and the distraction of a peace treaty would only capture the attention of Silantus for so long.

They had to break into the city at nightfall. Or they may as well give up and surrender their bodies to the northern snow.

As content with their preparation as Peronikh was ever going to be, he ventured into the camp's hub to gauge the mood of the soldiers. He discovered that a calm aura bound them in utter silence. A calm so relaxing that it was almost unsettling. Did they realise the importance of their mission? The consequences, should they fail?

Knots appeared in his sides, a nervous energy consuming him. For weeks now, troubled thoughts had plagued him. But never to this extent. His stomach churned violently as the sun dipped below the frost-capped mountain ranges.

Night came. Peronikh stirred himself to the present, where he would need to remain if their expedition into the valley below was to have any meaning. Everyone was ready, everything in place. The walled metropolis of Hattusha awaited them.

Merkhet, Taharva, and the brave, brave herald awaited them.

To descend upon Hattusha, the Egyptian army had to first navigate the treacherous cliffs enclosing the city.

Peronikh lingered at the rear of the silent movement. Every nocturnal creak and squawk triggered his alertness into momentary overdrive. He couldn't relax. He was on edge—they all were. The distant flicker of the flames lining the parapet guided them down the mountain trail and closer to Hattusha. Closer to the unknown fate of their quest.

At the base of the cliffs, their pace quickened, no longer hindered by the worry of losing their footing on the slippery slope. They powered towards Hattusha now, the fate of Egypt hanging in the balance. Peronikh asserted his presence among their ranks, marching through to join the battle commanders at the head of the army. He encouragingly slapped the soldiers on the back as he passed them, wishing to boost their morale and control his own fluctuating nerves.

Peronikh issued non-verbal commands, directing the soldiers into formation. A tedious but necessary exercise. When the troops were in position, Peronikh surrounded himself with his commanders and the hand-picked soldiers, tasked with duping the primary defence of Hattusha.

'The soldiers are ready, Your Worship,' one of the commanders said. His voice was raspy and his tone curt, as if to suggest: *are you?*

Peronikh returned a nod. Their food was so scarce, their situation so dire, they could not afford any further delays, or they would be returning home to nothing. 'Yes, it is time.' Raising his right arm into the air as high as he could reach, he swiftly swung it down.

The five Egyptian men, disguised as bedraggled Hittites, responded immediately. They bolted for the main gate of Hattusha, the one at the apex of the pyramid. They trampled through the snow-capped grass as they went, releasing agonising groans with every step. Panicked and shaken, blood smeared along their extremities and face, they climbed the stairs of the pyramid, their movements laboured and exaggerated. At the summit, they collapsed outside the city gate in spectacular fashion.

They wailed in unison, the feigned pain emanating from their hurried voices, capable of fooling anyone.

Meanwhile, the rest of the soldiers shuffled into place, moving stealthily under the night shadows. Peronikh observed their advances, swelling with pride. They were so courageous, following his command— and without contempt. The scene played out before him in slow motion, but strangely, the order of events was difficult to track. The scuffling of hurried feet, the muddled shouting, and other indiscernible noises arose from beyond the city walls, joining the chorus of howls of the fallen *Hittite* soldiers at the gate. Peronikh waited with drawn breath. As if his mind had unlocked a new threshold of power, the gate swung outward, exposing Hattusha.

A couple of Hittites raced from within to assist their wounded brethren. Peronikh could barely contain his glee. He struggled against an overwhelming impulse to let forth a resounding victory cry. Thankfully, his soldiers were more composed than he, surging forward in numbers. The helpful Hittites realised the magnitude of their error but not until after it was too late. An assortment of weapons pierced through their sides, and swarms of Egyptian soldiers poured through the gate.

They had breached the infamous Hattushan walls, the ones lauded from map's end to map's end as impenetrable. Peronikh chased after his soldiers, readying himself with sword in hand. Upon clearing the gates, he saw the carnage they had already inflicted upon the unsuspecting Hattushan defenders.

The Hittite resistance was ineffectual though. So few were there numbers, Peronikh lowered his sword. It was obvious they had no contingency plan for an invasion. They relied—and relied heavily—on their external wall for protection.

A booming horn sounded from the other side of the city. Peronikh feared the return of the Hittite masses, commanding a couple of his nearby soldiers to close the gates at once. When it thudded shut, he and the commanders set up a base of operation adjacent to the main gate. The soldiers were ordered to split into groups of ten, to cover the length and breadth of the massive city.

The units roamed for what must have been an hour, scouring the city in search of their compatriots. Merkhet, Taharva, and the herald—wherever they may be. Some groups returned intermittently with exotic treasures, information about the layout of the city, and the odd captive for questioning. The foreigners presented to Peronikh were as stubborn his mother. They would not willingly reveal any secrets, no matter how much he snarled at them in their own language. He lost interest in trying to coerce them and didn't want to waste time resorting to unsavoury torture methods.

Peronikh was surprised at the lack of life in the outer city. No women. No children. Where were they all hiding? Every time a unit reported to their established base, his heart skipped a beat. However, they all told the same story. The city was blocked off. There was no way through the internal wall into the inner sanctum, save for maybe scaling it. Merkhet and Taharva were nowhere to be found.

'What news do you have for us?' Peronikh asked, greeting the latest of many units to have come before him.

The unit's assigned leader stepped forward to speak. 'Your Worship, we may have found a way through. You are going to want to see this for yourself.'

'Show me.'

The man, accompanied by his unit, led him to an obscure gate covered in indecipherable markings. It blocked their entry into the inner sanctum. Peronikh studied the gate, trying to make sense of it. Constructed out of the same heavy timber, as used on all the others, except this one was half as thick. If they applied enough force, there was a chance they could push their way through.

'Round up the other units.' Peronikh said. 'We need all the bodies we can muster.'

The Egyptians huddled around the gate. So vast were their numbers in such a confined space, they formed a line twenty deep across the face of it. Still, thousands more hung back, unable to join the action.

Peronikh found a set of stairs to the side of the gate. He climbed halfway up, gaining enough elevation to project his voice. 'On my signal, lock in together and shove with everything you have. Buckle that gate and frolic in the spoils that await you on the other side.'

He issued the signal, and they rushed at the wooden barrier. It groaned louder than the collective exertion of the soldiers, resisting their initial efforts. The gate seemed to give way a little under the pressure of their strain, encouraging them to persist. Three more heaves and their efforts boiled over. The men and women stopped, panting, as they leaned on their neighbours.

'Again!' Peronikh urged them.

The soldiers inhaled, and then met the gate in a monumental collision. Its foundations emitted a deafening creak. The front line copped the brunt of it, but it did not deter their efforts. Yet the gateway still denied them entry. Frustration and impatience welled inside Peronikh.

'Swap out, swap out!' he yelled.

New faces lined up in their place, rested and eager to prove themselves.

'Push! Push! Push!'

They snapped into formation, launching themselves at the gate. This time its timber stoppers fractured, and the barrier buckled inward. The onlookers mostly cheered, some of them complaining aloud that they had done all the grunt work. Peronikh joined the scurry of soldiers bursting through into the unknown. They did not await orders from their commanders, nor did they need any. Their task had not changed: find their compatriots.

The inner sanctum of Hattusha was lavish with temples, upper-class houses, and an elaborate, striking castle at its centre. Clearly, the place where the noble Hittites gathered, it still embodied the same stone resonance as the rest of the city.

Peronikh ambled around the mysterious city, absorbing its intricate details. He longed to understand how they sourced water, how they survived the inclement weather in the sloping mountain ranges upon which Hattusha was built. But a series of bloodcurdling shrieks interrupted his journey through the cobbled streets.

The chilling cries came from somewhere back near the buckled gate. He asserted himself at the vanguard of soldiers scampering towards the commotion. Jogging around a bend, they were thrown immediately into the fray. A contingent of Hittite mercenaries must have crept behind the Egyptians and begun to slaughter them unawares.

Peronikh hadn't the faintest idea how the remaining Hittites had managed to catch them out, and he had no time to ponder. He raised his sword again, this time vowing to use it. Mangled Egyptian corpses decorated the street around him. His forces were in disarray. He tried to link up with the other Egyptian soldiers, but the Hittites intercepted his path. Although they were small in number—maybe one hundred—the Hittites were well organised. To Peronikh's dismay, they dictated the flow of battle. It could only last until they were overrun by the Egyptians. But how many brothers and sisters would he lose in that time?

A Hittite warrior rushed up at him, wielding an axe with a maddening glint in his eyes. Peronikh parried his first advance but stumbled backwards under the force of the blow. The axe packed a concentrated punch, unlike the eloquent dance of swordplay of which he was more accustomed. The axe's handle was short—his adversary's reach was limited. Peronikh leapt forward, stretching his opponent with a flurry of attacks. He struck low, high, and everywhere in between. The Hittite's eyes narrowed. He had underestimated the Egyptian.

Peronikh swung his sword overhead, bringing it

down with tremendous speed. The Hittite, slow to react, just managed to brace his axe up in front of his face. But in his haste to protect himself, he misjudged the parry. Peronikh's sword buried itself into the flesh gripping the axe.

The man howled in agony as blood spurted all over his face, soaking into his thick beard, and giving it a dark red hue. Peronikh wrestled the sword free from the axe's handle after it had sliced right through the man's fingers. After a few tussles, the sword was loose once again. Using it as a spear, Peronikh drove it through the chest of the Hittite, who staggered backwards, knocking over one of his comrades.

Glancing around, Peronikh saw the Egyptians were gaining control of the fight. He banded together with his closest allies. They cut their way through to a stubborn group of Hittites, keeping other fellow Egyptians at bay with their three-pronged spears. Their enemies had formed a tight ring, shoulder-to-shoulder, and no one could get near them. Peronikh stepped away from the onslaught, eager to provide direction to his valiant soldiers.

'Archers! Bows at the ready!'

At least ten archers nocked arrows and pulled their drawstrings tight.

'GROUND ON THREE,' Peronikh yelled above the clamour of battle. 'ONE. TWO. THREE!'

The Egyptian infantry collapsed to the stone floor, and the archers released their arrows. They whizzed through the air, hitting their mark. The Hittites lost their formation, and the Egyptians used the cold hard stone to propel themselves at the scattered enemy. The few remaining Hittites, although brave, were dealt with in quick succession.

The injured Egyptians were treated, and the dead were collected, while the living resumed their search of the city in wounded silence. They were warier now, harbouring a sense of guilt for the needless losses they had suffered.

Hattusha's inner sanctum was not as expansive as its outer — and before long — a unit located the prison cells. Near the castle, Peronikh followed them inside. They passed under a wooden archway and descended into a narrow hallway with a low ceiling. It was dimly lit by the faint glow of fading torches, mounted upon the wall. The cells had an ominous ambience to them, as if they themselves were captives.

Peronikh was at the vanguard of the unit now, following only the leader. He dragged his fingers along the cold wall, nerves coursing through him. What words could he summon to make Merkhet understand? They pressed on, down and down, in the faint light.

The cold became icy when suddenly, the unit leader turned towards a cell. Peronikh swelled with hope, drawing in a deep breath as he reached the cell. The moment of truth, on which Egypt's salvation hinged upon. He swivelled his gaze inside the darkened cell and could see a single lumped figure inside. When his eyes adjusted enough, he was able to make out who it was.

'Taharva!' Peronikh almost squealed with joy as he saw the hulking figure of the royal bodyguard within the dank stone cell. He pointed at two of the stouter soldiers. 'You two, over here. Break down this door.'

The wooden door resisted their initial crunching kicks, but it was weakening, and their persistence was soon rewarded. After a few more well-timed kicks, the door crashed open.

'Remove his binds at once,' Peronikh said.

The stockier soldier, who had bust down the cell door, obliged. He sliced through the thick rope binding Taharva's wrists together with ease.

The Nubian wore a grave expression. 'You are a sight for swollen eyes, Peronikh.'

Taharva gained his feet, stretching. He still appeared in good shape despite his stint in captivity.

'What's happened to your face?' Peronikh asked. 'Where is Merk? We have almost searched every cell and are yet to find him.'

Taharva exhaled—a heavy, heavy sigh. 'I don't know. I heard movement all through the night.'

Peronikh cursed. He wanted to cry. His perfect plan was almost perfect. *Almost*. A thousand times he dreamt of their crushing defeat at the gates of Hattusha but never this. The Hittite king must have taken Merkhet with him.

'Does this Silantus know of Merk's nobility?'

'No, Scrollworm concealed his identity.'

'We have no time to waste, then. We have to rescue him and crush the Hittites.'

'Should we leave some sentries behind to secure Hattusha?' Taharva asked.

'No, we are going to need everybody with us. Spread the word,' Peronikh said, turning to his soldiers. 'We leave for Aladaglar within the hour. Raid the city for warmer garments and enclosed footwear. We will not win a battle on the harsh winter slopes wearing sandals.'

Peronikh brimmed with excitement. It coursed

through him like a dose of the nip, just as toxic and twice as satisfying. They could still find Merkhet and return to Egypt. To satisfy his curiosity, Peronikh ventured down the corridor a little farther. More empty cells either side until he reached a dead-end with a single cell remaining in front of him. He peered into it and was ecstatic to find the herald sitting there, nursing a bloodied leg and covered in angry purple bruises.

A set of keys jingled from behind Peronikh.

'We found these, Your Worship,' a soldier said.

'The herald is here. Quick, unlock this cell.'

The soldier completed his bidding, and Peronikh entered the small space.

'Tell me what happened,' he said, encouraging the herald with a gentle pat on the shoulder. 'We saw that you were grabbed at the gates.'

'Yes,' the herald began. 'That surprised me. Came without warning. I called out for the king's counsel and sure enough the gates opened, but I guess you could say they weren't overly thrilled by my request.'

'Where did they take you?'

'Through to some chamber. It all happened so quick,' the herald said, his expression turning steely.

Peronikh encouraged him, worried that he might want to suppress some of the horrible details. 'Please, you must tell me everything.'

The herald nodded. 'I was dragged to the chamber. They tortured me, taking turns to beat me. Screamed at me as they rotated for additional beatings. Asking why I was really there and what our motives were. I thought it would never end, but eventually, I think my resolve beat them. They became convinced of our intentions to sign a treaty, and I was granted the king's audience.'

247

'What was he like? Never mind, sorry, please continue.'

'In his presence, I read the treaty proposal aloud. He didn't seem disbelieving at all. Not like I thought he would. He said: *"we will leave at dawn."*'

'Excellent, you have done great work for your country. Egyptians will be forever in your debt, but I must confess. I owe you an apology.'

'How so, Your Worship?'

'We have no intention of signing a peace treaty with the Hittites. I needed you to genuinely believe that we did, so they could not extract the true plan from you. For that I am sorry.'

If the herald was shocked by Peronikh's revelation, he concealed it well. 'I understand,' he said, probably biting down hard on his tongue.

'We will organise you some treatment on the way to Aladaglar.'

Peronikh embraced the relief washing over him. For the first time since they left Egypt, he could sense that a resolution was imminent.

Once they had dealt with the Hittites and rescued Merkhet, Peronikh would be able to return to Llora, return to his throne.

Chapter 31

An entire day passed, but there were still no signs of the Egyptians. The Hittites waited patiently. Merkhet less so.

He awoke that morning next to a sharp metal implement. Someone had honed its edge meticulously. Someone wanted him to be free, and the blade would have no issue slicing through the rope that bound him when the time was right. Merkhet slid it beneath his leg and waited.

From that moment on, he fidgeted in the chariot, unable to find comfort in its padding, which was starting to resemble the hardness of his cell in Hattusha. His woes were amplified by the constant throbbing of his blood-deprived hands. The rope dug into his skin, but he would not suffer the embarrassment of pleading to Silantus to loosen the bind, not when he could soon free himself.

All the while, the boisterous Hittite king made his rounds through the camp. Merkhet grew fonder of the man's jovial nature by the day. More than regaining his freedom, he hoped that the two empires may be able to establish a long-standing peace.

In anticipation of the Egyptians' arrival, the Hittites had climbed the winding ravine and established their camp on the plateau at its crest. The chariot was positioned at the highest point. Merkhet was privy to the movements of the entire camp. Confined to the chariot, near the king's tent, and left with no other option other than to watch, he did.

The Hittite camp was an endless hub of activity. They were wary, given the Egyptians' absence and delay to the outset of the treaty negotiations. Temporary armouries and weapon stores were erected, fire pits were constantly roasting the game captured from each morning's hunt, and the men and women moved with purpose all along the treacherous slope.

Silantus checked in on Merkhet regularly, sitting opposite him in the chariot. 'What are those wicked countrymen of yours up to, Jepsu?' he asked. 'We are at the summit of a mountain range and our sentries are always on duty. They can't possibly think to ambush us, and good luck to them if they try scaling these ragged cliffs behind us.'

'I don't know, Your Grace,' Merkhet said.

He wanted to know, to understand. Frustration welled from deep inside him. Peronikh needed to end this today. Merkhet wanted to go home. He missed his mother and how she could dissolve his problems until they were nothing at all. He missed Llora, her eyes the rarest and most precious sight in Egypt. The chance of one day reuniting with her was all that prevented him from freezing in the cold, miserable Anatolian lands.

'They could never dream to win a siege on the walls of Hattusha. Did you know that we have the most impenetrable city in all of the lands?'

Merkhet didn't get a chance to respond.

'There is no other fortification like it. The design of my very forefathers,' the king said, proudly boasting.

'It is rather impressive.' The usual conviction in Merkhet's tone was absent, his mind elsewhere. He was perched upon the terrace of the royal palace watching the serene flow of the Nile. A herd of gazelles bandied about the edge of the river, a bloat of hippopotamuses playfully splashed about in it. His father was still alive and in command of Egypt. Merkhet had not a worry in the world, as he absorbed the tranquil view. He opened up his soul to the life of the river and to the blissful scents that wafted up from it. The nostalgic scene faded. He was shifting back to the present by a high, drawn-out horn, cutting through the frosty morning air.

When the echo of its last shrill concluded, Silantus was as alert as Merkhet had ever seen him. 'About time. Hold tight, Jepsu. I will make quick work of your brothers and sisters. My seat will still be warm when I return,' he said, adding a cheeky smirk.

The king leapt from the chariot, clearly still amused by his own remark. His leather shoes landed on the frosty plateau with a heavy thud. He demonstrated superb dexterity to maintain his footing on the slippery surface, and then bounded off to mobilise his troops.

Merkhet peered out of the chariot, anxious to see the state of the Egyptian army. He would settle for a single glimpse of them, but they were not yet visible. Peronikh and the Egyptians had to be approaching. Nothing else could explain the Hittite camp springing to life so suddenly.

Hurried voices issued commands all around him. The Hittite soldiers responded with urgency, scurrying around the camp to complete their final preparations. They undid the belts that held their woollen tunics in place and lifted the tunics up over their heads to fasten the leather armour beneath. Merkhet stared at their woollen tunics and had never fostered such overwhelming envy as he did now, shivering at the mercy of the elements. They slotted their bronze battle axes into their belts and carried their shields and spears into their battle formations.

The blood pumped through Merkhet—an internal drumbeat—heightening his senses. The day of his first battle had finally arrived. From a young age he envisaged this very moment in a hundred different ways, against a hundred different enemies. Single combat. Full-scale infantry warfare. The clash of racing chariots.

He had envisioned it all. Even though conflict contradicted his compulsive diplomatic desires, the mind of a young, chubby prince still wandered in the direction of glory, fantasising about it over and over again. Now that the moment was here, he rued his incapacitation. Merkhet would be denied his chance of greatness on the battlefield, restricted to the infuriating role of subdued spectator.

While the Hittites proceeded into their positions, he suffocated under the weight of helplessness. Merkhet could do nothing to assist his people in this battle. His fate rested outside of his control, torturing him. Was it ever within his control? He clenched his bound fists and his sharp, untrimmed fingernails cut deep into his palm. Then Merkhet spotted a wall of soldiers in the distance. Rows and rows of them, men and women, marched towards the Hittite army, who waited static and patient.

The Egyptians—they had to be—inched forward, their shields forming an impenetrable barrier. Well, he suspected they were Egyptian, but they did not wear the standard white linen used in battles. Their clothes were the same as the Hittites. As they were getting closer, their sun-glistened skin and lack of facial hair set them apart from the mountain people.

What was Peronikh's strategy? They were outnumbered and fighting on unfamiliar terrain. Not to mention the slope they had to contend with or the cold that would slice through his sun-dwelling compatriots. The only saving grace was that the Hittites' chariotry were unable to function in the current climate and terrain. Infantry against infantry, archers against archers.

Merkhet struggled to imagine the scribes depicting this battle on the walls of a temple. The tactics were obscure, non-existent. Exasperated, he rested his head in his palm for a moment. He expected better of Peronikh and Silantus. The battle had all the signs of a quick encounter. A dreary, senseless onslaught, the kind Merkhet could prevent if he were given the opportunity to flex his diplomatic muscle.

The Egyptian army was poised just outside the range of the Hittite archers. The battlefield succumbed to eerie silence. The Hittites stared down the Egyptians, who returned a gaze as fierce as Horus'. It was near unbearable for Merkhet watching on. Any second now the battle would begin, and all he could do was stave off the nagging urge to blink.

Something glimmered in his peripherals, startling him. Merkhet had not noticed her clamber aboard the chariot, but Haliya, the stunning queen, sat across from him. The jewel encrusted pendant around her neck had caught his attention. He studied the transparent black stone that flirted with the tip of her cleavage, admiring its expert craftsmanship. She smiled at him, and he turned away, blushing.

The timing couldn't be more perfect. Peronikh, the blue War Crown of Egypt resting upon his head, broke through the ranks atop Abacca and emerged at the helm of the army. Jealousy, fused with anger, overcame Merkhet. His brother was on *his* horse, wearing *his* crown. He had known, somewhere deep down, that Peronikh would grace the Golden Throne after he was exiled. But confronting it in the flesh hurt even more than hearing the Hittite king speak of it.

Peronikh raised his sword towards the skies. In awe-striking clarity, he screamed, 'Osiris, we are not ready for you!'

'For Egypt!' the soldiers howled in response.

The Hittites charged forward with a deafening roar of their own. In turn, it was matched by a raucous clatter from the advancing Egyptians. Merkhet exhaled sharply, releasing a waft of breath in the form of a frost-like mist. The front lines rapidly closed in on each other. Self-preservation was granted little regard by either force as they met in a brutal collision. The clash of weapons rang out on that chilly morning, and arrows rained down through the misty fog, striking many victims unaware.

Merkhet observed the initial exchanges with great intent. His hands were sweating and itching as the fledgling desire to thrust a weapon in them matured into full-blown lust. Both sides suffered early casualties. The fight continued around their corpses. When a soldier fell, another entered the fray in their place. The front lines gave way to the strain of constant battery, and the Hittites and Egyptians spread all over the battlefield. Many pockets of warfare were created, voiding tactical formations altogether.

The Hittites boasted more soldiers and were plying that to their advantage. Distinguishable by the way they roamed through the sea of black in packs of fours and fives, their opponents were overwhelming the stranded Egyptian infantry. Countless comrades were undone in this manner, and Merkhet had reached his tether.

He couldn't just sit there and watch his people be slaughtered. What else could he do? The despair was crippling. Merkhet was almost resigned to closing his eyes and hoping for the best when he was drawn to a clearing of bodies forming halfway up the ravine. He shifted uncomfortably in the chariot, squinting to identify the figures at the centre of the clearing.

Peronikh, his bare chest unmistakable, and Silantus. Merkhet had lost track of his brother as soon as the battle began. He cursed under his breath. No matter the circumstances, Merkhet could never wish death upon his brother.

If Silantus' persona matched his combat skills, Peronikh was in mortal danger. His brother was a savage competitor in his own right, but Merkhet wasn't convinced he would be able to compete with the Hittite king. Some soldiers around them stopped fighting, eager to witness the clash.

The leaders appraised each other. Silantus wore a bronze crown, setting him apart from the other Hittites. His woollen tunic stretched to the top of his leather boots and a black cloak draped the length of his back. They stood several yards apart, weapons in hand, exercising great caution.

Perhaps both were aware, very aware, that their intimate skirmish could determine the battle's outcome. Merkhet's heart burned with fierce desire, dispelling the worry from his thoughts. He willed his brother on to victory. The confusing circumstances surrounding his exile and his absurd fondness for the Hittite king, seemed distant now. The man had possibly—if not definitely—orchestrated the deaths of his two greatest companions.

Egypt was coming to say sorry, calling Merkhet home, and he would forgive his country at once.

Silantus pounced forward, raising his spear high and whirling it like a sword, but Merkhet was snapped back to the present.

'Well,' the Hittite queen said. 'Are you going to free yourself or not?'

Chapter 32

'You?' Merkhet gasped, finally managing to say something. 'Why?'

Haliya didn't say anything, but a faint smile lingered as she watched him. He shifted his legs and reached for the sharp blade laying beneath his thigh. In the clamour and fury of the battle, he had forgotten all about it.

Merkhet twisted his wrists apart so that he could slice through the knotted rope binding them. Stretching on the ground, the triumph of freedom dulled his other senses momentarily. But it wasn't long before the wet surface compromised the woollen garments covering his feet. He would need to move. Merkhet bowed before the queen, thankful, despite not quite understanding her motives for assisting him.

A short way down the ravine, it sunk in just how vulnerable he was. Defenceless, he used the shelter of tents to hide his movements. A Hittite warrior hurried past him, and Merkhet was adamant the man must have seen him, but his strides continued up the slope and away from the Egyptian. The relief then, as Merkhet stumbled upon a gleaming pair of silver battle-axes on a weapon rack, was palpable. He helped himself, twirling the deceptively light axes through the crisp morning air. He marvelled at how comfortable they were in his grip—a razor-sharp extension of his arms.

His appreciation of the weapons was interrupted. Another Hittite warrior came scurrying up the ravine and this time Merkhet was not so fortunate. The man charged at him, fury harboured in his stern gaze, as he raised similar weapons of his own. Axe blade clinked into axe blade, and the reverberation was horrible. Merkhet almost lost both weapons in a matter of seconds but Montu, the glorious god of war, had other ideas.

Somehow Merkhet held onto them. His opponent was quick, swinging down hard with every strike. But the Hittite was also quick to tire. A heavy pant began to choke his every movement, and Merkhet found his opening. Stepping aside from a lazy attack, he let the man stumble past him before slashing back with both axes. They struck between ribs and hip, and the Hittite keeled over, blood soaking his garments. He did not attempt to get up.

Merkhet moved on. He did not get far before the hopelessness of the battle confronted him. Where the ravine levelled out and the main fight was taking place, the Egyptians were struggling. The advantage of the slope was giving the Hittites the edge, cutting and maiming Merkhet's countrymen with ease. They swarmed with alacrity at the Egyptians, and it would be all over soon unless something changed the course of the battle.

'I have missed you, Scrollworm.'

Merkhet was so startled by the gruff voice that he almost tumbled over. He turned away from the battle to find Taharva standing beside him.

'How—'

Taharva flashed a couple of miniature weapons, some sort of mining tools, and a cheeky grin. 'Found them in Hattusha.'

'I'm not asking how you were able to scale a cliff and sneak up on me ... Alive—how are you alive?'

The Nubian shrugged. 'I was near death for a time, but the Hittite king treated me and Peronikh found me, released me.'

'You truly are one of a kind,' Merkhet said, dragging his loyal companion in for a hug. He was beyond grateful that the captain was still present in this life and not lost on his way to the next. 'Where are we needed most?'

Taharva scanned the battlefield, studying it with something resembling a thousand years' experience. 'Follow me. Stay close!' he urged. 'Not like when you were younger and always streaked ahead.'

A hulking dark blur made its way through the ranks of the unsuspecting Hittites. Darting and weaving, Taharva wreaked havoc as he glided down the ravine. Numerous Hittite soldiers shaped up to his terrifying mass and all of them regretted it. With one or two quick lashes of a magnificent iron sword, he savagely dismantled them. Major arteries were torn asunder and limbs were cleaved aside.

Merkhet's personal guard was fixated on carving his way through the enemy army and was almost halfway down the slope, rushing to meet the main concentration of the Egyptian regiment. On the back of the uncertainty and disarray he inflicted upon the foreign forces, they were slowly clawing back the tide of momentum. The Hittites turned around to the shrieks of Taharva's victims, gifting other Egyptians the chance to recover valuable ground.

Merkhet was astounded at the shift of energy in the battle but had to cut his admiration short. Taharva was getting away from him, so Merkhet powered ahead, mindful to keep just clear of the Nubian's devastating reach.

The Hittites appeared cumbersome as if corrupted by contagion, unwilling or incapable to adapt to the change around them. The Egyptians rallied behind Taharva, spurred on by his recent surge through the opposing ranks. The fight was far from over though. Battles always tended to sway back and forth, some even hanging in the balance for days and weeks. But the Egyptians' odds were increasing with every slash of Taharva's blade. The size of the two armies drew closer to parity.

The Nubian stopped to wipe away the sweat on his brow, before striding back into the fray. Merkhet clicked his heels together and pursued at a gallant trot. Taharva slammed an unsuspecting infantry soldier and the man buckled to the floor. The captain then spun around and sliced down another enemy.

'Pay attention, Scrollworm,' he said, clipping Merkhet hard around the ear. 'Just one inattentive moment and you won't make it home, you hear me?'

Merkhet nodded, the aftermath of the whack stinging in the icy air. Ravenous, frenzied attacks were being launched from all sides. Danger loomed in every direction. In the heat of combat, the bone-deep chill retracted. His much anticipated first battle had finally arrived.

Taharva, not overcome with awe, defended the lunge of a desperate Hittite towards him. Merkhet raised his dual axes ready to fight, thankful for his Nubian guardian.

Continuing forth, a pitch-defying neigh temporarily drowned out the commotion of the raging battle, ringing loud with familiarity in Merkhet's ears. To his unbelieving delight, Abacca galloped towards him with remarkable pace. He transferred both axes into one hand and embraced the horse affectionately around her muzzle. She reciprocated the tender greeting, nestling in behind his head. Abacca's luscious coat radiated warmth, spreading swiftly down Merkhet's spine and energising him.

'Scrollworm, cut it out. Enough daydreaming on the battlefield.'

Merkhet met the Nubian's gaze and that was apology enough. 'Father,' he whispered, 'give me the strength to lead Egypt to victory and banish the chaos from our lands.'

Abacca stared deeply into his eyes, unblinking. She lowered her back for Merkhet to hoist himself onto the saddle. He climbed up on her, which was difficult with only one free hand.

'Let's go, girl. It is time we finish this,' he said, giving his companion's enchanting mane a reassuring rub.

Merkhet urged Abacca farther down the ravine, balancing caution against haste. She galloped through the battlefield, dodging the pockets of combat. Her speed kept increasing until they were at topflight. Merkhet guided his majestic mare to the area where he had last spotted Silantus and Peronikh engaged in arms.

Slowing to a canter, Abacca approached the general vicinity of where he had seen them fighting. He was overcome with relief when the visibly exhausted combatants came into view. The enthusiasm of their attacks had all but faded. Lacklustre offence met underwhelming defence. Yet they continued to toil, never daring to break eye contact. Mist wafted from them as their hot sweat met the cool morning air. They were spent beyond all recognition, and still, they taunted each other.

Merkhet dismounted Abacca, all awareness of his surroundings gone.

Peronikh was struggling. The outcome, whatever it may be, would happen soon. His muscles slumped closer to the ground with each parry. Silantus appeared to be faring the better of the two combatants—his breathing laboured but regular. The Hittite king created an opportunity, surging forward with a new wave of energy. He swung his spear hard at Peronikh, who parried with no great conviction.

In repelling the attack, his brother lost his footing and fell backwards. Catching his fall with his weak hand, he was scrambling to regain his feet. Silantus rushed in for the kill, landing a blow on Peronikh's side by feigning one way and then striking the other. Blood gushed out of the wound, and his brother lay helpless on the frosty ground.

The Hittite king loomed over Peronikh, swinging down at his neck with crazy strength. Slow to react, his brother, parried the blow just an inch from its target. Silantus' spear ricocheted off the sword.

Merkhet pelted into the fold, yelling nonsense, 'Phrawwww!'

The king abandoned his hunt on the flagging Peronikh, directing his attention to Merkhet. A thin, devious smile appeared on Silantus' face and his eyes narrowed, declaring that the prospect of battling his former captive did not perturb him. Merkhet tried to dispel any fondness he may still harness for Silantus and began channelling the skills that Taharva had taught him on how to defend against the lusty and unrelenting advances of a spear.

Merkhet ventured at the Hittite king, tightening his grip on the dual axes, and bracing for that first devastating impact. The initial clash of weapons would calm his erratic nerves and set the pace of the skirmish. They drifted closer to one another, the surrounding soldiers forming nothing more than a blur in his peripherals. A whirl of bladed silver flew through the air and a flurry of blows were exchanged before Merkhet could even acknowledge them. His instincts dominated his reaction—and his instincts were impeccable. He feared his prolonged captivity would work against him, but the Egyptian was up to the challenge, and Silantus knew it.

'What's the matter?' Merkhet asked him. 'You're not going to claim that you're too tired to fight, are you?'

'You know me better than that, young one.'

'Maybe. But you don't know me.'

'I know more than you think, Merkhet. The Cursed Pharaoh, isn't that what you're known as?'

Merkhet locked his jaws together and grunted through the small gap in his teeth. 'We'll see about that.'

He lunged at Silantus. The light weapons responded to his will as he attempted to cut through the Hittite king. Silantus was able to block the attack, but both of Merkhet's axes were locked into grooves of the spear. The overwhelming force of the assault pushed the spear back against the king's head, inflicting a cut on his cheek.

Silantus dabbed at the thin trickle of blood, smearing it on his face. The insult of suffering such a meagre wound must have infuriated him because his retaliation was immediate.

Merkhet dug his heels in the soft ground, preparing himself for the incoming assault. Rushing forward, Silantus' eyes spoke a tale that his playful banter did not. He would not stop until the Egyptian was dead. Maybe until all Egyptians were dead. The fearless glaze in those eyes transfixed Merkhet into darkness. He wouldn't return to Egypt. He couldn't be their saviour. Merkhet was the Cursed Pharaoh.

He twisted left to parry the vicious strike of the spear and watched it rebound off his axe. Again and again, the king came for him, and each time the fatal strike drew nearer. The weapons, once aerodynamic, started to weigh down on his arms, such was the fierceness of their encounter. How long could he maintain himself when Silantus operated on a seemingly endless supply of stamina?

As the Hittite king renewed his terrifying onslaught, Merkhet tried to banish the negative gloom overshadowing his mind. Taharva's wisdom came to the fore, and Merkhet started to identify a pattern to their duel.

Silantus attacked high left, feigned to the right, and then struck high left again, before a rapid low right, high right combination.

Merkhet's fear abated and newfound concentration directed him. Whether it was his own ability or divine intervention, it did not matter. He was up to the challenge of defeating the Hittite king, and he returned a swift response to rival what he had defended. Silantus met each block with gusto, but a pant, steady and labouring, crept into his breathing.

'So, you are human after all,' Merkhet said.

'No, humans can be defeated.'

Merkhet charged at Silantus. As he approached the point of impact, his sandals betrayed him, and he slipped beneath the menacing Hittite king. Merkhet fumbled to raise at least one of his axes in time. Fearing the worst, his eyes were shut when a harried neigh reverberated across the ravine, drowning out the sounds of battle.

Between peeking eyes, Silantus was rooted on the spot as Tendrence came bounding through the masses. Merkhet was most surprised, given the steed's embattled reputation of unreliability. Egyptian and Hittite soldiers alike, dived out of the stallion's way. All were desperate to avoid a grim demise beneath Tendrence's thunderous hooves as he sprinted at maximum speed towards Silantus. The king was paralysed with fright, perhaps for the first time in his life.

Tendrence leapt in the air, propelled forward with devastating velocity by his hind legs. The horse's front hooves crashed into Silantus' chest, whose ribcage cracked under the pressure of the steed's immense force. The Hittite king released a howl several pitches higher than the grotesque crack of his ribs. So vile the noise, everyone within earshot cringed as Tendrence scampered away, even quicker than he arrived.

Merkhet dashed forward—he would not miss his opportunity. Leading with his axes, in a flash, he found himself hovering over Silantus. The king was in a sorry state, propped up against a fallen soldier, blood oozing from his gaping mouth. He choked on the sweet mountain air as he tried to ingest it.

Merkhet inhaled deeply, not to spite Silantus but to compose himself. 'Sorry, family always come first,' he said, lowering his voice so only the king could hear him.

Silantus accepted his fate, a bloody smile appearing on his pained face.

Merkhet, the strength of Egypt coursing through him, swung both weapons into the king's stomach.

Silantus gurgled as more crimson drops spilled from his mouth, before finally, collapsing to the ground.

'Egyptians!' Merkhet screamed at the height of his lungs. 'Form on me! By the strength and will of the gods, it is time we finish this!'

The Egyptian army—his army—responded to the plea, and the battle hurtled back into life. Silantus' death gave the Egyptian soldiers a renewed sense of optimism: they might just make it home after all.

The clusters of enemy resistance grew slimmer and irrevocably weaker with each slice and hack of Egyptian weaponry. Isolated from their comrades, some form of unsavoury brutality awaited each of the Hittites. Without their leader, they attempted to skirt around the Egyptians and retreat from the combat in their droves.

Merkhet was torn. Part of him wanted to decimate their forces without mercy. Yet his compassionate side appealed to his reasoning. The Hittites were genuine people just on the opposing faction of a tedious conflict. He called for his infantry to lower their weapons and allow the mountain people to pass.

At that moment, an unmissable opportunity presented itself. Haliya. She was crouched over the corpse of Silantus, silent and observing. Almost immediately, Merkhet had found a way to ensure that there would be no repercussions for the compassion he gifted the Hittites.

He tapped the shoulder of an Egyptian soldier next to him. 'Secure the queen. She will be returning with us to Thebes.'

The soldier nodded, enlisting the services of a fellow infantryman to assist him. The soldiers pulled Haliya from the ground and hauled her to the Egyptian encampments where she would be held. She did not resist, allowing the soldiers to lead her away.

Merkhet surveyed the rest of the battleground. The Egyptian troops had astutely started to sift through the abandoned Hittite supplies for anything that might assist their journey home. Merkhet was distracted though, unable to join in the looting, foraging, or relieved celebrations. He was forgetting something. Rather, *someone.* He ran to his brother's side.

'I—I'm—so sorry,' Peronikh said, spluttering.

'For what? You are here now.'

'You don't understand how sorry I am, Merk.'

'Will you hush a second, so we can get that wound treated?'

'I must tell you something.'

'Brother,' Merkhet said, 'whatever it is, it can wait.'

'I helped him. I'm ashamed, but it's true.'

'Helped who? Will you stop speaking in riddles?'

'I helped him,' Peronikh repeated.

'I don't care. You're losing blood fast and you're speaking nonsense.' Merkhet raised a solitary hand, attempting to hail some sort of treatment for his brother. The gesture went unnoticed amid the resounding victory cries.

'You don't understand. He is responsible for everything. And I helped him.'

'Helped him do what?'

'He set it in motion. The raft. Your exile.'

Merkhet's heart pounded in his chest. What was

his brother alluding to? 'Explain! Now!'

'Someone tampered with the burial raft. He did not want Nekhet to reach the Afterlife.'

'You mean our father.'

Peronikh looked up at him, and held his gaze, but didn't speak.

'Speak, or may the gods forever curse you! What evidence do you have to support your claims?'

'He tampered with Nekhet's burial raft.'

'Who is it you're protecting? Why didn't you stop him? And why do you keep calling him Nekhet? He was our father.'

'I couldn't stop him.' Peronikh said, faltering.

Merkhet maintained his silence, insisting that his wounded brother must continue.

'I helped him.'

'How, exactly? Seems more like you helped yourself to the Golden Throne.'

Merkhet's hands trembled. Rage. Fear. He wasn't even sure he had experienced anything like this ever before. His emotions bubbled and swirled all about him. If he didn't need to understand what had happened, what was happening, he would have already turned away.

'The administration did not support your reign,' Peronikh said. 'Their inaction has angered the gods.'

'To what end, dear brother? Egypt must be in ruins by now.'

'It can be saved. I know it can. You must hurry back. Egypt needs you.'

'Egypt had me. I wasn't good enough,' Merkhet said, unable to prevent his frustration spewing out of him.

'I didn't want to betray you. I didn't have a choice,' he said, verging on a beg.

Peronikh's eyes went watery and sullen, but something still wasn't right. A pathetic hunger, a lust for power, still lingered deep within those black pupils. His brother had always coveted the Golden Throne. The War Crown on his head confirmed it, and that innate desire would never leave him. Peronikh reached for something inside the woollen leggings he was wearing. He pulled out the Aten necklace—Merkhet's necklace—and held it in his upturned palms.

'Everyone has a choice, Peronikh. Your eyes do not lie.'

A strange calmness overcame Merkhet. No moment of indecision. No hesitation. The *true* pharaoh's curse—not the one scared citizens whispered of—burned bright in his mind. Making the impossible decisions for the betterment of Egypt.

Merkhet picked up his necklace from Peronikh's hands and removed the blue crown from his head. He paused a moment, then turned his back on his spluttering and bloodied brother, leaving him on the frost-covered ground. 'Sorry, brother. I didn't have a choice, either,' he whispered.

Thebes—the City of One Hundred Gates—was calling Merkhet home.

Chapter 33

Llora plodded herself down in the dried mud of the Nile's banks. Sitting in dimness, she concentrated on her breathing. Her hands rested on the small bump that formed in her stomach.

Thebes had held its breath for too long and was now just starting to exhale again, ready to take on new life. The sky had lightened even more in the preceding days, but the sun did not have the intensity with which Llora was accustomed. Any remaining fires dwindled to a smoulder, and then a pleasant gust cleared the lingering smoke and plagues away to the east. No sandstorms or earthquakes in weeks. But what did it all mean? If the improving conditions were signs from the gods that Egypt was once again on the path towards balance and order, when would the river return to life and the sun burn like it once did?

She brimmed with optimism, especially after some of the people who had deserted Thebes began to reappear. Who would come back next? Her brother, her mother, Peronikh, Merkhet, the army, the rest of the Thebans? Maybe some of them would never return.

The waiting hurt just as much as the uncertainty, and nothing could distract Llora from the judgement that would be headed her way before too long. Not now that her secret was there for everyone to see. She would need to find a way to set aside those concerns though. She knew who had taken Wuntu and possibly even where he was being kept. If she could just get the help of the pharaohship, there would be plenty of time to concern herself with everything else, once her brother was safely back at home, resting on the reed mat next to hers.

'Hello, Llora,' Merep said, joining her.

Llora's insides swirled. 'Hi,' she replied meekly. Merep knew—how could she not?

'I see a congratulations are in order.'

Llora buried her head in her hands, the truth confirmed.

'Don't even dare to try and convince my son to raise Peronikh's child when he returns home. Are we understood?'

'Yes,' Llora mumbled through her hands.

'Look at me and say it,' Merep said.

She raised her eyes to meet those of the once Great Royal Wife. They were usually cold but now a fire blazed in them. 'Yes, you have my word,' Llora said.

'Thank you. Please, take this, from one mother to another. It will protect your child in the womb.'

Llora accepted the Amulet of Bes and Merep left her, alone at the Nile.

Chapter 34

Merkhet led the Egyptian army back to Thebes.

Their journey was slow and strenuous, hindered by the necessity of carrying their fallen comrades. Abandoning them at Aladaglar and denying them an opportunity to reach the Afterlife was not an option. Not a single soldier questioned Merkhet's insistence on proper burials, despite many of them nursing serious injuries of their own.

The Egyptians may not have looked upon their battle wounds and scars with favour, but they could be thankful of the Hittites for replenishing their food stores and giving them the necessary sustenance to fuel their passage home. Their urgency to return to Thebes and escape the harsh wintry weather, demanded them to surrender many other treasures. The Hittite royal chariot, among others.

Merkhet could see the Egyptian border in the distance. A warm tingle traversed up and down his spine. *Home*. But what home was he heading to? The approaching skyline was dull, not dark, as he had heard the soldiers describe. However, it held a stark contrast with the beaming sunshine of the northern desert lands that lay between Egypt and Hattusha. Would Merkhet recognise Thebes when they arrived? He gritted his teeth and marched onward. The people behind him—and those waiting ahead—spurred him on.

Crossing the border back into Egypt, he clamped his eyes shut, fearing the immediate and vengeful response the gods may deliver him. Light, blissful light, crept through his eyelids. The sky above them lightened. A gloomy darkness still permeated the horizon, but the sky near him grew brighter and brighter.

Merkhet enjoyed Taharva's massive strides, ploughing effortlessly through the sand, as they matched his own. The Nubian had not mentioned Peronikh, not asked for an explanation or sought to cast judgement. Merkhet was thankful for that because he wasn't sure he had one.

'What is the first thing you will do?' the captain asked him.

'Haven't even thought about,' Merkhet said, not lying. He just had to get home. After that, what would be, would be.

The army had trudged their way through the lands for nearing on three months and barely a word was spoken. At the very height of their weariness, when they appeared ready to collapse and never get up, the ruins of Thebes came into view. Merkhet inspired and horrified by the sight, buoyed the disheartened soldiers from a begrudging walk into an emphatic trot. They were almost home.

Merkhet closed in on the city, the sullied army in tow. Thebans gathered outside the capital's walls, seemingly in a mood for celebration. Quite some time had passed without reason for festivities, and Merkhet traced his memory back to the most painful of all.

Long before his own tribulations, to the time when his father was murdered by the Hittites. In the confusion of dealing with Peronikh, he had lost the importance of what they had achieved at Aladaglar. The Hittites were defeated, and an unintentional consequence, his father avenged. How Merkhet wished the great man himself was around to swallow him in a hug, the safest place of all.

Shaking himself to his senses, Merkhet understood that the return of the army was more than a cause for celebration. It was the beginning of Ma'at's restoration, re-establishing the balance between chaos and order in the world. The gods had conveyed their discontent with the Egyptians, and the people had suffered through the underwhelming inundation, insect plagues, sandstorms, earthquakes, and the disappearance of the sun. Now with the army's arrival—and the skies around Thebes truly brightening—the people could envision a return to normality.

Merkhet guided the troops through the citizens. The soldier's families were all out to welcome the army home and many of them reconnected at once. He scanned the faces before him. Where was Llora? Why was she not waiting for him?

Dread spiralled through him but was quickly lost. Sprinting to his mother, Merkhet wrapped his arms around her as tight as he could. Merep was wearing her hair down again, like she had always done when he was growing up. She matched his hug, both doing their very best to suffocate each other under aeons of deprived affection. Her warm tears dripped down his upper arms. Merkhet didn't mind, not even in the slightest. He continued to hug her as his smile, buried deep in her neck, stretched from ear-to-ear. He clung to the moment. Reunited with his mother when he thought that they never would be.

Merkhet felt a spatter of droplets upon his head. He was ready to unleash a torrent of curses at the bird responsible when he realised that they were raindrops. It never rained in Egypt. The crowd cheered and danced under the drizzling clear blue sky.

'Praise the pharaoh, it rains,' several citizens chanted.

Many joined their chorus: *'praise the pharaoh, he has returned.'*

Perhaps Merkhet's return had touched more than the heart of his mother. Could it be that the gods were crying, too?

'Your father would be so proud,' Merep whispered in his ear. 'He set you a task before he died. I'm almost ready to share it with you.'

'What is it?'

'Soon, my dear, but not today.'

Merkhet lingered another moment in the sweet

embrace of his mother, gave her a peck on the cheek, and then turned to face the crowd. 'I know why the gods abandoned us.'

'Tell us,' the crowd demanded of him.

'I am not the Cursed Pharaoh, as some would have you believe, but I am not worthy of the Golden Throne, either. I have not passed the Pharaonic Trial.'

'Well, pass the trial,' someone shouted. It could have been Taharva.

As the crowd began to chant, '*pass the trial, pass the trial*,' Merkhet couldn't suppress a smile. After a moment, he raised his hand to silence them. 'Only a pharaoh can judge the trial.'

'*The gods will judge, the gods will judge*,' the chant continued.

Then Merkhet, light rain pattering on his head, was being herded to the Nile, where he would face a four-thousand-pound adult hippopotamus.

Merkhet was handed Horakhty and a dagger. He had missed his bow almost as much as Egypt itself.

The Nile gurgled rather than roared, and the enormity of expectation encased him. It had also silenced the Theban spectators, for their would-be pharaoh must confront a hideous river monster. Not only would Merkhet be required to stare down the hippopotamus, he would need to defeat it, in order to prove his worthiness as a true successor of the

Eighteenth Dynasty.

His quiver was full. Reaching over his shoulder several times, Merkhet ruffled the reed fletching as he counted all ten arrows. He would be permitted no more and no less to achieve victory, for that was the ancient law. But Merkhet buzzed with a sense of positivity unfamiliar to him. It drizzled upon his return to Thebes, and that had never happened before in his life.

He turned towards the Nile. A bloat of brown-grey hippopotamuses stood in the middle of the sad river, only half submerged in the low waters. Merkhet had witnessed his brother's trial several years earlier, which he was grateful for. He had a strategy. Separate the beast from the herd and do not miss. Do anything but miss.

His stomach churned violently. If it came to close combat, he wasn't sure his dagger would be of much use to him. He may as well close his eyes and pray to Isis because he would certainly be chomped in half by a pair of sharp, curled incisors.

The biggest hippopotamus, the brownest and greyest of the lot, ambled upstream against the meek current, isolating itself from the others. The indecisive Merkhet, the one who would wait so long for the opportune moment that it would pass him, was gone. He was the rightful pharaoh and would gladly demonstrate that for his people.

Stringing Horakhty quick, Merkhet steadied his arm, and released. The arrow sailed directly at the mammoth river beast's ear. A grazing shot, resulting in one angry Hippopotamus and only nine arrows with which to kill it.

Merkhet didn't wait to watch the beast charge at

him. Its haughty growl, so guttural and terrifying, was enough to send him into a dizzying sprint. His feet pounded along the mud-sand as he scrambled to nock another arrow.

Fumbling at every fletching, it sounded like the hippopotamus was almost escaping the shallows. Merkhet finally succeeded: nock, turn, shoot. The second arrow stuck better than the first, piercing the beast's left eye. Now he had one seriously angry half-blind hippopotamus to contend with.

An arrow protruding from its bloodied pupil, the beast entered a frenzy. It gained at least twenty feet on him in an instant, halving the distance between them. Whirring back to top speed, Merkhet tried to calm his breathing. One accurate shot and Egypt would be saved. A blind beast held no chance against the warrior he had become. All he needed to do was loose one more arrow. One more, just like his father had taught him.

Merkhet cradled his cherished bow as he stretched back for another arrow—the final one he would require. He grabbed it, bracing himself to deliver the shot. But he slipped over and crashed onto the banks. Horakhty slid from his grasp upon impact and a faint splash suggested some arrows were swallowed by the Nile.

He could not dwell on his misfortune. Merkhet rose to a crouch, not even having time to check the contents of his quiver. The hippopotamus was almost upon him and the grim fate of the Disgraced Pharaoh was near. Granted that it was less of a punishment than the river beast's rotten fish stench, which was already enveloping him, he still tumbled out of the way at the last second. Slashing behind him, Merkhet hoped to gouge the nearest leg and hamper its movement.

The dagger sunk into flesh, tearing through it. The blade tugged his arm as it sliced and sliced, but he was too afraid to look. The hippopotamus wailed so loud Merkhet was jolted back to his senses. Leaving the dagger lodged in the tough hide, he darted in the general direction of his bow. The beast, shaking the ground with every bounding movement, could not be far behind him. Still on the move, Merkhet was lucky enough to receive gushes of watery spittle all along his back. Had his efforts had any effect on the hippopotamus at all?

Merkhet retrieved his bow, scooping it up without slowing. He padded at the quiver's opening. Empty. He was beginning to panic. His lungs were ready to burst, and he was without a single arrow, without a dagger. What a fitting end—falling short at the last hurdle. But Merkhet's legs did not stop, even though they were running farther and farther from any hope of where he might find an arrow.

Then it came to him, beautiful and clear, bound tight with sentimental pain.

Flipping the bow to gauge its width, Merkhet smiled an unhappy smile. He leapt and twirled in mid-air, landing to face the charging hippopotamus. Ten feet. Five feet. He braced for the collision, which reminded him so much of the hyena in the desert. He didn't close his eyes this time, and the river beast's gaping jaws, opened even wider, as Merkhet shoved his bow inside the grotesque cavity. Slumping to the ground, the hippopotamus thundered over him, his head taking a knock from its torso. Somehow, he was not crushed beneath its enormous mass.

Dazed but alive, he heard a loud crunch. Horakhty fracturing into splinters. Back on his feet, Merkhet stumbled towards an agonising chomping demise. The beast had its back to him, and he was getting closer.

If for nothing else than any chance at saving his bow, he pulled on the dagger. Heaving it from the hide in one swift motion, Merkhet drew the blade across the hippopotamus' throat, where the skin was blubbery and not at all tough. A smooth and deep incision formed. Blood gurgled from it and the beast stopped chewing. It collapsed, one leg at a time, and so did he.

Merkhet allowed himself to blink a few times. It was over. He survived the Pharaonic Trial. He was the Pharaoh of Egypt, true and proper.

The crowd cheered as Taharva rushed over to hoist him to his feet. The Nubian proceeded to prise open the river beast's mouth. Merkhet received his mangled bow from his loyal friend, complete with snapped bow string. He gave Taharva an appreciative nod.

Lufu tried to hail Merkhet down. Moving through the people, he politely denied the vizier's request, hugging the remnants of his bow instead. The pharaoh had no time to spare. The restoration of Thebes would prove taxing and that wasn't even his most pressing endeavour.

'Lufu, organise a Heb-Sed festival for tomorrow morning.'

The vizier nodded and allowed him to pass.

Merkhet traversed the city, his destination set on the royal palace.

He ascended its familiar slopes and burst inside. He slowed as he reached the royal guards outside the throne room, wanting to settle his turbulent thoughts. He didn't know who would be waiting for him in there, just that someone would. Someone who thought it was fine to interfere in the proceedings of the Afterlife. Someone who thought it was acceptable to meddle in the affairs of the pharaohship.

Peering beyond the guards, Merkhet spotted Prahmun, exactly where he anticipated *someone* would be. Sitting upon the Golden Throne and enjoying the comforts of the royal palace. Or the slim remnants of those comforts.

At least the throne room had survived the chaos untarnished and was as immaculate as ever. Atop the throne, the vizier was oblivious to his surroundings. Merkhet sucked in as much air as his lungs would allow, taming his fury. He needed clarity for the impending confrontation. The deceit would end here.

Merkhet edged past the guards. 'I hope you aren't too comfortable on my throne, old friend.'

Prahmun paled, clearly startled by Merkhet's arrival. 'Your throne?' he asked, nursing the Double Crown in his lap. 'You were exiled from this very Egypt. How did you slime your way in here?'

'I must confess that I've heard some interesting stories in my absence. Tales my most trusted adviser must be eager to hear.'

'Indulge me,' Prahmun said, his arrogant tone

reminiscent of Merkhet's exile.

'Let's see, where should I begin?' Merkhet's heart raced, not knowing where he should start. So much needed to be said, and he desperately wanted to leave the throne room having swiped the smugness right off the vizier's face. 'The story I heard was that a certain vizier thought he could get away with sabotaging the pharaoh's burial raft.'

Prahmun squirmed on the throne.

'What I don't understand is what you had to gain from this? You were already the vizier and you could never be pharaoh. You do know that, right?'

'Of course I know that, you foolish boy. How could I expect you to understand? He's your father after all, in your eyes he is incapable of any wrongdoing.'

'Oh, please. Tell me all about how he has wronged you. While you're at it, you may as well explain your role in how I came to be exiled!'

'The weakling caved, did he? So much potential yet always so disappointing.'

'Who are you talking about?'

'Peronikh. Who else do you think? Where is he?' Prahmun asked.

'It is time you vacate my throne.'

'You have no right! It belongs to my son!'

'Your what?'

'Peronikh, my son,' he muttered.

Merkhet remained silent for a moment, uncertain. In the name of the gods, could just one thing in his life be simple? 'Explain.'

Prahmun let out a hideous laugh. 'Where should I begin? Perhaps you'd like to hear the tale of the day your father stole Samena from me? Forced her into the harem and forbade I ever saw her. We were so happy until your father ruined everything! He tore our family apart.'

'So, you've put the entire country at risk over a sob love story from forever ago? If she had a child, my father would never have admitted her into the harem.'

'The pompous fool did not know she was pregnant. His arrogance blinded his sense. Poor Samena had to conceal the truth for fear of consequence.'

'His arrogance? My father's supposed crimes are not for discussion on this day. Or any day. Who are you to question the will of the pharaoh? You sicken me.'

'You are just as heartless as him. I was right to abandon your rule. I grow weary of this trivial chatter. Where is my son?'

'He's not coming back to Thebes. I left him in the frost at Aladaglar. His betrayal of crown and country could not go unpunished.'

'What do you mean you left him? Tell me your tongue is full of lies or even the gods will not be able to stop my wrath.'

'I speak the truth,' Merkhet said.

'You imbecile!' Swelling and red, Prahmun's face looked as if it were about to burst. 'How could you? He was innocent. I convinced him he was the only one who could maintain Ma'at.'

'We all have choices. Peronikh made his and I have made mine.'

Prahmun slammed his fist in rage, making heavy contact with the throne. But he did not wince, nor display any sign of pain at all. If he did suffer, the vizier concealed it well.

Had Merkhet overreacted in the heat of the moment? Maybe Peronikh was coerced into sitting upon the throne. Merkhet crumbled under the weight of the unknown. He never considered there may be more details to uncover. Merkhet was teetering. Their lack of blood relation meant nothing. They were brothers.

'I can't believe your incompetence,' Prahmun said. 'Your family's insolence never ceases to amaze me. It is no wonder Llora never loved you.'

'What did you say?'

'She never loved you. She was just doing what she was told until you were exiled. Why don't you ask her about that necklace you're wearing?'

'You despicable man. You dare utter such lies as you await the gods' justice.'

Prahmun chuckled. You haven't seen her yet, have you?'

'Why does that make you so happy?'

'I cannot wait for this. It's probably a good thing you left Peronikh for dead.'

'What're you saying?'

'Nothing. I have said too much already. I wouldn't want to spoil the surprise. It's larger than life,' Prahmun said, a sickening grin spreading across his putrid face.

Merkhet had heard enough. The vizier's life was not safe if he remained in the throne room. The pharaoh snapped his fingers together, summoning the royal guards into the room. They detained Prahmun with ease, their brute strength too much for him to resist.

'Prahmun, you are to appear at the Judgements to

answer for your corruption. The day after tomorrow, the gods will judge you for what you are, a vile and treacherous being. Remove him from my sight. Leave the Double Crown on the war table.'

The crown was taken off Prahmun, and then he was dragged away by the guards. Merkhet was alone. Beset with raw hurt and confusion, he sat on his throne. When he had seen his mother's tears of joy and the jubilant crowd that gathered, he was relieved to be home, but now he was riddled with uncertainty.

Merkhet wasn't the one who had embarked on a deplorable quest for revenge, so why should he be burdened with guilt and blame? Why hadn't Peronikh revealed the true reason behind his actions?

Or maybe he tried and Merkhet didn't listen. So many questions still remained unanswered. Most disconcerting of all—what role had Llora played in his exile?

Rage coursed through him. Smoke, the dense and acrid kind that wafted from the great courtyard fires of Hattusha, was likely to bellow out of his ears and pores at any moment. Merkhet should have taken due time to collect himself in solitude, but he couldn't wait. He needed answers.

His enduring anger escalated to unimaginable heights when he found Llora in the adjacent dining hall. Her undeniable glamour—smooth, unblemished skin and mesmerising blue eyes—made it even more painful to look upon the impressive bump she fashioned.

Merkhet counted the approximate months of absence. It didn't matter, anyway. They had only ever kissed, and girls couldn't conceive from sloppy, inexperienced kisses.

'Why?' he demanded of her.

Llora did not speak and before he could stop himself, Merkhet tugged on the Aten pendant resting against his chest. The chain snapped easily, and he discarded her gift in disgust. It meant nothing to him now.

Unsatisfied, he reached for the amulet of Bes dangling around her neck, and its flimsy chain gave way. He pegged the amulet downward. The delicate gem, containing the miniature wooden symbolism of Bes, smashed into smithereens. The shards scattered across the floor. Outside of his luxurious gem home, the pathetic dwarf, with the braided mane of a lion, never appeared so insignificant.

Llora whimpered in disbelief. 'How could you destroy my unborn child's protection?'

'How could *I*? How could you!'

'Merkhet, I'm so sorry,' Llora said. 'You were gone for so long. How could I know if you were ever coming back? You have to understand that I didn't mean for this to happen.'

At once, Prahmun's teasing words about it being wise that he had left Peronikh at Aladaglar made sense. His brother—or whatever he was—had done him a great favour. Merkhet would dodge a wayward spear with this deceitful girl. Her eyes, once alluring, now promised him nothing more than pain and sorrow.

'Don't insult me with your petty excuses. With my brother of all people. Apparently, he's not even that anymore. Did you know about that, too?' he scolded her.

'Only as the army were leaving. I didn't know

before then, I swear.'

'What did you know?'

'Nothing,' Llora whelped, waves of tears streaming down her face. 'I was held to ransom. The man has my brother.'

'After all that you've done to hurt me, you're now going to lie to me as well?'

'I'm not! He has Wuntu. Please, you have to help.'

'That is not what I'm talking about. Why did you give that necklace to me? To have me exiled?'

'He made me get close to you, to distract you, but it was more than that to me. I'm so sorry that you were banished,' Llora said, wailing now.

'You think I care about being exiled? That would have happened without your help. Your betrayal cuts far deeper. We were planning to marry! Does that mean nothing to you?'

'It means everything.'

Merkhet regarded her protruding stomach. It couldn't be more than a few weeks, maybe a month, before she would give birth. 'Clearly not. I have no more words for you, Llora. I can't even look at you.'

Merkhet hurried to depart, not wanting an opportunity to arise where he might regret his harsh words. The Returned Pharaoh would be ruthless. Egypt needed that of him. He forced one last glance in her direction. The tears glistened on Llora's face—her beautiful face—and inexplicably, he wrestled with the idea of kissing her.

'Please, Merkhet. You can't just leave me. What about my brother? He must be so scared down there. Please, don't let him suffer because of me.'

Merkhet turned his back on the peasant girl, the

one his mother had duly warned him about, and she cried, louder than ever. Storming out of the hall, he retired to the royal chambers. Entering them for the first time since his exile did little to relieve the torment that gnawed at him.

Merkhet stopped in front of the bed. Was this where it happened—where the betrayal occurred and the child was made? He strode to the open terrace doors and the infusion of emotion began to strangle him. Had Peronikh and Llora shared the sun's sensual journey, as she and Merkhet had once done?

When he was in Hattusha, Merkhet had pined for those afternoons with Llora. They were the pure source of shameless comfort he could enjoy after his father died. Once Nekhet passed, his life and Egypt's, were one big swirl of misfortune and tragedy. Merkhet missed the way the Tireless Warrior-Builder teased him, how everything was so easy in his presence.

The pain pounded in Merkhet's head, where images of everyone's hurtful actions joined forces. Those didn't even hurt the most. His own inexcusable actions replayed over and over, too. He shut his eyes so that Peronikh would disappear, but the scene didn't fade. It just grew more vibrant. Merkhet couldn't escape them. Even if he gouged out his own eyes, he would not be able to forget Peronikh's pleading face.

Merkhet opened himself to the unfamiliar and forbidden temptation of the nip, flirting with those dark and euphoric thoughts for most of the night.

Chapter 35

It was a long, sleepless night for Merkhet, but he was pleased that Ra completed the rebirth journey for the first time in many, many months.

The sun gleamed, twinkling as it rose, signalling a welcome return to order for the Egyptians. The gods shone their favour upon him once more. Or was it for the first time? It didn't matter. Today, the people would celebrate his return as the rightful pharaoh. Tomorrow, Merkhet would lead the reconstruction of Thebes.

The Heb-Sed festival, hosted in his honour, was to be held prematurely. Thousands of years of tradition dictated that it happen in the thirtieth year of a pharaoh's reign, as a means of rejuvenating their strength. Merkhet had no qualms in defying tradition.

After everything he had endured, had he not earned that right? Egypt needed to know that he wasn't the same quivering boy who was exiled from their lands. He had matured. Now he was a decisive leader, capable of commanding a prosperous empire.

Merkhet had grand intentions for the festival. In truth, it would serve as a means to honour someone other than himself. A person so deserving of recognition, he couldn't wait to announce it. After receiving a quick shave of his head and courtesy ponytail wash from an attentive servant, he exited his chambers. An escort of royal guards awaited him on the slope outside the palace entrance.

'Your Worship,' one of the guards said, 'what shall we do with the Hittite lady?'

Merkhet spotted Haliya lurking behind the guards. He had forgotten all about her in the wake of his trial. 'Restrain her in the throne room. I will deal with the queen later.'

At the conclusion of the festival's rituals and offerings to the gods, Merkhet would deliver his address to the faithful citizens. Tables and chairs lined the open space—unlike the coronation banquet—this was open to the public. They flocked in their thousands, possibly from far away outside the city walls. Bounties of food and drink were available for the event. The Hittite's food stores had replenished their own and the royal beer stocks were raided for the occasion. The Thebans had everything they required for a true Egyptian celebration.

Many familiar faces, some unfamiliar, pressed him for stories of his journey throughout the day. Most delivered him a sincere welcome home. It was uncharacteristic of the pharaoh, but he enjoyed mingling with the people. The day went fast, watching the children play games on the outskirts of the procession as the older guests indulged in the delicacies on offer.

Llora did not attend the festivities, and that distance allowed Merkhet's anger to subside. How could it not when he was surrounded by so many smiles and so much laughter? As he readied himself to address the masses, Merkhet couldn't help but smile himself. He did feel rejuvenated, like he'd had the most satisfying rest of his entire life. Despite not really sleeping at all, the Heb-Sed festival fulfilled its purpose. He was ready to take on whatever would come his way next.

Merkhet made his way onto the wooden platform. For some reason, a fire danced within the confines of a large ceramic pot. The boisterous chatter disappeared at once. 'The past thirty years certainly have gone quick.' The crowd laughed, easing any dormant tension he may have had. 'I would like to thank all of you for coming today. It has been a crazy journey, but I have returned and the sun shines once more.'

The crowd cheered, and Merkhet buried the last of the residual anger he harboured. The Egyptians were scared, and although it was disappointing that they were quick to entertain the rumour of the Cursed Pharaoh, there were other more sinister forces corrupting their views. The people were not to blame, not when the gods had shown their discontent with such striking clarity.

Unexpectedly, Raina clambered onto the platform beside him, drawing the attention of the crowd. She dumped a hefty wad of papyri scrolls into the fire, then faded into the background. Merkhet suspected those might be some of the official records produced since his father's death.

She guarded her writings like no other. Touched by the symbolism of her selfless gesture, he found the courage to continue. 'Today is less about renewing my strength, so much as admiring someone else's. Taharva, please come forth.'

Having been summoned onto the stage, Taharva stood next to Merkhet. Mighty and fierce and humble, as always.

'This man,' the pharaoh said, holding his arm out before the Nubian, 'is responsible for righting the favour of the gods. It was he who abandoned his post as Chief of the Royal Guard to accompany me in my exile. It was he who turned the tide of battle with the Hittites. He did so at great personal risk, and today we will all recognise the fortune-changing heroics of Turn-Tide Taharva.'

Merkhet pulled out a slither of red cotton, the exact same hue as the royal guard garb, from his linen top. He tied the cotton strip around Taharva's wrist, covering Nekhet's royal seal: the hunting bow. Even the strictest advocates of slavery didn't dare speak up and try to deny the Nubian his deserved freedom.

Merkhet hugged the big man. 'You have always been a loyal friend,' he whispered. 'I'm sorry this has taken so long.'

'Thank you, Scrollworm.'

'To freedom!' Merkhet shouted.

'To Egypt!' the masses joined him. 'To prosperity!'

'Everyone, please take the time to enjoy the feast.

Because tomorrow we must rebuild this great city of ours.'

Merkhet walked off the platform, and the true celebrations began. Beer sloshed from cups, more of it seeping into the sand than into mouths. Many times throughout the afternoon and evening, he tried to slip away from the festivities. Someone always spotted him and thrust him back into the centre of the celebrations with a drink in his hand. He didn't have the courage to argue with them.

The sun dipped but the party carried on, and Merkhet finally saw his opportunity to leave. He gave a curt nod to two of the royal guards overseeing the festival. They accompanied him to the palace, and he bid them farewell at the top of the ascent, where they would assume their post for the night.

Strolling into the throne room, Merkhet was relieved to finally have some time to himself. A chance to breathe and prepare himself for the strenuous days ahead. Except he wasn't alone. He had forgotten about her again.

Merkhet observed Haliya. A mysterious aura surrounded her, clouding his judgement. Or was that the gallon of beer he had drunk? She seemed oddly relaxed for someone bound around the waist to a pillar. Her captivity would ensure that the Hittites did not seek retaliation for their loss at Aladaglar.

'What am I going to do with you?' he pondered aloud.

Haliya shrugged away the question, 'Well, you are the pharaoh, are you not? You should do whatever you please with me.'

Her calmness mystified him, and she spoke

Egyptian! Merkhet bit down on his lip and twisted his head sideways, marvelling at the finer aspects of her exotic Hittite beauty. His mind was already lost to otherworldly desires when an unexpected figure loomed in his peripherals. Raina—where had she come from?

'Raina, you are dismissed for the evening. You didn't need to discard your writings about the beginning of my reign and all the chaos that ensued it, but I thank you for it.'

The scribe paused for a second, and she flashed him with the briefest of smiles. 'You're welcome,' she said.

Merkhet almost choked as he tried to get his next words out. But Raina's expression told him not to push it. She sauntered away, showing recognition of her dismissal.

He hesitated. What was the worst that could happen after everything he had already endured? Merkhet locked gaze with Beebee. The feline's lack of protest prevailed. He unsheathed one of the swords mounted on the wall and severed the rope binding, freeing the queen from the pillar.

Haliya rose from her seated position. The comely woman did not care to disguise the suggestive manner with which she stretched her legs. She faced Merkhet, shoving him firm in the chest.

Startled, he retreated a few steps. She drew nearer, pushing him again. A final prod and he was seated upon the Golden Throne, flabbergasted. Haliya pranced over to the war table and collected the Double Crown. She came back, placing it on his head and kissing him on the neck.

Chapter 36

Merkhet was still awake, somehow bursting with energy, when the sun rose the morning after his Heb-Sed festival. Especially surprising, given the unexpected events of the evening prior. He had consumed a near toxic volume of beer at the festival—and to his absolute dismay—did not secure a single wink of sleep.

A second consecutive sleepless night, but if they were all that much fun …

Merkhet made a deliberate effort to wipe the grin off his face. He couldn't. Rolling out of bed, Haliya did not stir. She could be graceful when she wanted to be.

He was not one to relish in vindictive behaviour, but at that moment, Merkhet could not contain his guilty elation at the thought of Prahmun's impending Judgement. Merkhet wanted his guileful former vizier to suffer a thousand times over for his actions. It was less than he deserved.

In some regards, Merkhet had already parted ways with the negativity from his harrowing exile. After a pleasant return to Egypt, he was even ready to forgive Llora.

First, he had to muster the strength to meet the hollow gaze of Prahmun at the Judgements and sentence him to a righteous death. The justice of Ma'at would always prevail while he was pharaoh.

His mother sat in the courtyard, beneath the acacia tree. She beckoned him to join her. Merkhet did not hesitate.

'I am ready to share with you,' she said, her voice sweet and homely, 'what your father envisioned of you, should you ever rule.'

'Yes, Mother?'

'Build a great city in the northern delta. A formidable city that will make our enemies weak and vulnerable at the very sight of it. It will be our greatest defence.'

'I will make it so,' he said. 'First, I must repair Thebes.'

'You are a good son,' Merep said. 'Now, go, do what you must.'

'It is so good to see you again, Mother.'

Smiling, Merkhet departed the palace, where towards the bottom of the enclosed descent, Lufu stopped him. 'Your Worship,' he said, bowing. 'I'm sorry it has taken me this long to see you.'

Merkhet waved the vizier's worries away. 'I have

been preoccupied.'

'It was wrong of me to ever give audience to their antics. I hope you can forgive me,' the vizier said, struggling to sustain eye contact.

'You were only doing what you thought was right, to please the gods and maintain Ma'at.'

'You are too kind, Your Worship.' Lufu nodded towards Thekla, positioned a few feet away. 'It is with great regret I need to inform that your father's tomb has been compromised.'

Had Merkhet's final tribute to his father, the flax defence, worked? He ran his hand along the top of his ponytail. 'Is that so?'

'The sarcophagus is intact, and the thieves did not acquire much, but I thought it best to protect the most important relics until such a time as the tomb seal can be restored.'

'Thank you, Lufu.'

'Perhaps one day,' the vizier said, 'you would like to hear the origins of your father's prized weapon?'

'Enough with your grovelling, tell the tale now. The Judgements aren't going to begin without me,' Merkhet said, smirking.

Lufu smiled. 'In that case, do you know who Thekla was crafted for?'

'Strangely enough, I know nothing of its origins.'

'It was a diplomatic gift to your grandfather, Turkhet, from the Nubians. They possessed advanced smelting techniques and were crafting weapons we could scarcely imagine at the time. We weren't always hostile with them, you know.'

Merkhet nodded, keen to hear the rest of the story.

'The Nubians insisted that the Master Diplomat's

blood be forged within the weapon, granting it special properties.'

'What special properties?' Merkhet asked.

'Did you ever try and lift it as a child?'

'I couldn't. I wasn't strong enough.'

'Try it now.'

Merkhet lifted the golden war hammer with ease. 'But now I am?'

'Sort of,' the vizier said with a gentle laugh. 'The weapon is truly unique. The strongest man in the world could not lift it by himself unless he had your grandfather's blood coursing through his veins.'

'So why couldn't I lift it as a child, then?'

'Exactly that, you were only a child. It still has a physical presence. Thekla's weight is tremendous. It was just too heavy for you back then.'

Merkhet withdrew Thekla and twirled it in his hands, amazed by the weapon and its startling origin. 'Thank you, Lufu, that is some useful insight. Will you be attending the Judgements?'

'I might give it a miss. The reconstruction of Thebes should not be delayed, and the gods know that I should return to Memphis soon.'

'Excellent. I shall check in with your progress later.'

'Also, Your Worship. You look just like him. Your father, I mean. The ponytail is especially impressive. I think it could rival his, even in his prime.'

Merkhet smiled. He bid the vizier farewell and collected his royal guard escort, all while still wielding Thekla. They boarded the royal chariot, departing for Prahmun's Judgement.

When Merkhet arrived at the Judgements, the crowd were huddled close together in anticipation.

Word of the vizier's involvement in the spread of chaos had circulated quicker than the news of his father's death. The people deserved to witness the gods' justice.

Merkhet raised Thekla high above his head, and the murmuring faded. 'Bring forth the accused,' he commanded in a resounding voice.

An administrative official handed him the maatebes. Merkhet fiddled with them as Prahmun was dragged by two guards into the centre of the elliptical arena.

'Prahmun, you are accused of betraying your pharaoh, betraying Egypt, and thereby inviting the infernal legions of chaos into our humble lands. The gods will pursue justice and decide whether you are innocent or guilty. In the gods, we trust.'

Merkhet cast the maatebes high, hoping that Horus may kiss them with the gods' verdict. Up they went, soaring higher and higher, before plunging into the sand. Two suns faced the sky. The crowd gasped, disbelieving. Merkhet's blood ran hot. How could this be?

Prahmun jumped in the air, a declaration of emphatic victory. Looking at that supreme smugness, knots formed in Merkhet's stomach, churning tighter and tighter. He didn't realise his first challenge as the rejuvenated ruler of Egypt would come so soon. How was he meant to interpret the will of the gods?

When he thought his resolve might waver or even abandon him entirely, a faint roar entered his ears. Merkhet tilted his head to listen, and the crowd, having heard it too, followed his lead.

The roar grew louder, carrying with it fury and understanding. The pharaoh smiled as the gush of the inundation awed the crowd. The Nile would be their lifeblood once again, and the gods had shown him the path of justice. Another test, and this time he would pass it. Merkhet refused to create a legacy as a timid pharaoh. The people would know his strength. They would fear it, respect it, and understand that he was a living embodiment of the gods. He alone would administer their will.

'Two suns,' Merkhet announced.

The spectators were drawn to the drama, speechless, and craning to see what would happen next.

'Excellent! The gods have spoken,' Prahmun said, 'release me from these binds at once.'

'You are right, the gods have spoken. But I alone can interpret their will. They have deemed death too easy of an escape for your heinous crimes. They have reminded me of the true meaning of punishment.'

Prahmun halted mid-victory dance, the colour draining from his face. 'But there are clearly two suns. Look! Two suns mean freedom! My freedom!'

'The gods have judged you guilty for your crimes, Prahmun. A death sentence would be too lenient a punishment, even though the Afterlife will not have you. After you are stoned, our greatest physicians will treat your cuts, bruises, and wounds. You will thank them before being subjected to the blazing hot fury of Ra. But our physicians will apply salve to your burns and the stoning will commence again. Welcome to your new life. Let it stand to reason that no one should seek to replicate your wrongdoings. The gods are always watching us.'

The crowd applauded, cheered, and hurled abuse at the disgraced vizier.

Merkhet, proud of his courage to provide a just ruling, exhaled a massive sigh of relief. 'Commence the stoning!'

The guards taunted the former vizier, feigning to throw and laughing every time Prahmun flinched. They marched up to his face, shouting obscenities. The crowd jeered them on, wanting blood. When did they not?

Merkhet watched on, enjoying the spectacle against his better nature, and vowing to ensure that the guards responsible were fed beyond their wildest dreams. The guards gave in to the demands of the bloodthirsty spectators. Stones came in a flurry. As did Prahmun's howls of agony. His torture echoed off the wall of spectators, and their ceaseless roar was a fitting approval. The vizier's blood sprayed across the sand.

Still, there was a nagging suspicion that his punishment didn't match the crime.

When Prahmun could only manage to whimper, Merkhet called a cease to the stoning. 'Treat his wounds, strip off his robe, and send him into the desert, where Ra will have no trouble finding him.'

Neglecting the chariot, Merkhet strolled towards the nearby river, after collecting the crown from the rear carriage. As he walked with it in hand, he contemplated the difficult rebuilding phase that lie ahead. First, he would need to make amends with Llora and apologise for his harsh words, for he would not be able to concentrate until that was resolved. Merkhet lowered himself to his haunches and admired the rush of the Nile. The brown-green liquid rushed by him and set him at complete ease.

He positioned the Double Crown on his head. After a quick adjustment, it was comfortable, and Merkhet could finally accept its presence. Once he restored Thebes, he would do as his father would have done. Assert Egypt's authority, making certain no foreign forces ever dare challenge them again, but Pharaoh Merkhet would do so through his own means.

Acknowledgements

To those who know me, I would assume it is common knowledge how much this writing journey means to me and will continue to do so. Yet, it means even more to me the people who have helped me reach this pivotal checkpoint: a published book.

So, in very deliberate order, some acknowledgements are required:

Mum and Dad. Thank you for gifting me an understanding of the importance of education (and for not judging too harshly when I left a fantastic job to pursue travel and writing).

My brother, Shane, and best mate, Dino (pronounced Dean-o). Thank you for reading through the early drivel and encouraging me to keep going anyway.

Sarah, Greeny, Kessey, Jon, Leigh, Moody, and Noddy. Thank you for your generous support of a premature book launch on Patreon. It did not go unnoticed.

Finally, to all my friends and family, who bought the kindle version of *The Pharaoh's Curse* even though reading is not your thing. Thank you.

PS: Don't worry, Hannah, I did not forget you. Thank you for your unwavering support and for giving me the space to chase this dream. You are a gem, a rare one.

Free Story Download

Turn-Tide Taharva is back!

How does he become a slave of the Egyptian Empire?

How does he rise to Captain of the Royal Guard despite this?

Collect your free story at www.cjboomer.com and be the first to hear about all the author's latest releases.

About the Author

C.J. has been writing steady for four years and draws much of his inspiration from the wonders of past civilisations. If he is not planning his next trip to visit one of them, he is writing about them. Pompeii and the view of the Bay of Naples from atop Mount Vesuvius ... wow, just wow!

Reading wide and far, he also coordinates a writing club at a local high school, where C.J. introduces students to the discipline and skills required to progress from idea to publication.

He currently has 2 works-in-progress and can't wait to set them free in the world.